LOVE NEVER FAILS

A PRIDE & PREJUDICE VARIATION

JENNIFER JOY

"Love Never Fails: A Pride & Prejudice Variation"

Published by Jennifer Joy

Email: contact@jenniferjoywrites.com

ISBN-13: 978-1-944795-90-0

I love you, Dad!

CONTENTS

FREE EXTRA SCENES

Want access to free bonus scenes?
Join Jennifer's New Release Newsletter here!

PROLOGUE

They buried Father. Two farmhands wielding shovels piled the moist earth on top of his coffin until they smothered the scent of pine, and it disappeared under the ground.

A few of the tenants and some friends had come to pay their respects. Elizabeth Bennet had not expected many. Mother was not there. Her nerves and a convenient sense of propriety prevented her from joining her elder daughters in their hiding place behind a tree at a discreet distance from the funeral service they were not allowed to attend until after the mourners had gone. Lydia and Kitty, Elizabeth's younger sisters, stayed at home with Mother so they might wail together in the privacy of their rooms as proper females were supposed to do. Elizabeth did not want to be proper. She wanted to be next to her father.

Elizabeth stood between Jane and Mary, her arms linked through theirs on either side as they approached Father's grave. Her knees nearly buckled as the final person left, but she forced herself to stand. Exhaustion poured over her like a wave. Her eyes burned, but she could not indulge in a good cry. Not yet. Not when her sisters relied on her to keep their family together through the trials which were yet to come.

Jane looked at her. “Come, Lizzy. You must rest.”

She was not ready to leave. Her limbs stiffened, and a numbness which had helped her through the past two days swept over her, so that she did not know if she would ever be able to move again.

“Just a moment longer. I…” She cut her words short, feeling like a puppet in her own skin. How could she explain that no number of goodbyes were sufficient for her to accept that Father was gone? She still looked for him when she rounded a corner or entered his study. Though she had helped the manservant with what she could to prepare Father for burial, Mother being in too poor a state to offer any assistance, she held the fading hope that this was all a horrible nightmare from which she could not wake.

In the distance, the last retreating figure turned back to look at the heap of fresh dirt marking Father’s final resting place. Elizabeth did not recognize him with his black great-coat and dark hat, but that did not signify. It would be difficult to recognize anyone through the blurry haze of the dark day.

"I never thought anything could happen to Father." Jane sniffed and reached her hand up to wipe her cheeks.

Elizabeth had not either. Yet, there they stood at the top of a grassy knoll where generations of Bennets lay under the stark autumn branches of an ash tree.

Mary said, "Blessed are they that mourn: for they shall be comforted."

Her words brought Elizabeth no comfort. It was unjust that Father’s death would mean that they could barely continue to live. Their home was no longer theirs, but would go to a distant cousin they had not yet met. Their income was so much reduced, they could not afford to live elsewhere. Her hands clenched into fists, and she hated herself for thinking of their troubles so soon. But someone had to do something. Elizabeth, her sisters, and Mother must live.

"Thank you, Mary," she said through her clenched jaw. "Let us return to the house and comfort our mother." The house. Not their home anymore.

HE LOOKED BACK AGAIN at the three ladies standing beside Mr. Bennet's grave. They would feel his loss greatly. Especially his favorite daughter, Miss Elizabeth. "My Lizzy" he had called her. She must be the one in the middle, her sisters' arms looped through hers, leaning on her petite frame for support. It was just as Mr. Bennet had predicted.

He would have to find a way to speak with her. He was honor bound to do so.

Slowly, the ladies turned to walk away from the grave. Miss Elizabeth glanced over her shoulder, and he recognized the look in her face all too well. The weight of responsibility, the grief of mourning, the burden of being stronger for the weak, the determination to hold on to those remaining, the fear of losing them too.... The distance could not disguise her emotions. He had felt them five years before when his father died. He understood their power.

Fitzwilliam Darcy turned back toward Netherfield Park. Now was not the time to reveal secrets. His honesty would cast propriety aside to reveal what shamed him at that very moment, but he determined within himself to respect her grief and wait.

SHRILL WAILS and lamentations greeted them before they even entered the house.

"I will ask for some tea to be sent up to Mother," said Jane. If anyone could bring comfort to her, it was Jane. But after three days of caring for the never ending demands of Mother and their younger sisters, Jane's eyes were surrounded with dark circles. If Elizabeth did not ease her load, she worried that Jane might fall ill.

"Do not rush yourself. I will tell Mother that cook had to fetch some dandelion root," Elizabeth said.

"She will not like it," sighed Jane.

"What else is there when we have no more tea leaves to reuse?"

Elizabeth continued upstairs with Mary. Lydia and Kitty knelt beside Mother's fainting couch, sobbing into her black skirts in the dark room.

The floor creaked as Elizabeth opened the curtains, then took her place next to Mother.

She lifted her head. Her eyes were red and puffy from tears.

"Oh, Lizzy," Mother said as she grasped her hand. "How unfortunate Mr. Bennet should pass away the same evening of the Meryton Assembly. He was to introduce you to Mr. Bingley! Now, how are we to meet him when we are not allowed to make calls and with no one to introduce us?"

Disappointed that Mother's chief concern was less about losing Father and more about missing out on a diverting evening at a ball, Elizabeth pulled her hand into her lap.

"I so dearly wanted to dance," sighed Lydia.

Kitty said, "Just think how dreadful it would have been had Father died at the Assembly."

Elizabeth clutched her hands in her skirt. Did they care for nothing other than dancing?

Mother fanned herself. "At least you would have been

introduced to Mr. Bingley and the other gentleman my sister told me was there. He had a commanding sort of name, though I cannot remember it now."

"Mr. Darcy of Pemberley," Elizabeth mumbled, only content to keep the line of conversation going because of the calming effect it seemed to have on Mother.

"Esther said that he was a rather serious gentleman. He did not dance at all, though there was a lack of gentlemen in the room and he never would have wanted for a partner. However disagreeable Mr. Darcy is, he is still a gentleman of means and could have married one of my daughters. Oh, if only Mr. Bennet had not died just before the assembly!" Mother's face crumpled under the pressure of a new round of sobs.

So much for calming Mother. No wonder Jane was worn to the bone. Trying again, lest Jane come upstairs to another emotional disaster of which she would take it upon herself to calm, Elizabeth said, "Tell us, what else did Aunt Phillips say about the gentlemen? Perhaps we should meet them in passing." Such an event was unlikely, but the idea would give Mother hope.

Mother dabbed her face with a handkerchief, letting her fan dangle from the black ribbon tied around her wrist. "Esther described Mr. Bingley as an affable gentleman. He danced with every lady in the room, though he did not dance with any certain lady more than once. Surely, if he sees Jane, he will want to marry her… though he may have his pick amongst my girls. If only Mr. Bennet had done his duty by us—"

"What of Mr. Darcy? Did Aunt give any indication as to why he did not dance?" Elizabeth interrupted through her agitated breath. She would not stand anyone— not even Mother— speaking negatively of Father.

Mother pinched her lips in disapproval of the interruption. "Of Mr. Darcy she did not say much other than that he did not dance at all for the entire evening. Can you imagine that?"

Kitty and Lydia exclaimed, "What? Not dance at a ball?"

Mary, who had sat quietly by the window, said, "The rewards of observation and reflection are far greater. I take little pleasure in a ball." As usual, she was met with blank stares. Lydia tossed a pillow at her.

"According to Esther, his manners were so off-putting, she determined him to be too proud to mix in company with the villagers present. Sir William tried to converse with Mr. Darcy and encourage him to dance, but it was for naught. Or so I hear," said Mother.

"If Aunt Phillips said it, it is as good as the gospel," Elizabeth said, too annoyed with the present conversation to attempt to change it and determined to think Mr. Darcy a good man just to be contrary. Aunt was known to exaggerate her stories to better suit Mother's craving for drama and intrigue. Her account only proved it. What gentleman would behave so abominably at an assembly? No, it must be an exaggeration.

"What bothers me most is that we are not free to socialize with Mr. Bingley or Mr. Darcy. How are they to marry two of my daughters if we cannot attend any social functions for several months at least?" Mother picked at her black crape dress.

"I think the black is striking against the silver streaks of hair at your temples," offered Kitty.

Mother reached up to touch her hair above her ears. "Do you think so? Striking, you say? Kitty, bring me a mirror."

Looking from side to side, examining her face and hair against her widow's weeds, she finally sniffed and handed the mirror back to Kitty. "Not too bad, I must say."

Mary said, "The hoary head is a crown of glory."

Lydia gasped. "Do not be so simple, Mary. Who would call their head hoary? That sounds dreadful."

"Gray, then?" Mary suggested.

Kitty said, "Silver is infinitely better than drab gray and I would never call Mother's hair dull."

"It is in the scriptures," said Mary, her chin jutted out.

Lydia twirled her hair around her finger. "Lor, whoever wrote that got it wrong. Silver is infinitely more beautiful than a hoary head."

"Father always said you were handsome." Elizabeth whispered the words, needing to talk about him even though it made her eyes brim and would upset Mother.

Bracing herself for another bout of tears, Elizabeth was surprised when Lydia sat taller and smiled. "Perhaps you will marry again soon!"

Fortunately for Lydia or Mother, who preened even more, Jane arrived with the tea. Elizabeth felt like a kettle about to boil over. Before the grass had time to grow over Father's grave, Lydia dared say that Mother might replace him! It was wrong.

Mother sipped her tea, her face contorting in disgust. "This is awful! Has cook decided to poison us all?"

Elizabeth looked at Jane apologetically. "I forgot to mention the dandelion roots, Jane. I am sorry." No matter how she tried, Elizabeth's efforts to appease her mother always went awry and her guilt increased when she saw how Jane gracefully soothed her while her own frustration intensified.

Pulling some papers out of her pocket, Jane said, "I found these on Father's desk. There appears to be some correspondence and someone should look through them." She held them out to Mother.

"Give them to Lizzy. I am unlikely to understand them anyhow. Is there no sugar to sweeten this vile liquid?"

Mother asked, not wanting to be bothered with any of the decisions which needed to be made unless it brought her comfort or lead a daughter to the marriage altar.

Jane persisted. “Is not Mr. Collins the name of Father’s cousin who is to inherit?” As if she could forget. The name Collins had become synonymous with dread in their household.

“That did not arrive recently, did it? I expect he will write soon,” Mother said.

Jane blushed. “I did not mean to look, but I did notice that it is dated the day before Father…”

Snatching the letter out of Jane’s hand, Mother poured over its contents, mumbling as she read. A large smile cheered her face and she fanned herself with the pages she rotated through her hands. “He means to marry one of you! We are saved!”

CHAPTER 1

Mr. Collins was gracious enough to delay his visit some months, but as winter crawled along and spring drew near, he descended upon them like an unwelcome guest. His delicacy insisted that he reside apart from the houseful of females, but he was a plague that would not go away during the days that mercilessly grew in length.

Jane was safe. She had fallen ill the previous month and, even had she been in excellent health, Mother had better plans for her. "She cannot be so beautiful for nothing," she said.

Mary, too, was spared from Mr. Collins' attentions though she was the only one among them to appreciate his mind-numbing confabulations.

Kitty and Lydia were fortunate enough to be considered too young for his notice.

He reached for Elizabeth's hand after clearing the breakfast room of all its occupants. She moved her chair away.

Undeterred, he said, "Cousin Elizabeth, you can hardly mistake my attentions and the little compliments I have showered upon you over these past few weeks. I have made it no secret that my aim, imposed upon me by my good patroness, Lady Catherine de Bourgh, who I praise for her superior wisdom in matters of matrimonial happiness…" He paused, no doubt losing the purpose of his soliloquy in the abundance of superfluous words. Clearing his throat and wringing his stumpy fingers, he said, "It is my aim to take a wife and, Cousin Elizabeth," he inched forward in his chair and reached for her hand, which she buried in the folds of her dress, "I have chosen you."

Elizabeth swallowed the bile stinging her throat.

So pleased with himself and so certain of her response, Mr. Collins never waited for her answer.

"I am quite comfortable in my current position and enjoy the condescension of my esteemed patroness, so that I am willing to continue in Hunsford for a time so that we might benefit from Lady Catherine's advice as we settle into our new roles as husband and wife."

His face turned red and he wiped his forehead. There was no circumstance in the world which would entice Elizabeth to allow him to touch her with those sweaty palms. She leaned back until the wood frame of her chair pressed against her through the upholstered cushion.

He took a large breath, no doubt in preparation for another windy speech and Elizabeth knew it was absolutely necessary to interrupt him.

"You forget, sir, that I have made no answer. Accept my thanks for the compliment you are paying me— I am very sensible of the honor of your proposals— but it is impossible for me to do otherwise than decline them." There, that sounded polite but firm.

Not discouraged in the least, he waved his hand—sweeping her refusal aside as insignificant and exasperating Elizabeth further when he expressed as much aloud.

Interrupting again, she said more firmly than before, "Sir, I am perfectly serious in my refusal. You could not make me happy, and I am convinced that I am the last woman in the world who would make you so."

His sweaty brows knit together and he squirmed in his chair, for the first time uncertain. "Need I remind you, Cousin, that you have little choice in the matter? I am in need of a wife and you are in need of a home. I humbly extend my generosity to your mother and sisters by offering them security on the condition that we marry. My situation in life, my connections with the family of de Bourgh, and my relationship to your own are circumstances highly in its favor. You should take it into consideration that in spite of your manifold attractions, it is by no means certain that another offer of marriage may ever be made you. Your portion is unhappily so small that it will in all likelihood undo the effects of your loveliness and amiable qualifications in the eyes of a lesser gentleman."

Wanting nothing more than to leave the room and the sickening presence of Mr. Collins, she controlled her breath so that she might speak clearly. "You must give me leave to choose my own future and pay me the compliment of believing what I say. I wish you very happy with whomever else you choose as a wife. In making me the offer, you must have satisfied the delicacy of your feelings with regard to my family and may take possession of Longbourn estate without any self-reproach. This matter may be considered, therefore, as finally settled."

She rose from her chair before he could utter another word and stormed into the peace of Father's study. Closing the heavy door a touch more resolutely than required, she leaned back against it and held her breath until she determined that she had not been followed into Father's sanctuary.

There were times she still expected to see him sitting behind his desk, engrossed in a book and smoking his pipe. The smell of tobacco and the intoxicating aroma of books filled her senses and she closed her eyes so she could see him. How she wished he was there to reassure her. He would never make her marry a ridiculous man to preserve their home. But why did she feel so guilty?

Slumping her shoulders, she opened her eyes to look at his empty chair. A chair he would never occupy again. The shelves of books he had taken such pride in collecting would never again pass through his hands. It was impossible to foresee a time when she could look at a book without a large lump choking her throat.

Elizabeth walked around his desk, letting her fingers run across the worn edge of the wood. It was as soft as cream from its years of use. Falling into his faded brown leather chair, she rested her heated forehead against the coolness of the oak desk and braced herself to face Mother.

SHE FOUND her in the garden.

Mother balled her fists and plunked them on her round hips. "I do not understand you, Elizabeth Bennet. It is in our best interest for you to marry Mr. Collins, yet you declare that you will not have him!"

"No, Mother, I will not have him and Father would never have expected me to marry him." She held on to that belief with a tenacity stronger than her self-reproach.

"Mr. Collins has been kind enough to allow us to stay here though Longbourn is now his to do with as he pleases. Surely, you could learn to think more kindly toward him given a sufficient amount of time. Need I remind you that our family's security depends upon his generosity? The least you can do is marry him."

Mother spoke of marriage as if it were the solution to all life's problems. Her sole wish was to see her five daughters married well and, while Elizabeth was not averse to the idea, she wanted more. So much more. She refused to settle for a man she could not respect. She craved good conversation. With Father gone, she had no one to talk to. Nobody who understood her humor, not that she exceeded in smiles lately. How could she make Mother understand?

"I cannot marry Mr. Collins. Can you not see how unsuited to each other we are? Father never—"

Mother raised her finger into the air. "Do not mention your father. He is not here, and had he done his duty by us, we would not be in this dreadful situation. I will not have you speak of him when he was so often wrong in these matters. Had he allowed me..." Her lips pinched and she huffed out her flared nostrils. Mother's anger at Father, though deserved in her view, pained Elizabeth more than she could know.

"Do you not think it inappropriate for Mr. Collins to court me while I am yet in mourning?" Elizabeth stood on shaky ground. Mother would be the first to set propriety aside if it meant that one of her daughters could marry.

"These are desperate times for us, Lizzy. If you do not marry Mr. Collins, he will have every right to cast us out of our home. Is that what you want?"

Elizabeth closed her eyes and exhaled deeply. She could not marry Mr. Collins. In the weeks since his arrival, every day brought a new reason for her to refuse him. He was ridiculous. Though politeness and indifference had tamed her sarcastic comments, Mr. Collins was the brunt of many scathing remarks made in her mind. A wife should want for her husband to hold her hand. She ought to feel her heart flutter when he looked at her. Elizabeth had been so repulsed by his touch, she could still taste the bile in her mouth.

Crossing her arms to strengthen her resolve, Elizabeth repeated, "I cannot marry him. I am decided."

Mother crossed her arms, mirroring Elizabeth's determination. "Then I shall never speak to you again. Do you understand me, Elizabeth Bennet? If you refuse to marry Mr. Collins, not a word toward you shall cross my lips. Your selfish disregard for your family is not the work of a daughter deserving of a loving mother."

Elizabeth's gut wrenched, squeezing her firm resolve until she ached. She would do everything in her power to prove her loyalty to her family and minimize the consequences of her decision, but she would not marry a man she could not respect... much less love. Father would not have made her do it, she repeated over and over in her mind.

Shaking her head slowly, Elizabeth whispered once again, "I cannot do it. I am sorry."

Pinching her lips so tightly, they turned white, Mother said, "It is your choice. If you would have me treat you as a stranger, then so be it." Throwing her hands into the air, she turned on her heel to leave Elizabeth standing alone in the middle of the garden.

The wind swirled around her, prickling her skin and sending chills up and down her limbs. Elizabeth wrapped her arms around herself, bunching her shoulders up to her ears to warm her neck. Lowering her chin, she shivered as another blast of wind reminded her of how alone she was. There would be no warming embrace to soothe her aching heart. Nobody would pat her shoulder and tell her that everything would turn out well. Elizabeth's arms fell to her sides as she realized the futility of her solo embrace.

Unable to return inside to Jane, who would gladly bear

Elizabeth's burdens on top of her own to her failing health, she turned toward the fields and walked.

There was a fallen tree on the edge of a grove where she often sought solace. The surrounding trees protected her from the sharp wind and it had a lovely view of Netherfield Park in the distance.

Sitting with her hands clutched together so that they would stop shaking, she let herself feel all the emotions she had tried to subdue at Longbourn. At first, no tears came, though they pooled together to drown her. She reached up to her mouth, gasping for breath, her fingers pressing against her lips. The pressure in her chest grew unbearable until, with a cry, the defensive walls she had worked so diligently building over the past months crumbled under the weight of her tears. Having no witnesses to her grief in the sheltered grove, she buried her arm in her spencer and sobbed as if she might never be able to stop.

BINGLEY HAD LEFT Darcy minutes ago, complaining of the chill in the air. Darcy welcomed the crisp breeze. It reminded him of his home in Pemberley. He rode on, keeping within view of the house lest it began to rain. He looked toward the top of a hill that afforded a view of Longbourn. Which of the Bennet sisters would Mr. Collins propose to? If he were to believe the gossip, Miss Elizabeth would soon be engaged. Not that she had much choice in the matter. It would take an incredibly strong-willed woman to refuse his offer and such ladies were hardly common. Guilt pricked his conscience, but he pushed it aside. He had done what he could.

Darcy rode up the incline, giving his stallion free rein. The blast of wind invigorated his senses and whistled through the trees nearby. Slowing to a canter as he neared the grove, Darcy pulled his mount up short. A young lady sat weeping at a short distance. The sound of their approach startled her and she wiped at her eyes with the sleeve of her coat. This was the closest he had seen her. Slowly, he nudged his mount forward. She was much more handsome than he had supposed. The tears shone off gold flecks in her eyes, lending them a brightness unique to her.

They had not been formally introduced, but Darcy would recognize Miss Elizabeth Bennet anywhere. His gut clenched for her. She looked so lonely and vulnerable sitting alone amongst the evergreens.

Without a word or a second thought, he dismounted. Careful not to alarm her, he gently reached into his pocket to pull out his handkerchief. She needed it much more than he did.

Walking closer to her with his arm extended, he silently offered the only comfort he could give.

Her lips parted to speak and she looked up at him questioningly. Had Mr. Phillips delivered his letter to her family? Had she forgiven him? They had not attempted to communicate with him as he had invited them to do, and he dared not call if he was unwelcome. Was she engaged?

A droplet of tear stuck to her dark eyelashes. His inclination was to wipe it away and fold her in his arms in an embrace so that he might absorb some of the pain she felt. The shock of his tender reaction to her intensified as her fingers touched his to accept the bit of white linen in his hand. She buried her face in it, turning to the side.

He wished he could stay, but he would not embarrass her more than he already must have. Not even his little sister, Georgiana, allowed him to see her weep. But he could not very well leave her alone.

Looking about and down over the other side of the hill, he saw a figure approaching. She bore what looked like a blanket. Her features, though much thinner than he remembered, were that of the eldest Miss Bennet.

Feeling awkward and intrusive, he waited until Miss Elizabeth saw her sister before he bowed, mounted his horse, and rode back to the stables. He wanted to look back at her again. Darcy left her clutching his handkerchief in her trembling hands. He hoped she would keep it.

CHAPTER 2

Jane looked as stunned as Elizabeth felt. "Who was that?" Jane asked, sitting so near Elizabeth, she could rest her head on Jane's shoulder.

Elizabeth straightened out the handkerchief and traced the stitched initials in the corner with her fingernail. The letters FD were embroidered in shiny, silk thread. "He must be Mr. Fitzwilliam Darcy." She pulled part of the blanket out to wrap it around Jane. "It is not good for you to be out so soon after your illness, Jane. You need time to gain your strength."

"The fever was over a month ago," persisted Jane. "He lent you his handkerchief? Surely, he must have said something."

Now that Elizabeth thought about it, their encounter was an odd one. However, it had been precisely what she had needed. She dried her cheeks and tucked the handkerchief into her pocket. She wished she could keep it. "He must have seen me crying and came over to lend me his handkerchief. That is all. You came and he left." Elizabeth shrugged her shoulders and sighed. "I am glad you came." Straightening up and clasping her hands together, she said, "I refused Mr. Collins' offer."

"I had not expected you would be able to accept him, Lizzy. You love too deeply." Looping her arm through Elizabeth's, they stared out over the rolling fields leading down to Netherfield Park.

"Would that I could be more practical, yet I do not really wish to change. I cannot fathom living a life of cold complacency, though there are times when I wish I could settle for less."

Jane squeezed her arm. "We will learn to cope with these contradictory emotions. I would not have you change, though it might ease your grief and… guilt."

Elizabeth nodded. "I do feel guilty. I cannot yet laugh for guilt that I should be too happy. It does not seem right with Father gone. I cannot offer security to my family because the man who extends the very things we need to survive is repulsive to me. How am I not to feel guilty?" She pulled the handkerchief out of her pocket and rubbed the soft linen against her fingers.

"Lizzy, that is in the past now and you should not choose to live in it. Remember it only for what you can learn and for the memories which bring you pleasure. That life is gone and if we are ever to be happy again, we must create a new one. In the end, you will wish you had spent more time living and less time grieving."

Elizabeth's breath caught in her throat. Jane spoke like Father would have when his mind took a philosophical bend. "Sickness has made you wise," she smiled weakly.

"That happens when one is closer to death than life. It becomes easier to see things clearly. Oh, Lizzy, do not cry! I am well and improving every day, otherwise I would never have ventured out. I only want to see you happy again."

Tears came easily to Elizabeth, but Jane's thoughtful

words and gentleness cast a rainbow over her despair of earlier and she smiled between sobs.

"Another basket arrived at the back door this morning. Mother is pleased because it had some fresh tea leaves and sugar in it besides some beef and baked rolls."

The good news calmed Elizabeth. "Mr. Collins takes credit for it, but I have my doubts. I suppose we will know for sure if the provisions stop coming and the repairs around the estate cease after having refused him."

"Would it not be romantic to have an admirer as our benefactor? I do wonder at the secrecy though. No notes have been left and nothing is ever said to indicate who is responsible." Jane stood and held her hand out to Elizabeth.

"So long as it keeps good food on the table, I will respect the gentleman or lady's secrecy and if his or her identity is ever revealed, I will thank the individual wholeheartedly." Elizabeth took Jane's hand for their walk home. She only looked over her shoulder once toward the house at Netherfield Park. No horseman was in sight. More was the pity.

THERE HAD BEEN moments in Elizabeth's life when she had desired Mother's silence. After three days of it, she wished Mother would say something. Anything. Even a shout would be better than her indifference. Her apathy did more to burden Elizabeth's heavy heart than a thousand rebukes.

Taking solace outside, Elizabeth sat near the garden pondering how best to continue. Mr. Collins had made it apparent that his interest did not extend to Mary, a hope she had cultivated. They would make a wonderful match. Mary's solemn manners and religious inclination would serve as an advantage to any parson. However, as surely as Elizabeth did not want Mr. Collins, Mr. Collins did not want Mary.

"Lizzy," called a voice Elizabeth had not heard in what felt like ages.

She reached her hands out, but Charlotte sat beside her, wrapping her arms around her best friend. For someone who did not indulge in emotional demonstrations, Elizabeth appreciated her gesture. Elizabeth rested her head against Charlotte's shoulder briefly, then pulled away before her friend grew uncomfortable.

"I am so happy to see you, dearest friend." Elizabeth pressed Charlotte's hand between her own.

"And I, you. How are you?"

"The passing of time is softening the grief."

"I am glad to hear it." Charlotte looked down at her lap and picked at an embroidered flower on her skirt. She looked at Elizabeth, her eyebrows bunched together, then looked back down.

"Charlotte, is something wrong? Have you a complaint against Mr. Collins? I was worried when he announced his intention to accept your father's hospitality and stay at Lucas Lodge that he might make himself a bother..." Elizabeth had been grateful for his absence and had applauded his decision to quit Longbourn after she had refused him. Though the Lucases welcomed him with open arms, she feared that his pompous manners would wear on them after the first evening.

"No," she replied softly. Taking a deep breath, she looked Elizabeth in the eyes. "I know that you will disapprove of what I am about to tell you, but Lizzy, I hope that someday you might come to understand my reasons."

Charlotte would never do anything nonsensical. What could she possibly mean?

Sucking in another breath, she said, "Last evening, Mr. Collins proposed to me."

So he had made a bother of himself. Poor Charlotte. Elizabeth reached out to touch her hand in reassurance. After all, refusing any gentleman was disturbing work— even a gentleman like Mr. Collins.

"Oh, Charlotte, I am so sorry he presumed—"

"I accepted him," she blurted out before Elizabeth could finish.

All she could do was stare. She knew her jaw was open but was too astounded to bother to close it. After some seconds, Elizabeth grasped at the first words which came to her. "I… I do not know what to say…"

"Lizzy, please be happy for me. I am not romantic like you. My needs are simple. I only want for a home of my own. His proposal is a blessing for me as I will no longer be a burden to my family. I am content."

She spoke so confidently, Elizabeth was almost convinced. Almost.

"But he is ridiculous!" she exclaimed, finally unscrambling the garbled words swirling in her mind.

"He may be to you but, to me, he is my way of securing my own home."

Her own home... "Longbourn..." escaped Elizabeth's lips on an exhale and she felt sick.

"Now, Lizzy, do not concern yourself. I have already discussed this with Mr. Collins and he agreed with me completely. We would not dream of you leaving your home while you are in mourning. When the year of Mrs. Bennet's mourning comes to its conclusion, I think that we can discuss the matter with clearer heads and will be able to come to an agreeable solution for all. Even then, if you feel you need more time, I am certain I can persuade Mr. Collins to be understanding." The words tumbled out of Charlotte like a snowball rolling down a hill, faster and faster.

Hope sprung up in Elizabeth's heart like a sailor spotting

land after months at sea. They still had a home! "You would do that for us?"

Charlotte relaxed her posture. "Of course. You are my dearest friend. You would never cast me out of my home, and I could never do so to you either. I know how difficult these past four months have been on you and the last thing I want is to add to your anxiety." Charlotte paused, looking out over the gloomy afternoon. "This solves so many problems for me, and maybe I am selfish in asking my best friend to be happy for me, but it would mean the world to me for you to be happy too. Not just for me, but for you."

Had four months passed? She counted the days. How was it possible for the same amount of time to have passed by so quickly and so slowly?

Shaking her head and willing herself to sound cheerful, Elizabeth clasped her hands together and forced a smile which deepened when she saw the earnest concern in Charlotte's face. She had been nervous to speak. Did she worry that in accepting Mr. Collins' proposal, she would thus put an end to their friendship? Unwilling to lose anyone else close to her, Elizabeth said, "I am happy for you, Charlotte. I do not understand it, I will admit, but I wish for you to have everything you seek in a marriage."

She stood. "Thank you, Lizzy. I know I should not feel guilty, but I do."

"You have no reason to feel guilt. Had I taken the security of my family more seriously, it would be me who would inform you of my engagement to Mr. Collins." There. She admitted it aloud. Elizabeth's family would lose their home because she could not overcome her aversion to the gentleman who held their future in his hands. Charlotte would soon recover from the guilt she felt because it was unfounded. Elizabeth wished she could say the same for herself. And now it was too late. If only Father were there to tell her that she had made the right decision, she could feel some peace.

"If there is anything I can do to help, please send a message. I will come." Charlotte stared at her intently, waiting for an answer.

Elizabeth nodded her head, unable to speak. If only Father were here!

Charlotte walked away. Elizabeth was glad she did not attempt to inform Mother of her news. The hysterical cries would have been heard in Meryton and she already had enough on her mind.

The corner of Mr. Darcy's handkerchief poked out from inside the sleeve where Elizabeth kept it. She had yet to have an opportunity to return it. She pulled it out and rubbed the soft fabric against her cheek. It smelled of sandalwood and soap. His wordless offer soothed her as surely as his handkerchief glided over her cheek. She tucked it up her sleeve again, where it would stay until she could return it to him.

With a sigh, she turned toward the house. It was time to go inside and weather the storm. It would be far better for Mother to hear the news from her than from Aunt Phillips. Since Mother had not spoken to Elizabeth these three days, their relationship could not get much worse.

Mother sat in the drawing room looking out of the window wistfully— as if she wished to be anywhere else but where she presently was. Elizabeth could not blame her.

Mary practiced dirges on the pianoforte. Lydia and Kitty wiped tears from their cheeks between tangled embroidery stitches. Jane clutched a book of poetry within her hands, but stared absently at the pages.

"Mother," Elizabeth called.

She flinched, but she said nothing. Only when Elizabeth sat beside her did Mother look at her.

"Mother, I have some news." Elizabeth swallowed hard,

her bravado of minutes ago abandoning her. With a deep breath, she let out, "Mr. Collins is engaged to Charlotte."

Mary stopped in the middle of her melody. Elizabeth felt their eyes upon her, but what else could be said?

Mother recovered first. "Miss Lucas is to inherit our home?" She snapped her fan open.

Elizabeth inhaled again. "She told me that she and Mr. Collins are happy to stay at Hunsford until your mourning is through. Is that not thoughtful of them?" She held her breath.

"The home I have lived in since the day I married your father, the home I bore my five daughters in... is lost to me." Mother pressed her hand against her forehead.

The look she gave over the top of her fan added to Elizabeth's guilt, yet she knew that all her reasons for refusing Mr. Collins' offer would be affirmed within five minutes of her being in his company again. Father never would have made her marry him. Elizabeth clung to that belief as if her life depended upon it.

Lydia said, "I had always thought Miss Lucas would be left on the shelf." She shrugged her shoulders and blindly stabbed her needle into her embroidery loop.

In a huff, Mother said, "No, now it will be Lizzy who is left on the shelf."

"Mother, please do not say such things," begged Jane.

Lydia pulled up on her needle, poking her finger in the process, and tangling the thread worse than it was before. "Better her than me, I say. I would much rather marry a dashing soldier. What a pity we cannot mingle with the regiment stationed in Meryton. Instead, we must stay home dressed in drab clothes and have no diversions." As if she did not accompany Elizabeth every time she walked into Meryton to see Uncle Phillips on business.

Kitty added, "When we are free, I shall wear my best white frock every day with different colored ribbons just because I can. I shall never choose to spend a day indoors when we are allowed to make calls."

"You speak of mourning as if it were a punishment, but I cherish the time I have to reflect on our father as well as my conduct before God." Mary, who gratefully had yet to resume playing her instrument, contributed.

Mother sat too quietly, her fan moving violently back and forth.

Wanting to be helpful and knowing full well that the responsibility fell to her, Elizabeth suggested, "We have more time before we need to leave Longbourn. I will be more vigilant in writing to family, friends… even acquaintances to see about a small residence we might be able to occupy. Would it not be wonderful to live in a comfortable cottage on the coast?" Elizabeth did not think it so wonderful to leave the home of her youth, but she knew it would be well-received.

Exclamations of delight filled the room, but the noise did nothing to distract Mother from her thoughts. She pinched her chin and chewed on the corner of her mouth.

When she finally did look at up, her eyes were clear. In a determined voice, she said, "I will not stay in this house for another month. It is no longer ours and I will not watch as it is taken over by someone else. We will leave as soon as I can make the arrangements."

Elizabeth's pulse raced and she looked at Jane in panic.

CHAPTER 3

Elizabeth wrote letters well into the night, spending more time scrounging for paper than in putting a pen to it. The simplest things had become objects of luxury and the search did nothing to ease Elizabeth's anxiety that she and her family could afford to live together comfortably on their meager pittance.

The following morning, she woke to the sounds of scrapes and bumps coming from downstairs. Wrapping a shawl around her shoulders, she tip-toed out of her room and down the hallway— though why she bothered to be quiet, she could not justify with all the noise coming from the drawing room.

Mother stood with the maid in front of a pile of mahogany furniture. Assorted samplers, silhouettes, ceramic figurines, and her bronze candelabra littered the floor. The maid's face was as red as the carpet and a trickle of sweat ran down her forehead to drip onto the floor as she leaned over to move what Mother pointed to.

"What is this?" Elizabeth asked. The drawing room was in

complete disorder. Pillows, tablecloths, and slipcovers were piled so highly on top of a chair, they looked like they would topple over if one made the mistake of breathing on them.

"I keep hoping that Mr. Bennet had enough sense to hide money somewhere. It is our lot to leave our home, but I refuse to leave it with anything that does not truly belong to the estate. Mr. Collins can keep the ancient furniture, but I will not leave anything of mine." She tapped her fingers against her chin and looked about the room.

Finding no fault with Mother's reasoning, but questioning her method and timing, Elizabeth asked, "And what are we to do with what you would take with us until it is time to leave?" She indicated the modest-sized pile in the middle of the room.

"I shall have it moved into the study. That room sees no use, and it will not be in anyone's way hidden away there."

Elizabeth cringed at the idea of Father's study being reduced to nothing more than a storage room. "Is there nowhere else?"

Mother ignored her remark.

"I am walking into Meryton to post some letters. Is there anything you need me to see to?" The maid looked up wistfully. No doubt, she would much rather walk into the village than move heavy objects around the house for Mother to inspect. Elizabeth was only too happy to escape the desecration which would take place in Father's study.

"Take your time, dear. I shall be much occupied and the fewer people milling about, the better," Mother said staring into a corner of the room she had not yet pillaged.

Already forgotten, Elizabeth started to go upstairs when the maid called out. "Will you be needing your spencer, miss?"

The weather had been wet and cold lately. Elizabeth did

not need to look out of the window to know what weather awaited her out of doors. "I should think so."

The maid wrung her hands together. "I had started the wash when I was called away."

That was unfortunate. "Did you find anything in the sleeves?" she asked casually, not wanting Mother to know that she hid a gentleman's handkerchief there. She would assume too much.

The maid nodded. "Everything is in the washtub."

Elizabeth had hoped to take it with her on the slight chance that she might see Mr. Darcy in passing. She had already kept it too long.

Borrowing Jane's spencer and an additional shawl, Elizabeth left the house shortly afterward.

The ground sloshed with each step she took, coating her boots with mud and seeping water into the loose seams around the sole no matter how she tried to avoid it. Her hem suffered too. She would have to wash her own dirty hems when they left Longbourn. They could hardly afford to take servants with them.

Where would they live? She prayed for a small cottage on the coast, somewhere not too far away.

Elizabeth remembered a trip she had taken to the seaside with Father when she was a child. It had something to do with an exposition, but what she remembered and treasured was spending all day with him. He had bought her a piece of peppermint, and they had gone to a place which had a great many books to see. The shelves went all the way up to the ceiling, and she had become dizzy trying to see the top. It had been a wonderful day. Maybe they could live near there. Sweet sadness slowed her pace.

"Excuse me, miss," said a velvety voice to her left, jolting Elizabeth out of her thoughts and forcing her with a thud back to reality. Her vision cleared of the cobwebs of past memories, and she recognized the stables leading into Meryton.

"I apologize for startling you," he said. Mr. Darcy wore the same black greatcoat and hat he had worn when he had offered her his handkerchief. He was exceedingly more handsome than she remembered him being through her tear-blurred vision from three days before.

Transfixed by the firm cut of his jaw and the kindness emanating from his chocolate brown eyes she, for a moment, forgot how to speak.

Recovering enough to put her tongue to use, she said, "Good morning, sir. Please do not trouble yourself. Had I paid any heed to my surroundings, I would not have been so easily startled."

He bowed, bringing himself closer to her stature where she could appreciate his features all the better. "I am Mr. Fitzwilliam Darcy of Pemberley. I am a guest at Netherfield Park. Please let me express my condolences for your recent loss." He watched her intently as if he expected a certain reaction.

Then she remembered. Of course. His handkerchief. With a curtsy, she said, "My name is Elizabeth Bennet of Longbourn…" Wait, Longbourn was no longer her home. "Or… at least I am for the time being. Thank you for the loan of your handkerchief, Mr. Darcy. I only apologize that I am unable to return it now, as I did not carry it with me today."

Mr. Darcy's brows furled. "Miss Bennet, it is an honor to finally make your acquaintance— especially so if you are soon to depart Longbourn. As you surely know, I had the privilege of meeting your father shortly before joining Mr. Bingley at Netherfield Park. He spoke highly of you." He held out his palms apologetically.

Her hand clutched the collar at her throat. Something

much stronger than curiosity bubbled under her tongue as myriads of questions rushed into her mind, overshadowing his remorseful stance.

He continued, his hands still out. "I had the pleasure of meeting him at my aunt's estate near Hunsford. I believe your cousin, Mr. Collins, is the rector there?"

Ah. That explained it. He was not apologetic. He was hesitant. How was he to know if she did not possess the same vexatious qualities as Mr. Collins? "Yes, he inherited Longbourn. I fear your aunt might soon find herself in need of another parson to fill his place once he occupies our home." The bitter words sounded hollow, and as soon as they were uttered, Elizabeth wished them unsaid. She had no reason to confide in Mr. Darcy, but it grew increasingly important that he not judge her based on his knowledge of Mr. Collins. Her neck grew hot as the impropriety of her comment sunk in.

Her eyes flickered up to Mr. Darcy's face, hoping not to see disapproval. She wanted him to think amiably of her, for she had nothing but kind thoughts toward him. The empathy he had shown, the understanding he had displayed in one simple act, had won her good opinion.

His features revealed nothing.

"Pray forgive me for speaking out of turn—" she began.

He held up his hand and shook his head. "Let me allay you of your worries, Miss Bennet, and reassure you that I think no less of you for your frankness than I did before."

He had thought of her before? Had Father said something to him? Intrigued all the more, Elizabeth sorted through the questions in her mind for the most appropriate.

"Thank you, Mr. Darcy. I do not understand to what I owe your understanding—"

A high-pitched voice interrupted. "Mr. Darcy, what are you doing standing in the mud?"

The owner of the whiny voice, a young lady, dressed in a

bold blue riding habit with a feather poking out of the matching blue silk band of her tilted hat, dismounted. She was accompanied by a young man who must surely be her brother. Both of them had fair hair, perfectly straight noses, and pointy chins.

Mr. Darcy sighed, his shoulders bunched up to his ears, before he turned toward the two joining them.

"Miss Bennet, allow me to introduce you to Mr. Charles Bingley of London and his sister, Miss Caroline Bingley."

Elizabeth waited for him to complete introductions before asking, "You are the gentleman who let Netherfield Park?"

Mr. Bingley bowed again, sweeping his hat through the air. Through a large smile, he said, "The very one. I am pleased to make your acquaintance, Miss Bennet. Please accept my condolences."

She liked him already. His manners were open and kind, and she wished Jane had accompanied her.

"Condolences for whom?" asked Miss Bingley, looking at her brother.

Mr. Bingley's unforgiving skin flushed bright red.

Mr. Darcy frowned deeply. “Miss Bennet’s father passed away recently,” he said quickly and quietly.

His help emboldened Elizabeth. She added, "My father died the day of the Meryton Assembly. Otherwise, we should have become acquaintances months ago." She expected tears to prickle her eyes, but was relieved when they did not.

"I am sorry for your loss, Miss Bennet," said Miss Bingley in a display of decency that surprised Elizabeth. She did not seem to be the sort of lady to concern herself with anyone other than herself.

Tossing her nose up in the air so that Mr. Bingley had to lunge out of way of the feather in her hat or risk being poked in the eye, Miss Bingley said, "My sister, Louisa, and I have felt the lack of satisfactory female company since our arrival. I realize that it may be too soon for you to pay social calls, but now that we are introduced, perhaps we might grace you with our presence or risk perishing from boredom before we return to the diversions of London."

"Caroline, really…" Mr. Bingley stopped, at a loss for words.

Her initial impression of the lady and of her brother thus confirmed, Elizabeth said, "It is a pity my eldest sister, Jane, did not walk with me this morning. I am certain that you would approve of her company." She was certain Mr. Bingley would approve of her too. Even with the subdued colors covering her thin frame, Jane's beauty shone through. She was head and shoulders more agreeable than Miss Bingley.

"I have found little difference between the accomplishments of a lady set up in town and a lady in the country. If anything, the country promotes greater opportunities in practical knowledge and improvement of the mind with fewer distractions and demands on her time. Let us not detain Miss Bennet any longer," Mr. Darcy suggested to the Bingleys. To Elizabeth, who bit her cheeks to suppress her smile, he said, "You came into Meryton for a reason, and we will not keep you from accomplishing what you set out to do." His dark eyes warmed her in spite of the cold breeze. A tuft of curly hair fell rebelliously over his forehead when he bowed to depart— the only implication of anything being out of place on his entire person. And as quickly as that, he left, herding his friends away with him.

While Elizabeth appreciated how efficiently he had led Miss Bingley and her thoughtlessness away from her, she was sad he had to go. He was everything considerate and compassionate. If what Miss Bingley implied was true, they were to leave soon. Elizabeth may not see him again.

She looked down at her hands, trying to remember why

she had walked into Meryton. The letters. Right. She had letters to post. Letters which, she hoped, would prove more successful than the previous batch she had sent and would keep her family together in a comfortable, albeit cramped, situation.

A letter from Uncle Gardiner had arrived in the post for Mother. She hugged it to her chest, trusting that it brought good news and would bring cheer to Longbourn. Though trips to London were few and far between— and would be even more so now— a stay with Uncle and Aunt Gardiner was always a welcome respite.

Elizabeth's fingers twitched to crack the red wax seal and read the letter, but she controlled her curiosity. She would hurry home and sit next to Mother until she shared its news. Mother had developed the bad habit of sending correspondence she thought to be bills up the chimney in smoke. Her hope that they would disappear if she ignored them long enough had yet to realize. Bills still came.

Her thoughts turning to money, she considered what options were available to her. Could she work as a governess? Perhaps she could find a position which would allow her to live nearby… No, that would not work. If they lived in London, they could never afford to live near enough to a family who would require a governess. Nor did Elizabeth feel qualified. Mary's skill on the pianoforte far exceeded hers. She could not embroider as neatly as Kitty. Though Elizabeth moved with grace, she was not nearly so talented as Lydia, who was a veritable encyclopedia of dance. Jane, though she was never bold enough to show her drawings to anyone, painted beautifully.

Each of her sisters displayed an area of talent, which, if put together, would make one formidable, accomplished lady. However, the talents they had were self-taught and lacked the polish of tutelage under the masters. And Elizabeth had yet to think of any great skill in her possession. Father had always complimented her intelligence— for all the good it did. If it was her great wit which had caused her to refuse Mr. Collins and lose her family's home, then surely she must be the wisest of homeless women.

CHAPTER 4

She must leave? Longbourn— her home— was lost? She must not have accepted Mr. Collins' offer after all. While Darcy's mind questioned her decision for practical purposes, his heart praised her refusal of a marriage of convenience. Could it be that she sought for the same, stout love he did? If only Miss Bingley had not called out and interrupted their conversation.

Darcy trudged across the muddy street. The less time he spent in Meryton, the better. He had no peace wherever he went. He had left Netherfield early to avoid Miss Bingley's irksome company, knowing full well that he might have to see Wickham, who had been stationed in Meryton for the winter. This stay in Hertfordshire grew more unpleasant as the days passed by, and if Bingley was inclined to leave, he would not dissuade him.

The only person he had hoped to see was Miss Elizabeth Bennet, and Miss Bingley had managed to ruin their conversation just when he was about to ask her about his letter. He would call at Mr. Phillips' office to ensure it had been sent.

At least they were introduced, albeit informally, and they

could speak more comfortably if they met again. He would not force his company on the Bennets unless he received reassurance from Mrs. Bennet that he would be welcome. He would respect her wishes and those of her daughters after what he had done.

"What are you pondering so intensely, Mr. Darcy?" Miss Bingley asked from behind him.

He turned back to see her panting to keep up with his long strides.

"Gracious, Darcy, but you walk with a purpose," commented Bingley.

Darcy stopped. Perhaps it would be considered rude to simply walk away, but he had learned long ago that being pleasant only encouraged those who were blind to his dislike. For Bingley's sake, he would endure.

"I have some letters to send and would like to see Mr. Phillips on a business matter while my stallion is shod. I had not planned to stay long in Meryton and was unaware of your plans to ride into the village or I should have waited for you. What brings you here?" he asked Bingley. He knew what— or rather who— brought Miss Bingley there.

"A need to get out of the house. The incessant rain has finally let up, and I felt that I should burst if I could not spend some time out of doors."

Darcy understood. He preferred open spaces as well.

"What is this about you thinking of leaving so soon after taking up residence at Netherfield?" Darcy asked.

Bingley looked accusingly at his sister. "Wishful thinking, I should think. Although, I have yet to see anything to keep me here. I do not yet feel attached to the place as I had hoped."

"Anything? Or anyone?" Darcy asked with a smile.

Flushing bright red, Bingley shuffled his feet. "You know

my reason for coming here. Yet, I have not found what I am looking for."

Pressing, Darcy asked, "And what might that be?" He knew the answer well, but wished for Bingley to speak decisively in front of his sister. Otherwise, she would have her way with no discussion.

"I have every intention of finding a wife with whom I may lead a quiet life in the country with the occasional trip into town."

Miss Bingley scoffed. "You would have much more success in your endeavor in town. Aside from Miss Bennet, whom we only recently met, there is a sore lack of accomplished ladies present. And I would not necessarily include Miss Bennet in that esteemed group. Did you see how muddy her boots were?" She looked quickly at Darcy with her chin up at a proud angle. Miss Bingley was proud of her accomplishments and considered herself to be a catch. Only no one had taken the bait as yet, much to her chagrin.

"I thought the exercise enhanced her lovely features. The fact that her boots were muddy says nothing about her accomplishments, but rather reveals a love of nature and healthy habits which every accomplished lady should possess," said Darcy.

Miss Bingley crossed her arms and harrumphed.

Ignoring her, Darcy asked Bingley, "I am curious as to what your plans are. Do you really intend to leave so soon?"

"I hardly know what to do, Darcy. What do you advise?" Bingley asked, scratching his head and further disheveling his wavy hair.

"We ought to return to town, Charles. There is nothing here to keep us." Miss Bingley rolled her eyes and threw her nose into the air, much too grand for the likes of Meryton and its surrounding estates.

Darcy grimaced at her interruption, though there was

truth in her statement. "I would suggest that you stay until you wish to leave. If the quiet life is what you crave, Netherfield Park is where you will choose to be. If marriage is your aim, you may choose to return to town where I hope you will meet with greater success during the season. I see no reason to make a hasty decision today."

"Capital idea! It is only one more month to the beginning of the season. If I find no reason to continue at Netherfield in a month's time, we shall depart for London. If, however, I do find sufficient reason to stay, I will be glad to have given Netherfield more time."

In a merrier mood, Bingley went in search of new acquaintances and friends among the officers in the regiment. It occurred to Darcy as he watched Miss Bingley reluctantly follow her brother that Bingley hoped to find a match for his sister as well as himself. It would suit Bingley for her to marry before he settled with a wife. An officer would be a good choice. Someone unafraid of confrontation and with a head for dealing with a conniving and oftentimes manipulative opponent. A picture of his cousin, Colonel Richard Fitzwilliam, loomed in his mind. He shivered it away. He would not wish that on his favorite cousin.

Looking over his shoulder down the road, Darcy wondered about Miss Elizabeth's character. He knew her to be hard-working, resourceful, and independent. Not the qualities he had thought would appeal to him.... And she was not engaged.

ELIZABETH WALKED HOME MORE SLOWLY than normal. Though the letter from Uncle Gardiner should have sped her steps, her thoughts of Mr. Darcy tempered her anticipation of his news. There was no denying that he was a handsome man—

tall, with a face of a gentleman and the solid body of a man who worked. Elizabeth welcomed the cold blast of breeze against her hot face.

That he showed a genuine depth of feeling was evident in his treatment of her. He had known loss intimately, of that she was certain. He knew how to console with a look, a simple gesture, and few words because he understood what it was to suffer.

At another time, she would be tempted to encourage his attention. As it was, she did not have the luxury of looking for romance. She needed to see to her family's immediate needs and keep them together. If she were blessed enough to find love, it would have to wait. She would see her sisters marry first. It was the penitence she would pay for refusing Mr. Collins and losing Longbourn. It was a small price to pay for her freedom. She was young, resourceful, and determined in her purpose. By this time, next year, she hoped to be in a better position to pursue her happiness freely.

Feeling as optimistic as a self-imposed martyr could, she paused as she entered the drive leading up to her front door. There was a cart full of crates blocking her path. Two men, each holding an end of a heavy wooden crate, heaved their burden onto the back of the cart and hurried back inside before she could ask what their business was.

Her body understood before her mind could comprehend what was happening. Her breath became shallow and she felt light-headed.

Jane rushed out of the house, wrapping her arms around Elizabeth. "I am so sorry I could not prevent this. I tried to talk her out of it," Jane cried into her neck.

CHAPTER 5

Breathing deeply to slow her heart before it leaped out of her chest, she grasped Jane on either arm.

"Jane?" she asked, desiring to understand, but afraid of the answer.

Without a word, Jane grabbed her hand and pulled her inside the house. Father's study door gaped open.

Elizabeth's stomach clenched and a wave of nausea rolled through her. She skimmed the bookshelves until her eyes burned. They were empty.

One final crate, the last, sat waiting for a stranger to cart it outside with the rest. When the man came inside to haul it away, Elizabeth moved to sit on top of it. But Jane, reading her thoughts, clung to her arm and held her back.

"Where are you taking my father's books?" she shouted through the hammer pounding in her head.

The man looked at her with large eyes and Jane tightened her grip on Elizabeth's arm.

"Lizzy, we must let him take the books. They are no longer ours. Even if Mother had not sold them, they would have to stay with the estate."

"But Father's books..." Elizabeth's voice choked into silence as the last crate disappeared through the front door never to be seen by her again. Never again could she run her fingers over the smooth covers; never again could she read her father's thoughts written in the margins; never again could she take comfort in the books which had bonded her to Father. She felt like she had lost him again.

Her eyes felt hot, but no tears would come. There were none left to shed. The room was as empty as she felt.

Bolting to the desk, she pulled open the drawers. Nothing. Her pulse throbbed through her. Clenching her jaw to spare Jane from the brunt of her anger, she asked, "Where is Father's journal?"

Jane's uncertain silence was all the answer she needed.

Elizabeth's nails bit into her palms as she tightened her fists and set out in search of her mother. Jane followed closely behind.

"Calm yourself, Lizzy. Please do not say anything you will later regret."

Elizabeth did not answer.

"Lizzy, slow down. Calm yourself, I beg of you," entreated Jane from behind her. She grabbed Elizabeth's hand to hold her back.

Stealing her hand away, Elizabeth charged up the stairs to Mother's room, where she would no doubt be found fanning herself in a senseless fit of nerves.

Her eyes trained on the fainting couch as she burst through the door, Elizabeth was taken aback to see that Mother was not resting leisurely. Rather, she stood giving directions to the housekeeper, a healthy, pink glow on her face. She looked as if she were planning a coming out ball or some grand social event which would put her daughters in the way of eligible gentlemen of fortune. She looked much too happy and Elizabeth's ire burned inside her.

Catching her eye, Mother waved her over to join them. "It is good that you are here, Lizzy. I have been giving instructions on what to pack. It makes me sad to leave all the servants behind, but I trust that Mr. Collins can keep them on the estate." She spat his name out like a dirty word she would scold Lydia for saying. "I want to move our household to London. I realize the difficulties and the expense involved, but I have sold some items to help."

Elizabeth gasped. "London? Is that why you sold Father's books? So that you may set yourself up in London to live out all of your silly fancies? How could you?" She lashed out, knowing her words would hurt.

Jane dropped into a chair, her hands at her temples.

Rubbing her hands together and pursing her lips, Mother said, "I have my reasons, Elizabeth. You may call them silly— it is what Mr. Bennet would have done— but I am your mother, and I am acting for your benefit whether you realize it or not. We shall be uncomfortable for a time, but it is the best place for us to be during the season."

Of course. She would marry off her girls as she had always dreamed of doing. A marriage of convenience had been sufficient for her, and now she expected her daughters to follow her example. Elizabeth would rather seek employment than suffer in an unequal marriage.

"Is that why you sold Father's books? For the coin?"

"I had no choice. I found no money hidden, though I searched through and poked into every nook and cranny in the house. Mr. Bennet's books were one of the items with the most value in our home. You know how dear books are. I am surprised you should ask."

Had Mother completely lost her senses? "They were not ours to sell. What will Mr. Collins say?" Never mind her emotional attachment to the precious tomes. Mother would never understand that. She may as well speak Latin to her for all the good it would do.

Mother waved away her argument. Before she could answer, a knock sounded on the door.

"Mrs. Phillips is here for you, ma'am," Martha announced. She hardly had time to move out of the doorway when in walked Aunt Phillips.

"Fanny, how are you doing today? You have a lovely flush to your complexion. I do declare that you look ten years younger than when I last saw you. Mr. Phillips wanted me to inquire if the man's servants were able to take the books off your hands as was arranged?"

Aunt Phillips' eyebrows shot up in twin question marks.

With an unperturbed look at Elizabeth, Mother said, "Yes, everything has been handled to our satisfaction. So long as Mr. Phillips received the price agreed upon, I am content."

Bobbing her head up and down, Aunt Phillips said, "Of course. The gentleman who purchased the library has been most honorable and did not argue over the price."

Sensing an opportunity to undo the damage done by Mother, Elizabeth demanded, "Who purchased Father's books?" Perhaps, just perhaps, there was the smallest chance Elizabeth might persuade the new owner to part with one book for her to remember Father by. At the least she would recover his diary.

"You know that Mr. Phillips is the pinnacle of discretion, dear. Though he speaks in a general manner of his business affairs, as a responsible attorney, he never mentions names nor specifics to me." She shook her head at the suggestion that Uncle might have been so untoward as to discuss something which might have been so helpful to Elizabeth. She crossed her arms and planned. She would need to return to Meryton and speak with Uncle directly.

Taking a seat next to Mother, Aunt Phillips asked, "Fanny,

has your tea been packed? I am positively parched! I have rearranged my guest rooms to suit Mary and Kitty, and the work has been fatiguing."

Elizabeth tensed. "Mary and Kitty? Why would you prepare rooms for them at your house?" She placed a hand over her heart to calm the pounding. Jane appeared every bit as confused as she was.

Mother and Aunt Phillips exchanged a look. Mother was not pleased, but it was she who spoke. "Your dear aunt has offered to keep Mary and Kitty with her while we move on to London. The advantages she and Mr. Phillips can offer the girls far outweigh any advantage they might have in London with us."

Elizabeth sucked air into her lungs, but it was so heavy around her, she may as well have breathed in water. This day could not get worse. Had she not gone completely numb, Elizabeth would have pinched herself. This could not be real.

Quickly, Mother added, "It is understood by all concerned that if we establish ourselves successfully, they are to join us. I only meant to give them a stable home on the small chance that it does not fare so well with us."

Elizabeth clasped her shaking hands together.

The tea had not been brought up yet, and Aunt Phillips still had news to share, but Elizabeth could not stand to stay in the room any longer. Mother looked excited— as if the loss of Father led her to a new life full of adventure and thrilling prospects. It made Elizabeth sick. She needed to get away.

If they noticed her leave, they did not say anything. She made it down the stairs and outside before she bent over with her hands on her knees to gasp for breath just as she had after a strong run as a child. Only, this was so different. Instead of recovering her breath, it drew more difficult as the seconds passed.

Pressed from all sides and hating herself for being so weak when she must be the strong one, she started walking toward Meryton. If Aunt Phillips refused to cooperate, then she would appeal to Uncle Phillips.

Raising her head and squaring her shoulders, Elizabeth marched on, her vision closing in on the path before her.

CHAPTER 6

Miss Elizabeth marched like she was on a mission. Her cheeks flamed red and her eyes flashed with an intensity which made it difficult for him to wrench his gaze away from her. Before he could stop himself, he called out to her from atop his horse. "Miss Bennet!"

She slowed, shaking her head as if waking from a dream. But she did not stop.

Waving his hand in front of him, he repeated, "Miss Bennet!" before he could stop himself. He touched his heels to the side of his borrowed horse to move closer.

He ought to have let her go. Riding a loaned horse while his mount's hooves were attended to at the farrier's, he remembered what the man at the stables had warned him about. It was too late.

Jolting forward, directly toward Miss Elizabeth, the brute reared up on his hind legs with a shrill neigh. Turning to the side with no regard for his surroundings— only the desperate need to escape whatever had tickled his ribs— the stallion made to knock Miss Elizabeth over.

With a cry, she held her arms in front of her face, stepped back, and disappeared with shocking speed.

Holding the reins steady, Darcy kept control over the adrenaline surging through him and calmed the animal. He looked to the edge of the road where Miss Elizabeth had been walking, but found her sitting on a ridge where carriage wheels had carved a deep rut. She clasped her ankle and winced until she noticed him looking at her. Instantly, her face straightened and she attempted to stand.

Darcy's anger at himself rose as he dismounted to assist her. Why had he insisted on getting her attention when he ought to have let her continue her peaceful walk into the village? Why could he not leave Miss Elizabeth alone?

Her attempts to stand had only muddied her hands as she tried again and again with no success. Feeling more and more like a brute deserving of a lashing, he went to her.

"Miss Bennet, I apologize. My thoughtlessness caused you harm and I beg for your pardon. Please, let me assist you." Would there ever be a time he would not need to seek her forgiveness?

"No, Mr. Darcy. I am quite well," she insisted, trying to stand and failing for the fourth time.

"You are in pain," he said, cursing himself.

"It is not so bad. If I could only stand, I could walk," she insisted in vain.

"Miss Bennet, you are not well, and it is my doing. Please, allow me to help you. Do I have your permission to ascertain if there has been a break?" It was a bold question, but under the circumstances, there was no alternative. They were half-way between Longbourn and Meryton, surrounded only by fields. He gave her a look which he hoped would reassure her.

It must have worked, for after looking around herself for help and seeing that there was none, she nodded her head.

"I will have to remove your boot," he added as he knelt down at her feet. He would not dare touch her without her full permission.

She looked around again. He did too. Were anyone to chance upon them, it would be blasted awkward to explain what had happened.

Leaning back and sighing in resignation, she said, "I do not have much of a choice, do I? I have twisted my ankle before, but not badly enough to prevent me from standing."

Unlacing her boot, he removed it without disturbing her ankle overmuch. He imagined the angry, red swelling under her mended wool stocking. Just under her ankle bone her flesh was noticeably more swollen than it ought to have been. Gritting his teeth together, he willed himself to focus only on the task before him with the cold, calculating precision of one experienced in ascertaining an injury. Waving his hand to cool his fingers, he pressed his hand gently over the thin wool covering her hot, inflamed skin. She flinched, then relaxed as the coolness relieved some of her pain.

"Is that better?" he asked. He was not better, blast it all!

"Yes," she whispered through her breath.

He looked up at her. Her lips parted and she closed her eyes. Her dark eyelashes skimmed the tops of her flushed cheeks. He only realized he had been staring when she opened her eyes to lock with his.

Clearing his throat, he said, "I will have to touch the bones here." He skimmed his fingers over the swollen skin.

"Do what you must, but please hurry. I am more concerned at being seen in such a compromising position than I am in the pain."

Sensible lady. How many women had intentionally set up traps to compromise him since he had inherited Pemberley? Of course, they hardly knew each other. He had to remind himself that he knew a great deal more about her than she did of him. She would only know of his great fault against her father, and he still did not know if she had forgiven him.

She winced when he moved his hand. About to apologize yet again, she cut him short. "Please tell me how you became so knowledgeable in sprains and broken bones."

"I grew up near my male cousins."

He felt her ankle as quickly and thoroughly as he could, grateful for all the practice he had had over the years tending to wounds and scrapes with his Fitzwilliam cousins.

She attempted to smile. "I only have sisters, and we got into more than enough scrapes without the rougher play of boys."

Placing her boot unlaced on her petite foot, he said, "It is not broken, but you have suffered a sprain— one which will keep you off your feet for up to a week, I think."

She pinched her lips together and bunched up her chin. Punching the damp earth with a fist, she shook her head and cackled bitterly. "Now all I need is for it to rain and for my mother to drive by. I can think of no other way this day could get any worse."

Her frustration increased his guilt.

"Please allow me to see you safely home. You are in no condition to walk." He extended a hand out to her.

SHE LOOKED AROUND AGAIN, hoping that a carriage might cross their path. A carriage would be the best way to convey her to Uncle Phillips' and then home. Merely thinking of her ankle made it throb all the more. Very well then, she would have to forgo her trip to Uncle. She punched the ground next to her again. Father's books would be gone by the time she could get to him.

Mr. Darcy held his extended hand out steadily, with no

flinch of indecision. His expression inspired trust. He seemed to be just as embarrassed as she was, judging from the blush across his cheeks.

Taking his hand, she let him pull her up to stand on one foot. She hopped a few times to gain her balance, refusing to take his arm until her sensibility overcame her pride. Several preferable circumstances popped into her mind in which she would be proud to take his arm, but she dreaded for him to think her feeble. She did not know Mr. Darcy very well, but she knew enough about him to know that he was not weak. Nor would he appreciate weakness in others.

She looked between him and his horse, her voice trembling despite herself. "How do you intend to return me to Longbourn?" Please let it not be by horse... She held her breath.

"You shall ride my horse."

Attempting to disguise her panic with humor, she said, "That brute that nearly knocked me over?"

In a tone similar to her own, he responded, "Would you rather I carry you?"

"Yes!" she wished to say wholeheartedly, but she swallowed hard instead. "I understand your predicament, Mr. Darcy, and I thank you for your gentlemanly manners toward me. But...," she inhaled. "I have not sat on top of a horse these ten years," she said in a rush through her exhale.

Mr. Darcy turned in order to stare at her more directly. "Ten years? How is that possible?" The astonishment covering his handsome features made her smile to minimize her own ridiculousness.

In one final attempt she tried to put her foot down and was deeply sorry she did. Groaning in pain as the blood rushed to pulsate in her ankle, she doubled over at the waist while clinging to Mr. Darcy's arm for support.

"I fear I have no choice in the matter today," she said,

straightening up after the initial jolt turned into a steady throb. How she wished he would wrap his cool hands around it as he had earlier. His touch had sent chills up her limbs until she felt as if her hair stood on end. The memory of it made her reach up to smooth her coiffure.

Hopping toward the horse, her jaw tensing with every inch she drew closer to the saddle, she looked up at the stirrup. It looked so high, it seemed to be an impossible task to get up in the saddle. Why did gentlemen prefer such tall mounts? How on earth was she supposed to get up there? Why could they not ride ponies?

Looking up at Mr. Darcy, who stood head and shoulders above her, she nearly laughed at the image in her mind of his long legs touching the ground as he sat astride a pony.

"Is there something you find amusing, Miss Bennet?" he asked. Was he teasing her? She could not read his expression.

What had she to lose? Without a doubt, he must think her one of the most ridiculous women of his acquaintance. "I was wondering how I am supposed to get up there." She nudged her chin in the direction of the saddle. "And I was wishing that you had arrived riding on a pony so that I might have a chance of keeping my dignity intact while mounting."

His lips curled up on one side, revealing an appreciation for her odd sense of humor. "If only you knew, you would not tease me so."

With a deft swoop, he encircled his hands around her waist and plopped her on top of his horse. She closed her mouth to prevent her heart from leaping out of it, and scrambled to entwine her fingers in the stallion's mane before she toppled off. If she had bumped her ankle in the process, she did not know it. Her nerves were on fire.

Embarrassingly aware of how her skin burned at the forced intimacy Mr. Darcy had been obliged to take, she tried to remember what he had said before her thoughts evaporated into thin air. Ponies… It was something about a pony. Ah!

"If your intention in making such a comment was to distract me from the horse, it did not work, sir. If it was to pique my curiosity, then you have succeeded immensely."

Silently, he grabbed the reins and turned in the direction of Longbourn. The jolt as the horse took its first steps made Elizabeth yelp in fright before she could stop herself.

Mr. Darcy slowed his pace. "I will lead him slowly and steadily. I will not allow any more harm to come to you." His voice, lowered into a calm monotonous tone to calm both her and the horse, was reassuring. As was the intensity and confidence in his eyes as he spoke.

Loosening her hold on the mane, she sat up in her seat and nodded for Mr. Darcy to lead on. She trusted him.

They moved in silence for a short time, during which Elizabeth observed the gentleman in front of her. His dark hair curled up over his collar, reaching up as if it would push off his hat. He was taller than most men. He would never have difficulty reaching a book on the top shelf.

She sighed louder than she had meant to. It had been weeks since she had shed tears over losing Father. She thought she had begun to heal, but with his books gone, it felt as if the healing wound had been opened back up to leave her vulnerable and aching all over again. Why had Mother not consulted with her?

"Excuse me?" asked Mr. Darcy, who on top of his many compassionate qualities, apparently had excellent hearing.

"I merely remembered the reason why I wanted to walk into Meryton…" she paused, considering whether she should continue or not. Should she tell him? Or would he feel that she offered details much too intimate for such a recent acquaintance?

She tried to hold the words back, feeling it inappropriate

to unburden herself on a near stranger. But his posture changed. A slight tilt of the head and a relaxing of the shoulders invited her to continue.

"I was on my way to see my uncle. He is an attorney in the village and has been helping us arrange affairs after the death of my father." Her throat tightened, but she pressed on. "I am grateful for the support he and Aunt Phillips have given to us, but this morning, he assisted my mother in the sale of Father's books." Her voice cracked and she had to stop. Biting her lips to hold back the emotion which would embarrass her further, she sat quietly rocking atop the slowly moving horse. Her fingers reached for the handkerchief tucked up her sleeve before she remembered that she wore a borrowed spencer.

She looked out over the verdant fields, willing her eyes to focus through the unshed tears.

"It was the small things, the seemingly meaningless details which pained me the most after my mother and then my father died. There would come a day when I would think I had waded through the worst— that all would be well, and I could remember the past like a sweet memory. Then, it would happen. A favorite line of poetry shared, the blossoming of Mother's favorite flower in the middle of a field, a deep laugh that had me searching the room for my father..." His soft words melted into Elizabeth's heart. He understood.

He turned to look at her directly. "I am sorry for the loss of your books."

Elizabeth wished he would keep talking, but he turned and clicked his tongue at the horse to continue their slow walk back to Longbourn.

CHAPTER 7

It should not have surprised Elizabeth to learn firsthand that Mr. Darcy was a man of few words. After all, when he had given her his handkerchief at their first meeting, he had not said a word. He had not needed to.

Never lacking in conversation, and needing to do something other than sit silently and stew on Mother's many faults as he led his horse along, she decided to learn what she could about him, though very little it might be.

"Are you enjoying your stay in Hertfordshire?" she asked, starting with a safe topic. Next, she should mention the weather.

"The countryside is pleasant. I have enjoyed many long rides through the hills and the distance to London is not so great as to prevent frequent trips into town when necessary." He did not sound convinced, but she appreciated his effort.

"I love walking over the fields and roads around Longbourn. Only, I have not been able to go so often as I am accustomed to these past few months." What with estate affairs to see to and Jane's fever, she had not ventured out as much as she would like. Otherwise, she surely would have met Mr. Darcy before now. Oh, she almost forgot to mention the weather. “Is the weather to your liking?”

“It has rained a good deal.”

She looked down at her muddy boots. "If you do not mind me asking, how do you know my uncle?"

Looking to the side so she could hear him and see his profile, Mr. Darcy said, "Mr. Phillips has helped me recently in some business matters during my stay in Hertfordshire. I found it easier to speak with him directly than to arrange for my man in town to travel here. Your uncle has been efficient and conducts himself honestly in his dealings."

Smiling at the compliment to her relative, she said, "I am glad to hear that he has won your approval. Two of my younger sisters are to stay with him and Aunt while the rest of us leave for London." She bit her tongue, knowing she shared too much, but wanting to talk about how much her life had changed so badly. Someone who understood. Someone who would not pat her on the shoulder and unthinkingly repeat that everything would be all right.

"From what I know of the gentleman, I am certain that your sisters will feel the advantage of stability in his home." He looked over his shoulder at her and hesitated as if he would ask her more.

It was foolish of her to expect comfort from a stranger. Of course he would only see the practical. "I have never been separated from my family before, and I admit that my dearest wish is to keep everyone together. I know in my mind that they stand to benefit greatly, but perhaps it is my selfishness which clings to my desire to keep them near."

"It is never selfish to want to be close to the ones you love. London is not far," he said softly.

"It is very far indeed when you have no means to travel the distance. I know where my obligations lie, and I refuse to settle for anything less than what I am willing to fight for."

Her chest heaved up and down in the intensity of her passion, and she wished she possessed even a small fraction of the calm reserve Mr. Darcy mastered.

Slowing until they almost came to a stop, Mr. Darcy turned. "I can find no fault with that. Life is lived but once, and you should never complacently accept any fate other than the one you desire when it is within your reach to grasp for it. I wish you success with your endeavors… whatever they may be."

Elizabeth did not know what her endeavors were at the present, her efforts to keep her family together having been pulled out from under her feet. Here was a gentleman— a successful gentleman with a good grasp on reality— and he believed in her, yet every decision she had made had negatively affected her family. She ought to be proud to inspire such confidence. Instead, she felt the tears sting her eyes and stuff up her nose.

Mr. Darcy turned again, piercing her through with the intensity in his eyes. It was as if he saw through her. His eyebrows bunched together, casting a melancholy shadow over his face. "You do not seem to me to be one to allow yourself to dwell in sadness. The very tilt of your eyes suits itself more agreeably to amusement."

Could she hide nothing from the man? Sighing in surrender, she admitted, "I dearly loved to laugh. But now, I feel guilty. How can I feel happy when one I held dearest in my life will never laugh with me again? It feels like a sort of betrayal. I know it makes no sense, but I cannot make sense of death either. It happens every day— we are surrounded by it in nature— but it does not feel natural to me. Otherwise, I should be able to better manage these emotions which would crush me." She wiped at her eyes. How improperly she acted, yet she could not restrain herself. She tried to console herself with the idea that she had no reason to believe she would ever see Mr. Darcy again once they left Hertfordshire... if consolation meant yearning for conversation she would never have again, then her plan was perfect.

~

DARCY LED the horse at the speed of a snail's crawl. It was easy enough to justify. Miss Elizabeth was afraid of horses. She put on a brave show, but the white of her knuckles as she grasped the horse's mane belied her fear. With her injured ankle, he would do nothing to cause her further pain. However, the truth of the matter was that he enjoyed her company. He had been drawn to her before, but this singular opportunity borne of disaster gave him the chance to converse with her... and he liked her all the more as a result of it.

It was a sound he had no right to, but he dearly wished to hear her laugh. It was plain to see that her merry temperament felt crushed under the weight of her grief and guilt. Though, why she should feel guilty, he did not fully comprehend. He, on the other hand...

"Your father must have been a remarkable man. Please tell me: Would he approve of your self-imposed guilt?" he asked.

She answered without hesitation. "No. He would want me to be happy."

"Sensible man."

"Yes... in some ways. My father was a great thinker. He had a great sense for the ironic and ridiculous, and he taught me to appreciate them as well."

"You mentioned his library... What sort of books did he enjoy reading?"

A deep sigh escaped her. "He had books about everything which tickled his fancy. Philosophy, poetry, botany, even novels... I had hoped to secure one of his books to keep in memory of him. He always wrote notes in the margins and underlined the words he most enjoyed."

"A reasonable request. I take it that you were unable to secure a book before they were sold?"

Her silence answered the question as clearly as a direct answer.

"I see. You do not know who bought them?" he persisted.

"No. That was the purpose of my walk into the village to see my uncle. I meant to ask him who bought the books. I know it was a fruitless mission. I would have all of the books returned to Longbourn so that I could see them some day. Now, I do not know where the books are and have no hope of ever seeing them again."

It was the perfect opportunity to ask her opinion of his letter— or if Mrs. Bennet had bothered to share it. However, Mr. Phillips had assured him that his letter had been delivered discreetly. He would simply have to trust him. Miss Elizabeth needed comfort more than he needed reassurance.

"It is painful to part with something of great value, but it is also difficult to be surrounded by things which constantly remind you of your loss."

"I am sorry you have suffered."

He looked back to see her head bowed, her soft brown hair caressing her face in the breeze.

Though it had all happened years ago, he recalled the emotions as if it were yesterday. Time had softened them, but he remembered. "When my mother died, my father had a difficult time of it. We felt her presence in every room of the house and it pained us greatly to be reminded of her at every turn. Of course, with the passing of time, sentiments dull no matter how much you hold onto the grief. It is both a blessing and a curse to let go. There is some satisfaction in holding on to it, but living in the past does not bode well for a promising future."

She was quiet for so long, he looked over his shoulder. She looked as if she had been struck. Had he said too much? Blast it all! He ought to have kept his mouth shut. What made him think he could help her? Why did he even bother?

"Thank you." She spoke softly, putting an end to his self-rebukes.

She sniffed and the horse pricked his ears up and bobbed his head up and down when she shifted her weight in the saddle. “Enough melancholy conversation, Mr. Darcy. Let us talk about happier things. You mentioned a pony?”

Darcy groaned. The story was humiliating, but it was his mistake to have mentioned it at all. Diving in before he could change his mind, he said, "I trust you will share my secret with no one." He looked back to see Miss Elizabeth's curious face regarding him with an impish smile.

"I was desperate to see my little sister, Georgiana, smile again after our father had passed away. After some months of moping, I invited her out for a ride. She had a lovely pony which was suffering from neglect, and I hoped that she would find comfort in taking care of it. But as determined as I was to see Georgiana happy, she was equally determined to continue in her misery.” Nearing the embarrassing part, he took a deep breath to continue.

“I did what any brother would do in my circumstances. I lured her outside. My blood stallion stood saddled and ready next to her pony. When she refused to mount, I…” This was more difficult than he had thought.

“You what?” asked Miss Elizabeth, leaning forward in the saddle. The corner of her lip curled up into the promise of a smile.

Thus encouraged, Darcy continued, “I hopped onto her pony. She was so pleased to have someone to ride her, she took off at a run across the field. It was all I could do to stay astride in Georgiana’s sidesaddle. It was… jolting.”

He could have cut his pony ride short, but his little sister had made the most glorious sounds, so he endured until she lost her breath from laughing so much— the same glorious sounds which now emanated from Miss Elizabeth.

She did try to hold back, but when he grinned back at her, her delicacy of manners gave way to peals of laughter which washed away any shame he felt at telling the story just as Georgie's smile had when he rode her pony.

The jingling of mirth gave way to the jingle of chains and the clomping of nearing hooves. A carriage approached.

"Oh dear," Miss Elizabeth said, noticing the carriage as Darcy led the horse to the side of the road.

CHAPTER 8

Maybe the people in the carriage would take no note of her. Anyone living in, near, or within a day's walking distance of Meryton knew her aversion to horses. They would conjure up all sorts of unflattering explanations for her to be sitting on a horse led by a single gentleman. Not that the real explanation was entirely satisfactory either...

Now that they were so near Longbourn, she had held high hopes that she would go completely unseen.

"Whatever happens, Mr. Darcy, my mother must never know how you helped me."

He looked hurt. "Do you intend to hop all the way to your door? Miss Bennet, your mother may not wish to see me, but I cannot leave you like this."

Of course, none of that mattered if the people in the coach blabbed to Mother. She had planned to have Mr. Darcy leave her— no matter how much he would protest— on the gravel path leading to the house. It was partially hidden by the corner of the barn. She would have hobbled to the door, or hopped the distance on one foot if necessary, but she had no intention of her mother seeing her arrive with Mr. Darcy. Mother would draw all of the wrong conclusions and she would lose Mr. Darcy's friendship.

"It would only complicate matters if my mother were to see you, and I would rather not cause you any unnecessary trouble."

He closed his eyes and leaned his head down. In a low voice, he said, "Let us see what happens with the carriage before we make any plans. It could be that your worry is for naught."

The carriage drew nearer, and she did her best to appear as if nothing were untoward. She was participating in an activity which was enjoyed by young ladies all over England. Of course, she had not heard of any who required a gentleman to lead their horse for them, but that was beside the point.

"Lizzy!" a masculine voice called out from behind her, making her cringe before awareness dawned.

"Could it be?" She turned as far as she dared without falling off the side of the horse.

"Lizzy!" called a feminine voice. Elizabeth was certain now.

"Thank goodness," she said under her breath for the benefit of Mr. Darcy, who looked every bit as nervous as she had felt before recognizing the familiar calls of her relatives.

The carriage stopped next to them and Mr. Darcy led the horse back to the path. The door opened and Uncle Gardiner stepped out. Aunt Gardiner peeked out of the door, her body leaning out into the open space.

"Uncle Gardiner! Aunt Gardiner! How glad I am to see you! Are you on your way to Longbourn? I did not know to expect you."

It puzzled her to see the look her aunt and uncle exchanged.

"Why, Lizzy, we came today as agreed upon with Fanny... excuse me, Mrs. Bennet...," he said, acknowledging Mr. Darcy.

"Pardon my manners. Please let me introduce you to Mr. Darcy." After introductions, she offered a brief explanation, "I took a fall in the road and twisted my ankle. Mr. Darcy has been so kind as to assist me home."

That brought understanding nods from her relatives, although the quizzical looks remained.

"Your mother did not tell you that we would arrive today to convey you and Jane to London?" asked Uncle Gardiner.

Elizabeth went numb, and she rubbed her fingers together to warm them. They felt like ice.

"No. We only received a letter from you this morning. I did not open it since it was addressed to Mother. We are to leave Longbourn today?" She looked around her. Could it be that she would be forced to leave her home so soon? "Mother said that we would leave before the end of the month, but I had no idea that she had arranged for us to leave so soon."

Uncle shook his head, his shoulders slumped. "I knew we should have written to you as well, Lizzy. I am sorry. Your mother has been busy making plans and arrangements and, knowing my sister as I do, I feel confident in implying that she simply forgot to communicate her plans to you."

Mother had made arrangements without her? What of all the people she had written to about the possibility of renting a cottage? Both shocked that Mother had taken the initiative and hurt that she had done so apart from Elizabeth's knowledge, she gaped speechlessly at Uncle.

"Come, Lizzy, let us take you home to London with us. I have missed you dearly and your little cousins have missed Jane. They eagerly await our return on the morrow." Aunt Gardiner spoke in a friendly tone.

Under any other circumstance, Elizabeth would be

thrilled to leave with them. However, this was different. This time, when she left, she had no guarantee that she could ever come back. It felt like such a great step to take. Like a commitment she was unprepared for and was being forced to make.

Unprepared to give an answer at that moment, she addressed Mr. Darcy, who stood patiently holding the head of his horse.

"Mr. Darcy, I thank you for seeing me this far. I think it best for all concerned if my uncle saw me the rest of the way home. The fewer times we have to explain the happenings of this afternoon, the better." She smiled, hoping that he would not insist on seeing her home or ask any questions.

"Of course, Miss Bennet. Mr. Gardiner, can you please help her down and between both of us, we can assist her into the carriage? Take care of her right ankle. It is badly sprained."

Elizabeth watched for any sign that he regretted the interruption to their time together, but he revealed nothing. Really, it was for the best. Had she not been scheming how to arrive at Longbourn without Mother seeing Mr. Darcy? She ought to be pleased.

Uncle reached up to help her slide down the side of the horse. His effort was not executed nearly so smoothly as Mr. Darcy's had been when he lifted her onto the saddle as if she weighed no more than a feather. Stabbing pain shot up her leg as her foot touched the ground. Mr. Darcy reached out to take her side opposite Uncle Gardiner and between the two men, she hopped to the carriage.

Getting into the carriage was another ordeal entirely, but between her relatives and Mr. Darcy, she was finally able to sit with her injured ankle propped up on the seat in front of her.

Mr. Darcy and Uncle had a brief exchange, and all too

soon, Elizabeth found herself traveling the short distance remaining to her home. She looked out of the window to see if Mr. Darcy was in view. She had enjoyed his conversation. She would miss seeing him.

~

Mrs. Bennet had read his letter and she did not wish to see him. It was as he suspected, but he had held out some hope that she might forgive him. However, by all appearances, Miss Elizabeth thought no worse of him. She was too honest to hide it, and why should she? He had wronged her father abominably. He could only conclude that Miss Elizabeth Bennet was a far better person than he, and he would do everything in his power to deserve her good opinion.

He reached into his pocket and pulled out Mr. Gardiner's card to look at his address. Gracechurch Street, London. Darcy did not have any acquaintances in that part of town. Perhaps it was time to widen out in his friendships. After all, Bingley was a man of trade, and he had proved himself to be a good and loyal friend over the years.

Patting the stable horse on the neck, he mounted to return to Netherfield Park. He looked back at the road just as the coach disappeared from view. It was for the best that the Gardiners had shown up when they had. He was beginning to like Miss Elizabeth. Very much. She spoke freely and he could tell what her mood was at a glance. Her honesty drew him in as surely as Miss Bingley's coquetries repelled him.

Drawing nearer to Netherfield Park, Darcy braced himself for another encounter with Miss Bingley. It was a pity to see a lady disposed toward a strong character weaken herself out of a desire to exalt herself in the eyes of others or flatter them. She ought not give importance to the opinions of others. Darcy certainly did not care for what others thought of him. He was fairly certain that Miss Elizabeth did not either. For one so young and inexperienced in the world, she spoke her opinions freely. Darcy's doubts of her forgiveness diminished. If she held him responsible for her father's death, she never would have spoken so openly with him. She would not have allowed him to help her— no matter how badly she was in need. She was too honest to act duplicitously.

As the grass turned to gravel, Darcy tightened his hold on the reins, slowing his horse from a canter to a walk. A stable boy immediately came out to take the horse away.

"Mr. Darcy, is your horse well?" the boy asked, confusion across his face.

"It was time for him to be clipped and shod. Instead of waiting, I decided to borrow this horse until the farrier could finish his work. Would you see that he gets an apple before the groom returns him to the stables in Meryton?" Except for his ticklish ribs, the horse had behaved gently with Miss Elizabeth on his back. Such behavior deserved a reward.

"Aye, sir." The boy scrambled off with the horse trotting behind him in search of a treat.

The front doors to the house were wide open, causing Darcy to pause at the bottom of the stairs.

In the entrance hall, he counted three trunks stacked on top of each other. Miss Bingley's maid scurried down the stairs, her arms full. Miss Bingley's penetrating voice trailed after her. "I have one more thing for you, Maria. I will not leave anything behind."

An inquiry to the butler as to Bingley's location led him upstairs where he found his friend standing in the middle of his room. Bingley's valet packed a travel trunk. "Shall I pack all of your things, sir?" he asked.

Bingley tugged at his hair and paced the room. "What am

I to do with her? She will be the death of me and she is twice my age!"

When he saw Darcy, he trudged over to the doorway where Darcy stood.

"She has done it this time, Darcy! This time Aunt Lavinia really has done it!"

CHAPTER 9

Darcy braced himself against the frame of the door and crossed his arms. Nothing would surprise him where Lady Lavinia Rutledge was involved.

Bingley paced and gesticulated wildly. "I received a message from Colonel Fitzwilliam only an hour ago."

Darcy stood at attention. “Richard? I do hope he has not involved himself in one of her schemes.” Richard had a soft spot for Lady Rutledge, as she did for him.

“Thank goodness he was there to control the damage my reckless aunt could have caused. As it is, no charges will be pressed, but I must return to London this evening. Father put me in charge of keeping an eye on her while he and Mother are away. I had no idea how much of a bother it would be." He ran his fingers through his hair. “I never should have left London, but she behaved well long enough that I let my guard down.”

Darcy walked in and took a seat in a chair just inside the room. He motioned for Bingley to join him. "Fretting will not help you. You must calm yourself and think with a level head. Obviously, your parents believed you capable of keeping Lady Rutledge safe from harm or else they would not have entrusted you with such a duty." While uttering the words, Darcy was secretly relieved he had not been charged with such an insurmountable task. He had thought when he heard of Mr. and Mrs. Bingley's departure to the New World to seek out partners in trade that they were going for the express purpose of escaping from Mr. Bingley's eldest sister.

"It is not Aunt's safety which gives me concern, but rather the safety of others who cross her path!"

Biting the insides of his cheeks to keep from smiling, Darcy asked, "What has she done now?"

Bingley fidgeted in his chair, bouncing first one knee up and down, then switching to the other between pulls of hair. "The real question is: What has she *not* done? I left her in good faith based on her reasonable conduct over the past few months, and now I worry that I shall not be able to depart from London again until Mother and Father's return... whenever that may be! I had expected them home by now." He leaned forward, elbows propped up on his knees, and massaged his temples.

"I doubt that your aunt sees the need for someone to watch over her constantly. She is, after all, a widow of means."

"That is part of the problem. Aunt has too much money and idle time."

Darcy could not keep himself from saying, "A most dangerous combination," with a grin.

Bingley ignored his jest. "I had hoped that with the passing of the years, she would settle, but that does not seem to be the case with her. She would sooner die in a carriage accident than peacefully of a ripe, good age in her own home."

Darcy sat up. "Is that what happened? Did she suffer an accident?"

Bingley pinched the back of his neck. When he lifted his head, he nodded. "That is precisely what happened."

"She is not harmed, I hope?" asked Darcy. He held Lady Rutledge in high esteem and would hate for her to suffer harm.

"No. She is well. The officer she ran down, on the other hand, had to be taken to the doctor."

Darcy had to lift his jaw to keep it from gaping. Of all her schemes, this was the worst he had heard of to date.

Bingley continued, "Fortunately for her, Colonel Fitzwilliam came upon the scene and was able to keep the damage to a minimum. He took charge and saw that the officer, who happened to be one of the men under his charge, was properly seen to."

Darcy shook his head and leaned back in his chair. "What happened?" This seemed far-fetched, even for Lady Rutledge.

"Aunt took her phaeton for a drive. She decided to go too fast and, with her vision not being what it once was, she ran over an officer who was walking arm-in-arm with a young lady along the path. The young lady escaped harm, but the officer's foot did not. I do not know the extent of the damage done, but Colonel Fitzwilliam seemed to be in high humor as he wrote the message, and that gives me reason to hope that he is not too badly injured."

That sounded like Richard. "Richard does appreciate the humor in any given situation. Did he request that you return at your earliest convenience?"

Bingley pulled on his sideburns, having done sufficient damage to his hair. "He did not, but he has his own responsibilities. He cannot watch my aunt too. I would not ask it of him though sometimes I think she would prefer him as a protector over me."

Darcy leaned forward. "This effectively settles your

doubts about staying in Hertfordshire." If the Bingleys left, he would to. And he knew exactly where he would go.

"Yes, I cannot leave her again. She has proved herself to be untrustworthy and I could never forgive myself if she suffered another accident or brought harm to anyone else. I must return to London where I will stay for the foreseeable future." He looked downcast. All of his illusions of being a property owner, marrying a country beauty, and settling into his own estate surrounded by a small army of children were shattered. Darcy could see it as plainly as writing on his face.

"I am sorry, Bingley. What can I do to lighten your load?"

Bingley considered. "My plan is to have Caroline stay with Aunt until we can find her a more suitable companion."

"What sort of companion do you think best?" he asked, trying to imagine the intrepid sort of valor a lady would need to fill the role of companion to Lady Lavinia Rutledge.

"She would need to be fairly young. My aunt has enough energy to tire even me. She would have to be strong-willed. Aunt thinks of the craziest schemes and will need someone of an equally strong mind to talk her out of them." Bingley slumped in his chair and threw his arms up into the air. "What I seek is the impossible! Ladies are bred to be docile and agreeable. Where in all of England will I find someone who could last more than a couple days with my aunt?"

The image of a young lady with soft brown hair and a devilish curl at the corner of her lips which no amount of sadness could erase hopping to the carriage one-footed came to mind. Her stubborn determination had been endearing, though quite inappropriate under the circumstances.

"I do not see anything to smile about," grumbled Bingley.

Darcy wiped his face of all expression. "I apologize, Bingley. Who you seek is a rare find. You should only be so fortunate as to find a lady with the qualities you describe. I will make some inquiries on arriving in town."

By all appearances, Miss Elizabeth Bennet would soon find herself in London against her own will. She would not take the decision, made for her by another, calmly. What awaited her in London? Would she be happy? There were too many unanswered questions, and though Darcy imagined that Miss Elizabeth would rather keep herself occupied than accept the charity of her relations— no matter how well-meaning and kind they may be— Darcy could not foresee a situation where she would allow others to continue to make decisions for her.

As a gentleman's daughter, he did not expect her to look for work, but perhaps she would benefit from an acquaintance with Lady Rutledge. He would see her more often if she became friends with the elderly lady.

"PLEASE MAKE no mention to Mother of Mr. Darcy, Uncle. I will never get answers from her if it is known that a single gentleman of fortune touched my ankle and lifted me up onto his horse."

Uncle looked down at Elizabeth. He held her in his arms, making her feel like she was a little girl again. Before she could protest or resume hopping to the front door after sliding ungracefully out of the carriage, he had scooped her up and carried her toward the front door.

Aunt's face lit up and she squeezed Elizabeth's shoulder. "He touched your ankle?" She gasped like a girl in knee skirts. "Do tell!"

Elizabeth looked nervously around her. Mother had an incredible sense of hearing and sight where single gentlemen were involved.

"I will tell you later in great detail, but let me assure you that it was necessary and Mr. Darcy behaved like a true gentleman would in a potentially compromising circumstance."

"I would assume so. I do not know much about Mr. Darcy, but I know enough to respect his caution. He has not allowed himself to be caught in some silly scheme by the conniving mothers of single daughters in search of fortune and position in society. Oh, Lizzy, if only you could see Pemberley. I visited the estate when I was a little girl and I remember thinking that it seemed more like a palace than a home. He is not what I would consider the most handsome man I have ever seen," Aunt said with a loving look at Uncle, "but he is much sought after by the members of the *ton*."

Uncle's arms shook, suppressing a laugh. "I love you, Madeline, but even I can see that Mr. Darcy has been blessed, not only in fortune, but in good looks. What say you, Lizzy? Do you think him handsome?"

Elizabeth felt hot all of a sudden and wished to be inside where she could sit near Mother and her ever-present fan.

It was impossible to hide being held so close to his face. "There is no denying it." Dearly wanting to change the subject before they entered the house, she added, "There is something so sympathizing and melancholy in his manners. For all that Mr. Darcy may have been blessed, he has suffered greatly."

Aunt's arched eyebrows and scheming expression unnerved Elizabeth. "Tis a pity he is here when you are to travel so soon to London with us. Your sprained ankle may turn out to be a blessing, dear. We would never expect you to travel while injured. We can put off our return for another week... give Mr. Darcy a chance to call?" She looked at Uncle, who agreed readily.

The last thing— and the only thing— Elizabeth wanted was for Mr. Darcy to call at Longbourn. Mother had no tact where her daughters were concerned, and she would ask him outright if he would marry her. She would pry the story out of them and would do her level best to see a compromise from which he ought to protect her reputation by making an offer.

On the other hand, Elizabeth would be lying to herself if she denied her wish for Mr. Darcy to call. His presence calmed her. And he was undeniably handsome. Were she ever to fall in love, she would hope to fall for someone similar to him. But what was she doing thinking of love? She ought not allow herself to feel such exalted emotions when she must concern herself with the security of her mother and sisters.

Feeling guilty, she winced as she realized that she had been smiling. Pain was much easier to handle right now than happiness.

"I am sorry, Lizzy," Uncle said as Hill opened the door for them to enter. "Let me set you in here," he said as he continued into the drawing room and set her down gently on a blanket on the couch.

Alerted to their arrival, footsteps were heard descending the stairs at a rapid pace.

Jane was the last to enter after Mother.

Hugs and greetings were exchanged by all— except for Jane, who immediately noticed Elizabeth sitting with her leg extended over the couch and her boot off.

Lydia made to slap Elizabeth's foot down from off the pillow she had arranged it on. "Oy, Lizzy, move your leg so that I may sit. You look like Cleopatra lounging on her couch. Shall I bring you some grapes and fan you while you eat them, your highness?" she teased.

Jane moved to block her blow. "Lydia, choose somewhere else to sit. Can you not see that she is hurt?"

Mother rushed over and moved Jane out of the way to

inspect the sprain. Elizabeth flinched when she poked the puffy skin where her ankle bone should have been.

Mother shooed Uncle out of the room.

"Take off your stocking, Lizzy. I want to see how bad it is," she insisted.

Elizabeth had hoped to avoid looking at her ankle. From the pounding, she knew it would not look pretty... and she was right. Already, she could see the stringy trails of blood vessels covering her inflamed skin. She would have an impressive bruise on the morrow.

Mother's hands flew to her face. "Oh, my dear. Whatever did you do to twist your ankle so badly?"

Elizabeth looked at Aunt, who pursed her lips and looked away. Reassured of her silence, Elizabeth chose to give Mother the truth. Well, most of it anyway. "I was walking heedlessly into Meryton and made a misstep. Fortunately, Aunt and Uncle drove by in their carriage and saw me safely home."

"That is all? One would think that a sprain this bad deserves a more glorious story!" said Lydia, clearly disappointed.

"How romantic it would have been had an officer of the regiment chanced upon you. He would have been duty bound to assist you home," said Kitty in a dreamy voice.

Elizabeth did not much like this turn in conversation. Jane already stared at her in such a way as convinced her that her story was not entirely believable. It was time to change the subject.

"Mother, Uncle tells me that the reason for their trip here is to convey Jane and me with them to London..." she let her words trail off, knowing that Mother would not let her finish her sentence anyway.

"That is so. I wrote to them the day Mr. Collins left here for Lucas Lodge. I had hoped that I could trust you to make better decisions, Lizzy, but after your complete disinterest in our future, I felt it best to take matters into my own hands."

Jane interrupted. "Mother!" She clasped her hands and looked down at the floor, embarrassed when all eyes turned to her.

Aunt Gardiner pulled the blanket gently around Elizabeth's foot and called Uncle in to join them. She sat by her in the small space remaining on the end of the couch, patting Jane's hands and smiling weakly at Elizabeth.

Uncle asked, "Is it as bad as that then?" He looked at Elizabeth.

"My ankle will heal. It is only that this news of leaving Longbourn so soon… I always enjoy your company and I am not surprised at your generous offer to take us in, Uncle, but… I have not yet left and I miss my home already."

Uncle's brow furled and he pinched his chin between his thumb and forefinger. "Fanny, how could you take it upon yourself to make these arrangements without first consulting with your girls?"

Mother looked shocked. "Did I not just give my reason? I could not trust Lizzy to put the needs of her family first after her refusal of Mr. Collins. Her choice meant the loss of our home! Now, I am not the sort to wallow in my misery. So, I wrote to you. If she and Jane are put in the way of more gentlemen in town, then perhaps she will find someone more to her liking. That is all I want— for my daughters to marry and be happy."

It was always about marriage with Mother. How many times had Father said, "… you have a mother who will make the best of it…" whenever a difficult situation occurred. He had been right. Her intentions were kind, if not misdirected and poorly executed.

Aunt Gardiner spoke. "Lizzy cannot travel in her condition. I suggest we stay for a week before journeying back to

London. She will be more comfortable that way." She looked at Elizabeth, a knowing glint in her eye.

Elizabeth smiled at her. She dreaded leaving Longbourn and an extra week was welcome. She had no reason to believe Mr. Darcy would call, so felt only a small amount of anticipation and anxiety that he might.

Mother nodded. "It is unfortunate, but it cannot be helped. I had so hoped to see my eldest girls settled before Lydia and I followed. Were you able to make the final arrangements for me, Edward?"

"Yes. The apartment is small, but it is furnished and it is affordable. It has a front room large enough to receive callers just as you requested."

Elizabeth looked between Mother and Uncle. What would Mother and Lydia need with an apartment? Surely, they would stay at Gracechurch Street with Aunt and Uncle.... Would they not?

Afraid to ask lest she be dealt another blow, she was relieved when Uncle noticed her confused expression.

Bunching up his cheeks and sighing deeply, he said, "Let me guess, Fanny. You have not told them your plans, have you?" It was more an accusation than a question.

Mother's face reddened. "I only look to do what is best for my girls. I have positioned them so that they might find the greatest success. Kitty will marry a regimental officer in Meryton. Mary will marry a clerk or a clergyman through the acquaintances of Mr. Phillips. Jane shall marry a gentleman of means in town. She cannot be that beautiful for nothing. Lizzy shall marry whomsoever she pleases, so long as she marries. With her being so fussy, I thought it best for her to have a wide selection from whom to choose."

"Thank you for your consideration," Elizabeth said sarcastically.

Mother slapped her fan in her hand. "That leaves Lydia

and myself to settle in a small apartment until such a time as our circumstances change."

Uncle stared at her with his mouth wide open. "You do have it all planned out, I see."

Elizabeth's chest felt heavy and it became difficult to breathe. "… until such a time as our circumstances change," Mother had said. What change did she seek? A sinking feeling threatened to leave her light-headed. She had to ask. "Mother, you have arranged our futures to the greatest advantage for what you consider success. What, pray, do you plan to do whilst in town?"

Mother fidgeted in her chair and vigorously fanned her face. "That does not concern you. Really, Lizzy, I have enough problems as it is without attempting to convince you to agree with me on every point. There are some things which I choose to keep to myself."

What was Mother up to? Uncle shrugged his shoulders and shook his head, as clueless as she was.

CHAPTER 10

Mr. Darcy did not call. She had worn the same long-sleeved dress to better conceal his handkerchief for naught.

Elizabeth spent the following three days rotating between her bed, a couch in the drawing room, and Father's chair in the study. She propped her foot up on his desk, imagined Mother's clutter out of the room and the books on the shelves where they belonged, and she would hear his voice in her memory until it faded. Would she forget Father more easily when she left Longbourn? The thought turned her cold.

She wandered through each room she limped to, memorizing every scratch on the wood floors where she and her sisters played as children; every peel in the wallpaper that Mother disguised behind cleverly placed pictures drawn inexpertly by her daughters; every stain on the rugs and furniture tapestry from a careless placing of a wine glass or saucer with coffee. Memories of happier times kept her company and filled her with gratitude and misery.

Jane, as Elizabeth expected, accepted her new fate with a cheerful resignation which ought to have pleased her more.

Mary and Kitty were already gone; their rooms empty and awaiting their next residents. They called every day full of news from Meryton and the latest gossip from Aunt Phillips. It was Mary who told them that Netherfield Park was empty once again. It did soothe Elizabeth's vanity to know that the gentleman was not present and therefore could not have called.

Kitty spoke of the regimental officers in their stylish red coats. She was pleased to bask in the many compliments she had received from multiple officers— much to the chagrin of Lydia, who could not imagine a world where Kitty deserved more compliments than she. Then, Lydia would remember that she was to go to London at the height of the Season where she would be flooded with far more compliments than Kitty— who would be stuck in the country. Poor thing.

Elizabeth stood in front of the couch in the drawing room, testing her weight on her ankle cautiously.

"My dear, what are you doing? You will make your injury worse." Uncle Gardiner entered the room wearing his great-coat and hat. Wherever he was going, Elizabeth wished she could go with him.

"I am much improved, Uncle. I was only testing to see when I might be able to move more." She took a step, favoring her right foot. It was uncomfortable, but not unbearable.

"Please sit down, Lizzy. You make me nervous."

With a deep sigh, Elizabeth took a step back and sunk into the couch behind her. The cushions molded to her in the familiar way they had developed over the past few days. "I have been sitting too much lately. I wish I could go with you," she grumbled.

Uncle smiled. "I really ought to visit Esther today, and I

am curious to see how Mary has settled, as well as Kitty. I have yet to see them in their new home as they have been so good to visit us here."

"Aunt Esther is happier than I have ever seen her. She feels that she has gained two daughters. I am happy she treats them thus…." A lump in Elizabeth's throat choked her words.

Uncle nodded in understanding. "But you miss them. It is to be expected, my dear. I prayed that your father would be able to live long enough to see his daughters happily settled. Of all of my nieces, I knew you would be the most affected by his loss."

Elizabeth nodded, still unable to speak.

Squeezing her shoulder, he said, "It will get easier as time passes. Maybe it will be good for you leave this place." Mr. Darcy had said as much three days ago.

Uncle took his gloves out of his coat pocket and slapped them against his open palm. "I must go. I want to post these letters before the carriage leaves for London." Pulling a blanket down from the back of the couch, he tucked it around Elizabeth. With a kiss on the top of her head, he left the room.

Elizabeth tried to read to pass the time. Thanks to Mother there were no books in the house, but Aunt had brought a novel with her and Elizabeth was grateful for the distraction.

What felt like hours had passed when she heard a horse's hooves speeding up the drive.

Hill was quick to open the door. It was a message for Aunt and Uncle.

Immediately searching for Aunt, who was helping Mother direct the packing of their remaining belongings, Hill went upstairs. Elizabeth strained her ears, but only heard silence. The longer the silence grew, the greater her worry intensified. Flinging the blanket off her legs, she limped over to the doorway in time to see Aunt Gardiner come downstairs. There was a flush in her cheeks and a sheen over her eyes. She acknowledged Elizabeth on her way to the door to send a returning message with the man waiting outside.

Her business done, she turned to Elizabeth. "I am so sorry, Lizzy, but we must leave today. Emma has a fever. Fanny and Jane are already packing your trunk. The rest of your things can come later as we had planned. We must leave as soon as Edward returns."

She left to make the necessary arrangements, and Elizabeth hopped up the stairs to help as much as she could.

THAT AFTERNOON, Elizabeth found herself seated next to Jane in Uncle's carriage. Her foot was propped up between Aunt and Uncle, and they did their best not to touch it during their jostling ride.

Elizabeth was more concerned with what she could see out of the window: the fields she had walked over countless times; the familiar curves and dips in the road she would not have need to travel anymore; the buildings in Meryton. She pressed her fingers against the cold glass and wished they could travel slower, but she dared not say anything. Aunt was anxious about Emma and Elizabeth would not dream of putting her nostalgia ahead of the needs of her cousin.

"Netherfield Park is empty once again. Mr. Bingley gave no indication that he would ever return," declared Uncle, startling Elizabeth out of her melancholy nostalgia.

"That is a pity. Mr.—" she started before remembering that Jane knew nothing of her incident involving Mr. Darcy. Nor did she intend for her to find out.

Aunt spoke. "It is a pity, and I was sad to hear of it. I have always held a special fondness for that estate. It is so well situated and has such convenient access from the road."

Uncle leaned back and stroked his whiskers. "I would have liked to have presented my card to Mr. Bingley. If he is who I think he is, his uncle did business on several occasions with an old partner of mine."

Aunt inclined her head. "Really? Which one was that?"

"Mr. Finley. Do you remember him? He has since moved on to the cotton trade up north, but he helped me immensely to establish myself in London. He used to brag of the runs they would do across the channel. It was all very quiet, you know. They dealt in spirits and munitions," he said under his breath, as if anyone outside the carriage could hear him.

"What is the name of the man you suppose is Mr. Bingley's uncle? Have I heard you speak of him?" asked Aunt, to Elizabeth's delight. The man sounded interesting. Elizabeth held on to the edge of her seat and leaned forward. She would not miss a word of this.

"Sir Alastair Rutledge was his name. He was bestowed a knighthood for his favors to the crown, and he married a young woman with flaming red hair and a personality to match. From what I heard, his years with her were the happiest and most diverting of his life. He died five years ago, leaving his fortune and a large house in St. James for his widow, Lady Rutledge. After his death, I never heard more of his family, not knowing them personally."

"That is all?" Elizabeth sank back into the cushion in disappointment.

Uncle chuckled. "It is all I know, but believe me that I aim to present my card to Mr. Bingley once I am reassured that Emma is well."

Jane commented, "How odd the Bingleys should leave so soon after letting the estate. Aunt Phillips told us that Mr. Bingley had brought his sisters with him, and I had hoped to make their acquaintance. I cannot believe everything Aunt said about his sisters and the other gentleman they had staying with them."

Elizabeth wondered where she had been when Aunt Phillips had revealed her thoughts on their neighbors. She could not recall. "What did she say?" she asked, trusting that Jane would soften Aunt's blows to suit her own forgiving nature.

"I do not feel comfortable repeating everything she said against them. It was most unflattering. Of Mr. Bingley, she had nothing but good to relate. Evidently, Miss Bingley refused to dance with any man she did not deem to be a gentleman at the Meryton Assembly. The gentleman with them, Mr. Darcy, refused to dance the entire evening though gentlemen were scarce in the room. Of that, you know, but I merely repeat it for Aunt's benefit. Aunt Phillips thinks that he is a most disagreeable man. However, I am certain they must have had cause to act the way they did and if asked, they would provide a reasonable explanation."

"I should think that someone like Mr. Darcy would find it uncomfortable to mingle with strangers at a public assembly. He is accustomed to refined company and familiar friends in his social circle," said Aunt with a flicker of her eyes at Elizabeth, who would have risen up in his defense had she been able to speak more freely to Jane.

What she heard ran contrary to the Mr. Darcy she knew. He had been all kindness and understanding in her limited experience. She pressed the handkerchief between her wrist and coat sleeve. "Do you think him a snob?" Elizabeth asked.

Aunt paused in thought, clearly mulling over her words. "It is not so much that, but rather that he is of a high social class which is unaccustomed to rubbing elbows with the working class. I cannot imagine that it would be easy for him to… blend in. I knew his mother when I lived in Lambton.

She was a gentle, soft-spoken woman. If he inherited her shyness, it would be easy to assume that he is proud. People often mistake shyness for pride."

Elizabeth could see that, but refusing to dance when partners were lacking went beyond shyness. On the other hand, would not a proud man avoid a public assembly, knowing that he would have to mingle with commoners?

"I dare say you can reserve your own judgments of Mr. Darcy and the Bingleys for when you meet them yourselves. Mr. Phillips told me that Mr. Bingley has returned to his home in London and Mr. Darcy will do so upon completing some business out of town." Uncle looked pointedly at Elizabeth.

Aunt noticed the exchange and, with an arched brow, she focused on Jane. "My love, once we are home and reassured that Emma is safe, I should like very much for you to call on Mr. Darcy. Perhaps, through him, we might arrange an introduction to the Bingleys. Miss Bingley might be a good friend to Jane and Lizzy. Sufficient time has passed to respectfully mourn, and I believe it will do my dear nieces more good to ease gently into society."

Elizabeth wanted nothing to do with society. She did not feel ready for company. But she would do anything for her sister. If that meant befriending Mr. Bingley's snobbish sister, then so be it. If it meant that she would more often be put into Mr. Darcy's company, then she could endure anything.

CHAPTER 11

"Uncle, I have made a decision and I seek your help," said Elizabeth before she lost her nerve.

He looked up from his morning paper. "Yes? Dare I ask what you have decided?" He motioned for her to sit next to him at the breakfast table.

"I have been here nearly two weeks now, and I appreciate the generosity you and Aunt have shown in taking Jane and me into your home and treating us as if we were your own daughters. I do not want to appear ungrateful in the least, but it has become apparent to me that I need an occupation." Taking a deep breath to calm her pounding heart, she continued, "Jane fits in so well here. She is a natural with the children, and she is content. I, on the other hand, feel useless."

Uncle folded up his paper. "But you play with them so well. They love the games you invent."

She would not back down now. "And I adore playing with them. It is just that...." She folded her hands together on top of the table. "I feel that I am not in charge of my own life. Things have happened, and decisions have been made for me." She held her hands up when Uncle made to protest. "I am fortunate that they have been mostly good decisions, but I feel restless and anxious. I must *do* something." She stopped, frustrated that she could not express her burning desire for independence better without giving cause for offense. Aunt and Uncle had been so kind, how could she tell them outright that she felt stifled in their home?

Uncle looked at her intently through his narrowed eyes. Only when he took a sip of his tea and sat back into his chair did Elizabeth breathe.

"I think I understand your meaning, dear girl, and I can find no fault with it given your upbringing. You were raised with a much greater amount of freedom than most ladies are allowed, and I daresay you would be much happier if you could find a purpose to suit you. Tell me, what do you think would satisfy you? We could hire a tutor to teach you a new instrument if you like..."

That was not at all what she had in mind. "I think it best for me to seek employment— something that will enable me to exercise my mind. I can be content with that, knowing that I am earning my keep." There would be no mindless needlework and empty accomplishments in her future.

Uncle abruptly set down his teacup, clattering in the saucer and spilling tea over the edge. "I do hope that we have never given you cause to believe yourself a burden in our home." His concern drew lines across his brow.

She was quick to reassure him. "No. Never! It is only that I would feel better about myself were I able to do something of value. I do not feel that I accomplish anything here that Jane is not completely and infinitely more qualified to do. I seek to be useful and fill my time with a worthwhile pursuit."

Uncle leaned back and lifted his teacup again. "I see. You feel the need to prove your worth, and you consider that the best way to do so is to work." Rotating the now empty cup in his hands, he said, "I will not have it said that a niece of mine had to seek employment. There are no options for a gently born lady that will not affect her prospects of marrying well."

Did Uncle believe, like Mother, that she was only useful as a wife? Her cheeks heated.

Covering her hand with his own, he said, "I know it is not what you wish to hear. I see it clearly on your face, Lizzy dear. However, you must consider what is expected of the daughter of a gentleman. You have certain advantages that my children will never have, being tainted by trade as they are, and I will not allow you to disregard them and ruin your chances at making a splendid match." He spoke sincerely, with no hint of the sarcasm she had when she thought of the injustices imposed upon them by the socially elite. Who were they to determine what would make her happy or to consider her uncle anything less than the gentleman she knew him to be?

She wanted to lash out at someone, but Uncle Gardiner's kind face did not allow him to be the victim. "I only need work to keep me busy until I feel whole again."

He patted her hand. "You do not seek to punish yourself for the loss of your father, do you?"

"No." Now, that was not completely true. She did punish herself. Only her guilt laid in what she had lost her mother and sisters. "I will not deny that I still miss him. Most likely I always will… but I know that he is gone and I no longer look for him." Mr. Darcy was right. Letting go was bitter and sweet; a relief and a misery.

"Yes, Lizzy?" Uncle encouraged her. "You were saying?"

Tugging her thoughts away from Mr. Darcy, she said, "It is not just Father. I feel as if my entire family is lost to me now. I will be the first to admit that I do not know entirely what I seek. I only know that I do not think that I can find it here." Tears burned her eyes. She felt so lonely at that moment. She even longed for her mother.

Uncle sighed again. "I will do my best to arrange something— a suitable employment we can keep amongst ourselves, my dear. I will discuss it with Madeline, and we will do our best. All we want is for you to be happy. It is what your father wanted too."

Elizabeth closed her eyes and whispered, "Thank you." She did not feel that Uncle understood her completely. She hardly understood. How could she possibly explain the empty want for something she could not express?

"You ought to eat, dear. You will need your strength." Uncle emphasized his point by requesting more tea to be brought in and placing a roll of bread on her plate.

She bit into the roll, not bothering to butter it or smother it with the fruit preserves he pushed in front of her.

He contemplated her as she chewed. Taking his spectacles off and placing them on top of the newspaper, he crossed his arms and tucked his chin into his chest. "Since we have arrived, I have neglected making any calls out of my concern for Emma. Her fever has passed, and I think it is high time I remedied that situation." Slapping his hands against the top of the table, he rose. "Yes, I think I know precisely where I must go today."

His manners changed drastically from one of deep concern to eager excitement.

"Where do you plan to go?" Elizabeth asked.

Aunt came into the breakfast room just as he neared the door. He grasped her by the arms and kissed her on the cheek. "Never you mind, Lizzy. I will tell you when I return if anything comes of it." With a wink at Aunt and a farewell nod to Elizabeth, he went upstairs to ready himself for wherever it was he had decided to go.

Aunt looked at Elizabeth. "What was that about?"

"He said he needed to start making some calls now that Emma has improved." She took another bite of bread.

Clapping her hands together and smiling at Elizabeth, Aunt said, "I think I know where he is going! Oh, I do think that you and Mr. Darcy would make a lovely match. And if he can arrange for Jane to meet Mr. Bingley, all of your troubles will soon be resolved."

The bite Elizabeth swallowed grew in her throat. Must marriage be the only solution to all of life's problems? She pushed her plate away, unable to eat any more. If a gentleman such as Mr. Darcy were to take notice of her, it must be on his terms. Anything else would be forced and humiliating.

DARCY DEARLY WANTED to laugh at the comedy playing out before him. For the past week and a half, Miss Bingley had been forced to serve as a temporary companion to Lady Rutledge after her aunt had chased two young ladies away. Each had lasted only a day. Darcy wished he could have witnessed it, but had only returned to London the evening before.

"I do not understand it, Darcy," said Bingley, tugging his fingers through his hair which, no doubt, had been in a constant state of disarray since his return to London ten days before. "The latest young lady I sent was extremely qualified. Her list of accomplishments was so impressive as to compare to the most elite amongst the *ton*. And she assured me that she was accustomed to temperamental individuals."

Miss Bingley snorted. "Temperamental?! Aunt Lavinia is beyond temperamental, Charles. I swear that if you do not find a replacement, my hair will be as white as hers by the end of the week. She is incorrigible."

Darcy turned toward the window, so they would not see him smile at their predicament. The very qualities he admired in Lady Rutledge were the same which often put her at odds with her socially sensitive niece. She spoke what was on her mind with an honest bluntness he could appreciate. She spoke as freely as he wished to— her fortune, status, and age giving her the freedom to do what she very well pleased. Not that she did not enjoy pushing the boundaries of propriety to the limits.

"Darcy, have you had any success in finding a qualified young lady to help keep our aunt out of mischief?" Bingley asked, not a little desperate.

"Qualified or not, we would hire a chambermaid at this point. Of what use are accomplishments if nobody will stay with her?" added Miss Bingley. "I cannot suffer through another day. Did you know that she put salt in my tea only this morning?"

Darcy suffered to keep a straight face. "An honest mistake. Anyone could mistake salt for sugar." He did not for a moment believe that it had been a mistake, but he felt the need to defend Lady Rutledge.

"Mistake, my eye!" complained Miss Bingley, more to herself than to anyone in particular.

The door to Darcy's parlor opened, and the butler announced the arrival of a visitor. "A Mr. Edward Gardiner is here to see you, sir. Shall I see him in or tell him that you are out?"

Bingley made to stand.

Darcy reached his hand out. "Do not leave just yet." To the butler, he said, "Please see Mr. Gardiner in."

Bingley looked questioningly at Darcy, but he settled back into his chair. Miss Bingley preened and rearranged her skirts to better effect, no doubt content that they had not been dismissed so easily.

Mr. Gardiner smiled when he saw Darcy and smiled even deeper when Bingley stood to bow. The rotund gentleman looked as if he would burst while Darcy made introductions.

"Excuse me for asking such a plain question, but is it possible that you are the nephew of Sir Alistair Rutledge? An old partner of mine did business with him many years ago."

Bingley's eyes widened. He knew how his uncle had gained his fortune, and he was in no hurry to acknowledge it. The accusations of piracy were overlooked because of the great favors Sir Alistair did for the crown, but Darcy could hardly blame Bingley for wanting to conceal his ancestor's colorful past.

"I am his nephew. Did you know my uncle Rutledge?" he asked hesitantly.

"Only of him. Please do not concern yourself on my account, Mr. Bingley. My partner only had the kindest of things to say about your uncle. He held him in high regard. I did see Lady Rutledge once before, and I must say that the family resemblance is striking." He looked at Miss Bingley.

She rolled her eyes. Darcy was uncertain if Mr. Gardiner saw her unladylike reaction.

Mr. Gardiner added, with a twinkle in his eye, "I have seen very few ladies since then to equal her beauty."

He had seen it.

Smiling at Mr. Gardiner in her sweetest manner, Miss Bingley said, "How delightful. You have a discerning eye, Mr. Gardiner."

"Really, it is fortuitous that you should be here today, for I have come seeking help," said Mr. Gardiner. "Due to circumstances beyond their control, two of my nieces are staying with my family. They are new to London and have few friends with whom to associate. They are gentry, and I aim to take special care to introduce them to the best people."

Darcy watched the Bingleys sit up in their seats simultaneously, their interest apparent.

“Please tell us about your nieces, Mr. Gardiner. Perhaps I shall decide to befriend them,” said Miss Bingley, as sweet as honey.

"They are from Hertfordshire. Their father passed away nearly six months ago, and we decided that it was time for them to visit us in town to enjoy a London Season."

Good for Mr. Gardiner for leaving out their unfavorable circumstances. Darcy had yet to determine Mrs. Bennet’s address so that he might continue to send baskets of provisions, but he would not let Mr. Gardiner leave without ensuring that all of her needs were seen to.

Bingley sat so close to the edge of his chair, he nearly toppled off. “You are the uncle to the Miss Bennets of Longbourn? I admit that not meeting Miss Bennet is my greatest regret in quitting Netherfield Park.”

“I had heard that you let the estate,” acknowledged Mr. Gardiner.

Bingley smiled. “We met Miss Elizabeth in passing. I am certain my sister is desirous of renewing their brief acquaintance.”

Miss Bingley's spine was so straight, a wisp of a draft would send her sprawling across the floor.

“I thank you, sir. It will benefit them greatly to occupy their time with new friends.”

Darcy watched the siblings. Bingley had heard of Miss Bennet’s beauty and grace. Of course he would want to meet her. Miss Bingley, on the other hand, smirked in her seat. Finally, she said, "I would love to invite you and your nieces over for tea, Mr. Gardiner. Does tomorrow suit your schedule?" Her words dripped with nectar. "I believe we can help one another. I will even include my aunt Lavinia in our party and Mr. Darcy, of course."

Darcy cringed. He made it a custom to decline invitations extended by Miss Bingley, but he could not refuse this one. He doubted her 'help' was what Mr. Gardiner sought. Nor did Darcy wish it for Miss Elizabeth. It would be good to see her again. It had been two weeks....

CHAPTER 12

The Gardiner house was abuzz with excitement and anticipation. "One of the gentlemen is bound to take a fancy to one of them," Uncle Gardiner was often heard saying to Aunt. Any pleasure Elizabeth had at the prospect of seeing Mr. Darcy again was dampened by their expectations. She would, however, finally have an opportunity to return his handkerchief. She had grown accustomed to carrying it inside her sleeve and would find a way to see it back discreetly to its rightful owner.

"What is Lady Rutledge like, Uncle?" she asked, attempting to distract him from thoughts of orange blossoms and lace.

"Lady Rutledge? Oh, you will find out soon enough. I only met her briefly when I was much younger, and since then I have only heard stories." He fussed with his cravat.

"Stories?" she pressed.

Uncle cleared his throat and shifted his weight on the carriage cushion.

Aunt answered. "Of what use is it to hear stories when we do not know for certain if they are true. She will be at the tea this afternoon, and you shall judge her character for yourself."

"I wish Jane had come with us," Elizabeth sighed. Mother would have been appalled, as Uncle had been, that her eldest daughter had preferred to stay behind when there would be at least two single gentlemen present. Mr. Bingley seemed like a pleasant fellow, and Elizabeth would have liked for Jane to meet him.

"I would rather her have come with us as well, but her reason for staying behind helps me feel easier. Emma is only now recovering from her fever and I would have been very anxious leaving her behind if not for Jane." Aunt crumpled her reticule in her hands.

Uncle squeezed her hand. "We do have a nurse, Madeline."

"I know it, and she is an excellent nurse, but… Jane cares so much more for the children, being a relation." Aunt's concern for her own child far outweighed her insistence that her nieces marry the first gentlemen put in their way. Elizabeth praised her sensibleness.

"Just promise me that you will not delegate Janey to the role of a nurse to the detriment of her future prospects. A young lady such as she ought to marry and have children of her own," insisted Uncle.

Adjusting the brooch on her dress, Aunt said, "You are quite right, my love. Perhaps I should have urged her more firmly to accompany us."

"Do not trouble yourself too much. It is my hope that there will be a next time." With an affectionate glance at Aunt, he clasped his hands together and focused his attention on Elizabeth. "Are you ready?" he asked.

Elizabeth forced the butterflies in her stomach down with a deep breath. Would Mr. Darcy be pleased to see her? She was nervous, but she would not own to it. "As ready as I imagine I could be."

The carriage lurched forward to a stop. "Here we are!" said Uncle in a cheerful voice.

The townhouse was favorably situated on a corner in a stylish neighborhood at St. James. Bright curtains adorned the wide windows, setting it apart from its somber neighbors. The clouds parted just as they descended the carriage to walk up the pathway leading to the front door. With the sun shining on the house, reflecting off the shiny glass and the light stones, it appeared as if the building were smiling. It ought not to have meant anything, but it did make Elizabeth feel better.

They were seen into a room styled in the Grecian fashion where a table was set up and arranged with all manner of repasts. Off to the side, there was a seating area where four figures stood when they entered the room. The Bingleys stood together and Mr. Darcy stood next to an older woman with silver hair. She bore a striking resemblance to her niece, Miss Bingley. She was as tall as Miss Bingley and thin. Her sharp eyes bore into her, and Elizabeth was certain nothing ever escaped the lady's notice.

She saw Mr. Darcy's lips curl up and felt her confidence increase. He was pleased to see her.

They had not even been presented yet, when Lady Rutledge said, "So, this is the young lady you told me about?"

Elizabeth stopped short, unsure whether to be flattered or alarmed to have been the center of a previous discussion. But one look at Mr. Darcy, holding his hand up to cover his smiling mouth, had her biting her lips to keep from smiling too.

"Aunt Lavinia, if you will allow me to make introductions, you shall soon find out," hissed Mr. Bingley with an embarrassed glance at Elizabeth and her party.

Introductions were made, and Lady Rutledge did not take her eyes off Elizabeth for a second. Elizabeth stood as tall as her reduced stature would allow, feeling as if the lady were measuring her.

They sat around the table, Lady Rutledge placing herself directly across from Elizabeth, so that she might examine her all the better. Mr. Darcy sat next to her and Miss Bingley flanked her on the other side.

Lady Rutledge was surprisingly quiet after her initial outburst, but her silence only put Elizabeth more on edge under her scrutinizing stare.

Between Uncle and Aunt Gardiner, Mr. Bingley, and Miss Bingley, the conversation never fell silent. Lively chatter filled the room, and her sense of foreboding increased. Miss Bingley was quick to agree with Uncle's praise of Elizabeth—a development which confused her further. She understood Uncle's reasons for doing so, but could not fathom Miss Bingley's motive.

How could she tell Uncle? She looked at him, but she could not think of a way to tactfully extricate herself from the increasingly uncomfortable room. If only Lady Rutledge would say something rather than stare at her from across the table.

Mr. Darcy, too, seemed to have come under Lady Rutledge's spell and sat silently contemplating Elizabeth. Though his gaze was agreeable, she wondered what he saw in her to capture his attention for so long. Stiffening her spine and lifting her chin, she traced the letters on his handkerchief hidden up her sleeve and tried to relax. Of course, unless Lady Rutledge quit scrutinizing her, she would have to keep it longer still.

"Mr. and Mrs. Gardiner, there is a matter of some delicacy of which I think I ought to seek your advice. We are among friends, so I will speak plainly," said Miss Bingley with a sweet smile.

Flattered by her compliment in including them as friends, they encouraged her to unburden herself.

Lady Rutledge narrowed her eyes until they were as thin as daggers.

"It has been incumbent on me to reside for a time with my aunt in her home, and I fear that my excessive obligations during this season prevent me from continuing there." She pulled her bottom lip out in a pretty pout. "Do you know of any young ladies of good birth and remarkable accomplishments who might serve as a sort of companion?"

Elizabeth understood her compliments then. Miss Bingley was careful not to look in her direction, but Elizabeth saw through her. Otherwise, why would she bother to compliment her— and in front of Mr. Darcy at that!

Looking at Lady Rutledge, who looked none too pleased at the topic of conversation, Elizabeth wondered what it was about the elegant widow that prevented her own niece from staying with her. Why would she seek a companion when her aunt clearly did not wish for one?

Uncle Gardiner stroked his sideburns, deep in thought. Aunt offered, "I cannot think of any eligible lady at this moment, but I will make inquiries immediately."

With a sigh that suggested resignation and a sharp voice that suggested rebellion, Lady Rutledge said, "You may as well save your breath, Mrs. Gardiner. I am an opinionated old widow, who causes so much trouble, my own niece has grown tired of my ways. There does not exist a young lady in all of London who would dare put up with me for more than a day." Her steely, gray eyes flashed at Elizabeth, laying down a challenge.

His wife thus addressed, Uncle took it upon himself to respond. "When you put it that way, I daresay you might have difficulty finding someone suitable. We will do our best to assist you where we can." He nodded in finality of that unpleasant topic. "Mr. Darcy, the last time you saw Miss Elizabeth, she had suffered an injury. I hope you find her well now."

It was a comment her mother would have made, and Elizabeth wished to crawl under the table.

"I did notice that Miss Bennet was able to walk independently. I apologize that I have not called sooner at your residence. A matter in Brighton kept me away from town until recently after leaving Netherfield Park." Mr. Darcy's polite answer made Elizabeth's ears burn.

"You are welcome any time," beamed Aunt.

"Yes, as is Mr. Bingley, of course. And Miss Bingley," added Uncle. He may as well have made Elizabeth wear a sign around her neck saying, "Please marry my niece!"

Grinding her teeth, Elizabeth looked away to see Lady Rutledge's smirk.

Uncle opened his mouth to speak again, and Elizabeth knew he would make another comment meant to make her look good before the gentlemen in their company. He meant well, but she would decide with whom she chose to spend the rest of her life. She did not appreciate his interference.

"I will do it," she blurted out. Elizabeth reached up to cover her mouth with her hand before she could say anything else she would regret, but stopped midair. Instead, she bit her tongue so hard, it hurt.

Uncle and Aunt were too stunned to reply. Maybe nobody had noticed...

Miss Bingley clasped her hands together. "How delightful! Oh, Charles, is Miss Eliza not perfect for the position?"

Drat.

Mr. Bingley mirrored Uncle's expression.

"Are you certain, Miss Bennet?" asked Mr. Darcy, his voice low.

What had she done? Would Mr. Darcy still be her friend

if she became a lowly companion? Rebelling at the ugly possibility, she straightened her spine and jutted out her chin. If he ceased being her friend because of her lowered position in society, then he was undeserving of her admiration. She searched his expression for the answer she wanted so badly.

Before Elizabeth could answer, Lady Rutledge snapped, "How old are you?"

"Old enough." She should not withhold information, but the woman's brusque manners grated on her.

"Humph. If you are old enough, as you say, then why are you not yet married? You are not ugly."

From the side, Elizabeth saw Mr. Darcy reach up to tug on his collar. Apparently she was not the only uncomfortable person in the room.

"Aunt Lavinia, what sort of question is that?" interjected Mr. Bingley, turning a rosy shade of pink.

Squinting her eyes at Lady Rutledge, Elizabeth smiled at Mr. Bingley. "It is a fair question, and I thank Lady Rutledge for the compliment."

“Do not be so sure it was,” Lady Rutledge said under her breath, but loudly enough for all to hear.

Focusing her full attention once again on Lady Rutledge until everyone else at the table blurred into nonexistence, Elizabeth said, "I have not married for the simple reason that I did not love the one gentleman who has asked. I find that I am incapable of accepting a proposal for anything less than the greatest of affection and admiration. I think love is worth waiting for and would not rush it."

A loud clatter broke her concentration on Lady Rutledge. Mr. Darcy’s teacup lay on its side. He grabbed a napkin to soak up the tea spreading over the tablecloth.

“Did the handle come off the teacup, Mr. Darcy? Caroline, you should not serve that cup to your guests,” chided

Lady Rutledge. She ignored Miss Bingley's adamant denial and stirred a measure of sugar into her tea, her expression softening with each turn of her spoon.

Holding her hand up to quiet her niece, Lady Rutledge said to Elizabeth, "I see. You refuse to settle, but you now find yourself in the uncomfortable position of needing to marry or remain dependent on your good relatives. Yet I sense that you have not given up hope. There will be times— many times, I daresay— when you will need such blinding optimism."

"Lady Rutledge, my niece has suffered great sadness recently, and her heightened emotions have made her speak in haste. She was, and always will be, welcome in my home. She is like a daughter to me," said Uncle Gardiner with a concerned smile at Elizabeth.

An eyebrow twitched up and Lady Rutledge brought a bejeweled hand up to pinch her chin. Her every movement was calculated to be stylish, much like her niece, Miss Bingley. Elizabeth wondered if she gave her lessons. "She has expressed herself clearly thus far, but let me ask some additional questions. Any lady who will not marry for convenience is of interest to me. Tell me, Miss Bennet, how did you come upon such modern ideas and why do you think I should agree to employ you as my companion?" She tilted her chin to the side, elongating her neck elegantly while communicating her interest in one becoming gesture.

Feeling more confident, Elizabeth answered. "My father encouraged me to have opinions and know how to express them. I get the sense that you, too, are a lady of opinions."

"Hmm," Lady Rutledge said noncommittally. "So you are entertaining at the dinner table, but can you play an instrument?"

"I manage well enough."

"Can you draw portraits?"

"Not well."

"Can you sing?"

"Hardly." Elizabeth could not help but smile at the ridiculousness of her situation. She had no qualifications, her ladylike accomplishments having been neglected over the years in favor of the improvement of her mind through extensive reading.

"You do not have much to recommend you, Miss Bennet."

Uncle Gardiner relaxed. Mr. Darcy smiled, though Elizabeth could hardly understand why.

Keeping her chin up and her sense of humor in place, she said, "Then I will return to my uncle's house, sure of their acceptance. I am not the one in need of a companion."

Aunt squeezed her hand in support, and Elizabeth practically felt the caress expressed in Uncle's kind face. Maybe she had spoken out of turn. There was nowhere she would rather be than with people who loved her unconditionally.

Mr. Darcy's smile deepened. She hoped he would call at Uncle's soon.

"I like you, Miss Bennet. Can you move your things to my house first thing in the morning? That is, of course, if your uncle does not object to it." Lady Rutledge's eyes danced over the top of her tea cup as she took another sip. It looked so much like Father when he looked over the top of his spectacles, it took Elizabeth's breath away. Lady Rutledge was not entirely what she seemed.

Swallowing hard, deeply regretting her impulsiveness, Elizabeth said, "I think we can manage that, Lady Rutledge. Can we not, Uncle?" She could not retract her offer now. Not when it was accepted.

Uncle Gardiner nodded, speechless.

In a snappy voice, Lady Rutledge added, "There is one thing we must get clear. You are to call me Aunt Lavinia. I will not be treated like a senile derelict in need of a nanny in my own home." She looked accusingly at Miss Bingley. "As far as anyone outside this room is concerned, you are a long-lost niece." She challenged everyone around the table with her pointy, extended finger and her piercing glare.

"Very well, Aunt Lavinia."

Satisfied, she said, "I shall call you Eliza."

CHAPTER 13

Darcy watched Miss Elizabeth leave with the Gardiners, anticipating the moments he would see her again. He would rather have called at the Gardiners to see her.

Patting his arm, Lady Rutledge stood beside him. "There is something quite extraordinary in Eliza, do you not agree, Darcy?" He could have embraced Lady Rutledge for ensuring Miss Elizabeth's standing in society by having her stand in as a niece.

Guarding his reserve, he nodded abruptly. "Quite. Nobody else would put up with you and your antics."

With a chuckle and a chastising whack of her fan on his forearm, she said, "You know me all too well. Tis a pity I am not thirty years younger, Darcy, or you would find yourself in grave danger of being trapped by me." Her eyes crinkled up on the side. The years had been kind to her, and she felt that age granted her the freedom to flirt with whomever she chose. Darcy knew better than to take her seriously.

"I doubt it. I have avoided the snares of many an ambitious lady, and I would have avoided yours as well— however cleverly crafted they might have been." He looked in the direction of Miss Bingley, who was the same age Lady Rutledge wished to be.

"You need someone who is full of life and vigor," Lady Rutledge said with another assault of her fan against his arm. "Someone who could not care less for conventions and restraints. Someone, dare I say it, very similar to your Miss Elizabeth…? I saw how closely you watched her." Her eyes glinted in mischief.

Darcy knew she merely sought to get a reaction from him, and he was determined not to bite her bait, though he was so warm, he wished to relieve himself of his coat.

"May I walk you home?" he asked, holding out his arm, desirous of the cooler outside air.

"That would be lovely," she said as they bid their farewells from the Bingleys and headed out of the door to walk the short distance to Rutledge House.

They were within sight of the house when Darcy saw a gentleman leaping across the muddy street, doing his utter best not to soil his polished boots. Lady Rutledge saw him too. He was difficult to miss in his military uniform with its shiny gold tassels and buttons.

"Colonel Fitzwilliam," smiled Lady Rutledge as she held her hand out toward him.

He bowed elegantly, swooping over her hand in a gallant fashion.

"Oh, Colonel, if I were thirty years younger, you would be in great danger from me," she said with a wink at Darcy.

Darcy shook his head at her coquetries.

"Of course, I know I should be cross with you," she continued with a pout. "It was your message to Charles that brought him back to London when I was only just beginning to divert myself."

Richard tilted his head in line with his lopsided grin. "It

will please you to know that the young officer you attempted to run down— an officer in my unit, I might add— suffered no further injury due to your... accident in the park. He would thank you personally for the new pair of boots you so kindly offered to replace the ones the wheel of your carriage ruined, but, as you can imagine, he is a bit hesitant." A smile spread over his entire face and Darcy chuckled inwardly.

Lady Rutledge jutted her chin up in the air and said haughtily, "That will teach the young man not to walk too near the driving paths with a young lady."

"And perhaps that will teach you to drive with your spectacles?" Richard suggested.

He may as well have suggested that she ride a horse astride in men's wear. "Absolutely not! I am not in need of spectacles, and I refuse to wear them," she lashed out.

"Every stylish lady of a mature age in society wears them," Richard said in an attempt to persuade her.

Darcy cringed. He did not claim any superior knowledge of the feminine sex, but he did know that any mention of age was a topic never to be touched. Not even with a long pole.

"Mature age? Just how old do you believe me to be, Colonel?"

Willing Richard to keep his mouth shut, Darcy clamped his lips closed in hopes that Richard would do the same. This was dangerous ground.

"Certainly not old enough to have a niece of marriageable age. I apologize, Lady Rutledge."

It was a clever maneuver to mention Miss Bingley. Lady Rutledge gave the impression of sternness and haughtiness, but she deeply cared for her friends and family. Miss Bingley had yet to care for anyone other than herself, but her aunt had not given up on her. Darcy's theory was that Lady Rutledge saw too much of herself in Miss Bingley to do so easily.

Richard continued when he saw Lady Rutledge's chin return to its proper place. "I do hope that Bingley was not too hard on you."

"That remains to be seen. I now have a niece who is obliged to stay with me. The following days will determine how much a punishment that is."

So she was serious about Miss Elizabeth posing as her niece to preserve her vanity. Good.

"Punishment? For whom— your niece or yourself?" asked Richard with a rakish grin.

"You have objections to your niece?" asked Darcy.

"Not as yet." She patted the arm she held with her free hand. "Time will tell. She is very thin and her demeanor is melancholy. I think she must have suffered greatly recently, and it is my aim to help her forget her sadness, or else she will not last long with me."

"Her father passed away nearly six months ago. She ought to still be in mourning, but circumstances have determined otherwise."

"As if a time limit could be placed on sadness..." A shadow crossed Lady Rutledge's face, but it was gone as quickly as it had passed. "That explains it. She must have been close to him." She continued walking, placing herself between the two young men so that she might be seen walking in style.

"Thank you for seeing me home, Darcy. And, Colonel, do try to keep your men in order. I should hate for their carelessness to cause them another unnecessary accident."

ELIZABETH COULD NOT SHAKE the stunned sensation all afternoon. She had said nothing of what she had done to Jane, knowing that she would not approve and would try to persuade her to stay amongst family. Now the decision was made, and it was too late to turn back. Would she never learn?

Uncle and Aunt supported her. But she knew they would. That was how they were. It was not what they had hoped for her, but neither could they expect a perfect man who was everything Elizabeth desired to fall from the sky and propose to her.

As her possessions were packed into a trunk and everything readied for her departure on the morrow, Elizabeth went to the nursery for Jane.

She opened the door to a tender sight. Jane knelt by Emma's bedside, softly humming and stroking the girl's flaxen hair. Elizabeth paused in the doorway, afraid she might wake Emma if she crossed the floorboards. Jane lifted a finger up to her lips, kissed Emma on the forehead, and slowly rose. She walked softly over to Elizabeth, as only one who knows where the creaks are from many times crossing the floor could do.

Closing the door behind her, Jane clasped Elizabeth's hands. "How was your tea?"

"It would have been better had you been able to accompany us. Mr. Bingley was present, and it struck me that your character would be very pleasing to him...." She bit her tongue, realizing how similar to Mother and Uncle she sounded— as if marriage was all that mattered.

"I know what you are thinking, Lizzy. You cannot hide it from me, so wipe that look from your face. You are every bit as stubborn as Mother is." Her face flushed and Elizabeth sought to calm her— especially before revealing her news.

"My sweet sister who speaks ill of no one calling me stubborn? Come, Jane. You cannot offend me when I am all too aware of my own faults. I am in a forgiving nature and shall even overlook your comparison of me with Mother, although I suppose that, at an extremely basic level, you are probably correct."

"Mother and Lydia called while you were away," said Jane.

Eager to hear about them, Elizabeth asked, "Are they well? Have they settled in?"

"Yes. They are happily settled and called to invite us for a simple dinner to celebrate."

"How lovely! Mother drives me to distraction sometimes, but I have missed her and Lydia. Does Uncle know we are to go there this evening?"

Jane shook her head. "No, Lizzy, we are not to go this evening, but rather tomorrow."

Elizabeth's stomach sank. Looking around for somewhere to sit in the hallway and finding nothing, she led Jane to her room.

Jane looked about her. "Lizzy, what is this? Where are your things?" She stared vacantly at the trunk in the middle of the floor.

"I have accepted employment with Mr. Bingley's aunt, Lady Lavinia Rutledge. She is in need of a companion, and I am to go to her tomorrow morning." There. She said it.

Jane said nothing, but felt behind her for a chair to fall into. Elizabeth sat next to her, searching her face. The roses left Jane's cheeks, leaving them a pasty white.

"You are leaving me?" she whispered. She may as well have reached into Elizabeth's chest and twisted her heart. Nothing she could have said could possibly hurt more.

Exhaling sharply, Elizabeth buried her face in her hands. "What have I done? Oh, Jane, I cannot go back on my word! I was so determined to occupy my time, and I let my emotions get the better of me. What am I to do?"

She felt Jane's hand on her shoulder, trying to console her when she ought to be the one consoling.

Sniffing her tears back, she lifted her head and clenched her hands together in her lap. "I am sorry."

Her face devoid of the judgment Elizabeth felt she deserved, Jane squeezed her shoulder and asked, "Why did you wish to leave?"

Twisting her fingers, Elizabeth said, "You fit in so perfectly here. You have found your place and have made yourself useful to the children. Aunt and Uncle feel as if they have gained another daughter."

"They feel the same way toward you."

"I know it, but I do not feel deserving of it. I have wandered about the house miserable since we arrived. I feel that I do not belong here, nor can Mother receive me in her cramped apartment with Lydia. I feel that I do not have a place, and I..." her throat tightened so much, the words dried up.

"You always have a place with your family. Lizzy, we are your family!"

Elizabeth nodded, still unable to speak. Dear Jane would always find a way to make herself loved wherever she went. That was her character. Elizabeth, on the other hand, felt alone in a room crowded with relatives. She was dreadfully unhappy. It was time to take her fate in her own hands and, come what may, be the master of her own future. Jane would never understand her reasons, but she craved her acceptance.

"I know it," she said in a tremor. She must make the best of her new situation. "And I know that you only wish me the best. I cannot understand it myself, Jane, but I feel a tremendous need to be busy, and I am too idle here. I need to *do* something."

Jane squeezed Elizabeth's hands between her own. After some moments in silence, she said, "I will give your regards to Mother tomorrow. And Lizzy..." she paused. "Lizzy, I hope that you find whatever it is that you seek."

CHAPTER 14

Elizabeth arrived at Lady Rutledge's house at the hour agreed upon. Surprisingly, it was only around the corner from the Bingley's residence. Its proximity somehow made Elizabeth feel better. She would see Mr. Darcy often. Also, Mr. Bingley was a jolly gentleman, and Elizabeth had every intention of introducing him to Jane at the first opportunity.

Lady Rutledge was already up and dressed when Elizabeth was shown to the room she would occupy. Soft carpet hushed her steps. This must be what it feels like to walk on clouds, Elizabeth thought as she walked across the powder blue carpet to the large canopy bed. Satin covers and a plethora of assorted shades and hues of blue pillows dripping with yellow tassels made Elizabeth gasp at the beauty and calmness of her new room. It was the size of Longbourn's hallway and drawing room combined.

A writing desk facing a window with a view out to the garden waited for her with several sheets of thick paper and a new quill pen waiting to be dipped into the fresh pot of ink next to it. She would not be able to go to Mother's for dinner, but she would send her a note describing everything surrounding her. Mother would be impressed, and it would soften her disappointment as much as it would appease Elizabeth's guilt at missing Mother's dinner— or so she hoped.

Her single trunk looked small in the room and Elizabeth realized that much of her allowance would need to be used for a wardrobe worthy of a so-called niece of Lady Rutledge.

A tap at the doorway sounded. Lady Rutledge stood there, tall and regal in a soft lavender gown and bold, purple jewels. The contrast against her silver hair was quite stunning, and she was well aware of it. She held her head high and at an angle.

"You are right on time," she said, entering the room. "Do you find your new room to your liking?"

Elizabeth hesitated before answering, not wishing to sound too eager, when in truth, this was the finest room she had ever set foot in. "It is beautiful."

"I am happy you approve. Now, I do hope that you are rested and ready to begin your duties. I intend to treat you as if you were my real niece to give credence to my story. I refuse to give others reason to speak against me as if I were unable to care for my own needs or go out for entertainment without someone to constantly watch over me." She rolled her eyes and huffed. The unladylike gesture caught Elizabeth off-guard, and she had to hold back her laughter. Lady Rutledge— nay, Aunt Lavinia— was full of surprises.

"You may laugh, Eliza. In fact, I encourage you to do more of that particular activity. It suits you much more than this morose mask of misery you wear." She took Elizabeth's face between her two hands and examined her features carefully. "Hmm. You are handsome, and there is something in your eyes which suggests a sharpness about you. I think we will get along well, but I will warn you about my real niece, Caroline. She is as sweet as honey when she wants something, but if she suspects that you might get in the way of what she has her eyes set on, she is capable of causing you a good deal of trouble."

She referred to Mr. Darcy— a gentleman who would not be persuaded to do anything he did not want to do, no matter what Miss Bingley may plan. Elizabeth was unconcerned. "I have no intention of getting in her way. I am aware of my position now and realize the consequences."

Lady Rutledge arched an eyebrow. "Ah, but you must be so much more than a companion. You are my niece now. Like it or not, as far as anyone else is concerned, we are family, and I depend on you to hold up your end of this farce. The consequences to you of not doing so are far worse than suffering the talk of the *ton*." Elizabeth heard the menace in her tone and resolved not to put her to the test.

"I do not care much for what others say. Only if I fall in my own esteem would I have reason to suffer shame."

Pinching Elizabeth's chin between her fingers, Lady Rutledge smiled, "That was what I wanted to hear. You shall succeed if you remember nothing else."

Elizabeth did not understand in what she was supposed to succeed. By every account, she was a failure. She had failed her family. She had lost their home. Her mother and sisters were scattered when they ought to have been together. Her father's books were long lost to her; the familiar curve of his writing forever gone to her. She had lowered herself to the position of a companion— even though the lady refused to acknowledge her as such.

Dropping her hand, Lady Rutledge said, "I should like to go for a drive in the open carriage in a short while. It is a fine day outside. Have you breakfasted?"

"Yes, ma'am." At the look she got, she corrected herself. "Yes, Aunt."

A cup of tea and half a scone had been all she could manage with her nervous stomach. And even that had been at Aunt Gardiner's insistence.

"Good. We will leave as soon as the carriage is ready. Is that your best dress?" she asked, looking with distaste at Elizabeth's gray gown.

Elizabeth pulled the fabric from her legs and looked down. She had not thought it a bad choice.

"A niece of mine would never allow herself to be seen in such an unflattering gown. We will see to that today, so that you are more properly attired before I present you to my friends." Spinning to leave and leaving a trail of perfume behind her as she went to leave, Lady Rutledge said over her shoulder, "I will leave you to settle for a few minutes. Then I think we will aim our carriage in the direction of Bond Street."

Elizabeth did not want to be left alone in this beautiful, but strange, house. Calling after Lady Rutledge before she disappeared from view, she asked, "Do you have a library?"

Her request met with a smile and Elizabeth took heart.

"Come," said Lady Rutledge, waving her fingers for Elizabeth to join her. "I am not surprised you asked. Tell me, which books do you prefer?"

Elizabeth started with the safer and more accepted works of Shakespeare and the popular poetry and novels she could recite off the tip of her tongue. As she felt Lady Rutledge's interest grow, she moved on to the lesser spoken of political satire her father had enjoyed, Greek philosophy, and a few scientific works on horticulture.

The last earned a surprised arch of the brow. "I understand from your diverse interests that someone very special had a tremendous influence in your reading? It is not often that a young lady, especially one so young as yourself, holds much interest in plants and politics."

Elizabeth shrugged her shoulders. She would not apologize for her taste in the written word. It had been her best means of education whilst at Longbourn, and Father had encouraged it. Elizabeth would have loved an opportunity to study with the masters and have more of the accomplishments a young lady would normally have. She knew that others would look down on her lack of fluidity at the pianoforte, her untrained voice when she attempted to sing, her stilted pencil marks at a sketch... but she would not allow them to intimidate her. Nobody could take away what she had learned over the years from the many books she had read— books which opened her mind and taught her to see things in a different light.

"My father read extensively, and he encouraged me to do the same," she said with pride.

“He was a wise man,” Lady Rutledge said in approval.

They arrived at a closed door, and Lady Rutledge opened it. A large window in the center of the room illuminated the floor to ceiling shelves lined with volumes, some shining in their newness, and some absorbing the light with their worn bindings— like old friends.

She gasped as she stepped into the room and felt the comfort that only a well-stocked library could bring. Walking to the nearest shelf, she lifted her fingers and let them run across the spines, resting against the polished mahogany.

"Those are the foreign books. My husband acquired quite a large collection during his extensive travels." She stood next to Elizabeth, pointing to each section and indicating what could be found. It would take several visits to remember where things belonged.

"You may select a book to read to me this evening. My

eyes sometimes fail me, and I have neglected my reading of late. I am in humor for a novel. Something with some romance in it." With that, Lady Rutledge stepped back as Elizabeth entered deeper to explore.

There were couches and cushioned chairs situated throughout the library, but the seat in front of the window beckoned to Elizabeth. She went to the area dedicated to novels and pulled one off the shelf to read later. *The Mysteries of Udolpho* by Ann Radcliffe. It was a novel she had read before and would enjoy reading again.

"You feel at home in the library," Lady Rutledge observed, watching Elizabeth's every move. Elizabeth knew she ought to feel self-conscious, but she did not. Nothing bad could happen in a library.

"It is my favorite room in any home."

"I see that I shall lose you to the first gentleman with a well-stocked library."

Elizabeth held her breath. She did not know what limits would be placed on her as a companion.

A knock at the door brought her back to the present. A visitor was announced. It was a name Elizabeth had not heard before. Mrs. Enid Wharton.

Lady Rutledge's spine stiffened. "Oh, how I wish it were Darcy calling instead of Mrs. Wharton. She is the most tiresome creature. She has her sights set on Colonel Fitzwilliam for her daughter. As if that was not fault enough, it was her son whom I ran down at Hyde Park," she said with a scowl.

Looking to cheer her, Elizabeth asked, "Who is Colonel Fitzwilliam?"

It worked. Lady Rutledge's face lit up like a sparkling chandelier. "He is a cousin to Darcy. Being the second son and heir presumptive, he will not inherit the title nor the fortune of his family unless his elder brother is so unfortunate as to die, but he is an honorable man and would make a wonderful husband for the right lady. So long as that lady is not Miss Wharton!" She huffed and Elizabeth, full of questions about Colonel Fitzwilliam, Mr. Darcy, and Mrs. Wharton, followed her into the front parlor.

CHAPTER 15

They received Mrs. Wharton, and Lady Rutledge rang for tea to be brought in, taking care to give specific instructions to the maid. Her manners toward the lady were so friendly, it was no wonder Mrs. Wharton was clueless as to how much she was disliked.

"How kind of you to call so early, Mrs. Wharton." Elizabeth thought she heard a hint of sarcasm in Lady Rutledge's voice.

"I had to be the first to welcome your niece. I did not know that you had another niece besides Miss Bingley..." News traveled fast! Clearly, Mrs. Wharton fished for information.

Elizabeth smiled as sweetly as Lady Rutledge, leaving it in her hands to do any explaining.

"Oh, yes. My late husband's family, you know," she said in a low voice as if it were a secret she only entrusted to her closest friends.

Mrs. Wharton's eyes brightened, and she sat back in her chair. "Of course." She looked at Elizabeth closely before declaring, "There is a strong family resemblance. I ought to have seen it."

Elizabeth bit her lips and looked out of the window to better compose herself.

"And how do you find London and your aunt, Miss Bennet?" Mrs. Wharton asked.

"Very well," she said, daring not to reveal anything more until she could get her story straight with 'Aunt' Lavinia.

Expertly coming to her assistance, Lady Rutledge said, "Elizabeth has lived all of her life in the country, which I am afraid is what accounts for her lacking wardrobe— something I aim to rectify today." She shook her head in distaste, and Mrs. Wharton clucked in agreement. "I have not seen her since she was an infant. Her father passed away some months ago, and I felt it was the best time to renew our acquaintance. The Season is upon us, and I hope to divert her mind with the whirl of activities available. How lovely it would be if she and Miss Wharton could become friends."

Mrs. Wharton narrowed her eyes. She was competition now.

"Of course," Lady Rutledge continued, "I will take it upon myself to see that she is well-positioned to marry into a fortune. We hold no aspirations for a title— apparent or presumptive."

And just like that, Mrs. Wharton's eyes softened and her warmth returned. "I shall have to introduce you to my daughter, Rosalind. I think you will be great friends."

"I should like nothing more," Elizabeth said politely, in doubt of Mrs. Wharton's sincerity.

The rosewood tea caddy and teapot were brought in and the small, round table was soon filled with china cups and saucers, silver spoons, cream, sugar, small cakes, bread and butter sandwiches, and assorted sweets which opened Elizabeth's appetite and made her mouth water.

Mrs. Wharton said, "You will never guess whom I saw on my way here." She paused, evidently hoping that someone would venture a guess. When nobody did, she continued, "I saw Colonel Fitzwilliam."

The teapot Lady Rutledge held in her hands paused only long enough for Elizabeth to notice. If Mrs. Wharton had cared to look at her hostess' face at that moment, she might have cut her visit short. Elizabeth watched the scene before her— for she was certain there would indeed be a scene.

Her senses heightened, Elizabeth heard Lady Rutledge exhale slowly as she continued pouring the tea. She looked at the sugar bowl.

"I hope you like Souchong. I prefer its deep, smoky flavor over the green teas." She motioned for Mrs. Wharton to help herself, a suggestion she took eagerly as she heaped three teaspoons of sugar into her teacup and stirred.

Lady Rutledge, also, stirred one level teaspoon of sugar into her tea.

When Elizabeth moved her hand toward the sugar bowl, Lady Rutledge covered the top with her hand. How strange. If sugar was to be denied her, she would indulge in a scone with cream. She had not had sugar in her tea since Lydia had used the last of it in what seemed like an eternity ago.

Her lips enclosed around the silky cream at the same time Mrs. Wharton took her first sip of tea. Elizabeth nearly choked as Mrs. Wharton's expression changed from one of elated satisfaction to that of a shriveled prune. Her eyes screwed shut, and her mouth pinched as her face contorted. When she finally opened her eyes, they were teary and glaring daggers at Lady Rutledge.

Lifting her teacup to sip delicately, Lady Rutledge lifted a plate of pastries and offered one to Mrs. Wharton, then took another sip of her steaming tea. "Hmm. Most refreshing. Please have a biscuit Mrs. Wharton. You look as if you need it. Is your tea too hot? Some consider Souchong to be an acquired taste."

Mrs. Wharton looked between Lady Rutledge and the teacup she drank from. So did Elizabeth. If the sugar had been replaced, as Elizabeth suspected it had, then Lady Rutledge did not seem to notice. She poured herself another cup and dropped another teaspoonful of 'sugar' into it.

With a groan, Mrs. Wharton reached for a biscuit. She looked with longing at the strawberry preserves, but thought better of it.

No more mention was made of Colonel Fitzwilliam, nor of any other subject for that matter. Mrs. Wharton clutched at her stomach and ate her biscuit as quickly as she could, occasionally licking her lips as if consumed by a great thirst. The remainder of her tea continued untouched in her cup.

Lady Rutledge reached over and rested her hand on Mrs. Wharton's arm. "Mrs. Wharton, you do not look well. Is there anything I can have fetched for you?"

Mrs. Wharton said, "Lady Rutledge, did you not taste anything… different… in your tea?"

Her eyes wide in innocence, Lady Rutledge took another sip out of her cup, savoring it in her mouth. "It tastes the same as always to me. Mrs. Wharton, shall I call for your carriage to be brought around? You really look unwell. Or would you rather I send for my doctor?"

"I think I will return home. Thank you, Lady Rutledge. It has been a pleasure to meet you, Miss Bennet." Her chair toppled as she hastily stood and, without further ado, she bustled out of the parlor with Lady Rutledge trailing behind her to ensure her safe entry into her carriage.

Now the sole occupant of the room, Elizabeth tasted a few of the white granules from the sugar bowl. It was as she suspected. Salt.

When Lady Rutledge returned to the parlor, she paused

when she saw Elizabeth watching her. She crossed her arms defensively.

"Why did you trade the sugar for salt?" Elizabeth asked, more curious than upset at her action.

When she did not reply, only moved her jaw back and forth as she tried not to look guilty, Elizabeth repeated, "What else do you have against Mrs. Wharton?"

"Realize, my good niece, that I am under no obligation to answer your questions but will do so because I have a tendency to like you."

Effectively put in her place and figuratively slapped on the wrist for her inquisitiveness, Elizabeth waited for a response.

"Mrs. Wharton has a daughter who came out at the same time as Caroline. Just like Caroline, she is a tradesman's daughter and in possession of a sizable dowry. She also stands to inherit a great deal when…, but that is beside the point."

Elizabeth could not help but notice how quickly Lady Rutledge changed the subject. Did she do so on her account? Was she sensitive enough to her feelings to avoid comparing the advantages some young ladies would have at their father's death when hers had left her, her mother, and her sisters destitute unless she married for convenience? Elizabeth felt it even if Lady Rutledge did not. Why had Father done nothing to improve their situation? How could he leave them as he did?

Feeling her cheeks burn, she heard Lady Rutledge continue, "… her son for making inappropriate advances on the young lady walking with him. Normally, I am happy to turn the other way and let young lovers have their stolen kiss, but she did not look as if she appreciated his attentions. For one lady to have two foolish children speaks volumes against her abilities as a parent. It serves him right that I flattened his foot!"

Elizabeth would have laughed if she had not been too shocked. She would take care never to make an enemy out of Lady Rutledge!

Her rant far from over about the many faults of the Whartons, Lady Rutledge added, "Imagine the nerve! She means to marry her daughter off to Colonel Fitzwilliam. They would be the worst mismatched couple in all of England. The colonel needs a lady with a strong mind— otherwise he would soon enough grow bored. He needs a woman to challenge him and keep him on his toes— as befits a man who has grown accustomed to excitement during his years in His Majesty's Army."

Elizabeth, happy to focus on anything but her own feelings, as uncomfortable and disagreeable as they were, said, "And you think that Miss Bingley would suit him better?"

Lady Rutledge shrugged her shoulders. "That remains to be seen. Caroline has had her eyes on Darcy for so long, it would take an act of God to change her target."

Elizabeth's gut wrenched unexpectedly. Clutching her stomach, she said, "If Miss Bingley is so determined, I do not see what prevents her from achieving her goal." She prayed that Lady Rutledge would give her a reason to doubt Miss Bingley's success. She had no right to expect that Mr. Darcy could love a lowly companion— he knew the truth of her situation. Not that she hoped he loved her. She certainly did not love him! Though she did admire him a great deal…

"It is true. Caroline will stop at nothing until she secures him. I just hate to see her sell herself short."

Speaking before she could stop herself, Elizabeth said, "Sell herself short? With Mr. Darcy?"

"Do not tell me that you, too, have your sights on him, Eliza. He would hardly look twice at a young lady in any form of service— however appropriate and well-disguised it may be. And in a competition with Caroline, I fear you would come out the loser, my dear. She has been working on him for too long now to so easily give up without a fight." Her speech was so matter-of-fact, it chided Elizabeth all the more to hear it.

It took all she had not to reply sarcastically about Miss Bingley's inability to catch the gentleman in her sights in a more reasonable amount of time, but she held her tongue. She sat up taller, remembering that she was a gentleman's daughter with nothing to be ashamed of.

Lady Rutledge poured the rest of her tea into a nearby plant. "You have no idea how difficult it was to swallow this vile beverage."

"Why did you do it?" She softened toward Lady Rutledge. She had, after all, prevented Elizabeth from stirring salt into her tea— a choice she did not take away from herself.

"It would have been horribly rude not to. Had I not put any in my own tea, she could have openly accused me of giving her salt. I gave her reason to doubt. Better her think she is crazy than slander me as a poor hostess. Besides, how was I to know it was not sugar? There must have been a blunder in the kitchen."

Unconvinced, Elizabeth pressed, "You did not know it was salt?"

Pouring another cup for both of them, Lady Rutledge said coolly, "Does it really matter?"

AFTER A LONG AFTERNOON of dress fittings, Elizabeth returned home with a day dress in sprigged muslin and an elegant dinner gown with green netting fit for events of a more social nature. Lady Rutledge had insisted that she have one, for she intended on inviting several friends over for a dinner party at the end of the week.

Now that her mourning period was over, she was in need of a few dresses. She could not wear gray, stripes, and black ribbons forever— especially with the London Season upon them. How had six months passed already? In some ways, it felt like an eternity had gone. So much had happened. So much had changed. Yet, it seemed that only yesterday Father had returned home from Hunsford. He had been in a merry mood and declared that he felt better than he had in the past few months. His optimism and high humor made his sudden death all the more devastating. It had been unexpected.

Fighting against the gloom of her sudden turn of thoughts, Elizabeth went to the library to sort her feelings. She would not be a good companion if she continued morose, but the struggle between joy and sorrow sometimes overwhelmed her. She hoped Lady Rutledge would include Uncle and Aunt Gardiner with Jane in her party.

She could, at least, take comfort that Mr. Darcy would be there.

CHAPTER 16

Elizabeth tensed when Mr. Darcy walked into to the room in his evening clothes. He stood half a head taller than the other gentlemen in the room. His hair curled around the tip of his high collar, just shy of his perfectly tied cravat. There was nothing outlandish in his dress. To the contrary. He wore doeskin breeches with a white shirt and cream waistcoat, topped with a fitted black coat that showed how wide his shoulders were. He was the most elegant man in the room full of young gentlemen and ladies dressed to catch one another's eye.

Mr. Bingley kissed his aunt on the cheek and paused when he faced Elizabeth, a look of consternation on his face. "I apologize, Cousin… Eliza… beth, for my uncertainty, but I do not quite know how to greet you."

Elizabeth understood his predicament well. "Seeing how we are really only recent acquaintances, I can only expect you to greet me as you would a recent friend. I am happy to see you this evening," she said, looking between Mr. and Miss Bingley. "There is much about my own family that I do not know," she added for the benefit of anyone listening. Lady Rutledge showed her approval with a smile.

Her answer pleased Mr. Bingley, and he bowed with such vigor, Elizabeth leaned back to avoid a collision. Miss Bingley, on the other hand, curtsied with her nose up in the air. All the better with which to look down at Elizabeth. "Are you well settled into your new…" she looked over to see if Mr. Darcy was paying attention before she added, "position, Miss Eliza?"

Lady Rutledge furled her brows at her niece. "If you are referring to her new position in society, I assure you, we shall have Eliza well set before the end of the Season," she answered in an icy tone. "I am relying on you especially, Caroline, to show your cousin the ins and outs of the *ton* and to help her make friends." She stared at Miss Bingley until the young lady flared her nostrils and jutted out her chin.

"Very well," she said in a manner which bode ill for Elizabeth. What a turn in attitude from their previous meeting!

Lady Rutledge held her hand out for Mr. Darcy to bow over, which he did with a warm smile, followed by a bow to Elizabeth. Miss Bingley hovered at listening distance.

"Mr. Darcy, how good of you to grace us with your presence. You so rarely come to these things, I half expected you not to show yourself." Lady Rutledge fluttered her fan as she did her eyelashes, clearly aware that the violet color of her fan complimented her eyes. Mother could learn a trick or two from her.

Miss Bingley added, her nose pointed up in the air, "Mr. Darcy is too grand to mix in company with just anyone. Of course he would come here to see his closest friends." Obviously, she considered herself a great deal more important to Mr. Darcy than he did. He ignored her comment completely.

The complaint against Mr. Darcy confused Elizabeth. He had never been anything but gentlemanly toward her, and she could not imagine him acting in a way to upset any lady. Surely, he must have had his reasons for not attending before.

With a glance at Elizabeth, he said, "I can only apologize for not tending to your requests earlier. When I am in town, I am afraid that business affairs take up a good deal of my time, and I am not always free to do as I would please."

Lady Rutledge waved her fan at him. "You are here now, and that is all that matters. Now, I have a special favor that I must ask of you. I have it on good authority that you and Eliza were formerly acquainted. Since she knows so few of my friends here tonight, would you do me the favor of escorting her into the dining room when dinner is served?" She looked haughtily in the direction of Miss Bingley, whose lips were pursed so tightly, they had lost all color.

"It would be my pleasure." He bowed his head toward Elizabeth, and a curl of hair once more fell over his forehead. A dimple on his cheek flashed as he pushed it away from his face. Was he as pleased as she was that she was to sit by him at dinner?

A man in an army coat came in, and Lady Rutledge not-so-graciously moved Mr. Darcy off to the side toward Elizabeth and away from Miss Bingley with a push from her fan. "Colonel Fitzwilliam! How delightful you could come!"

The colonel bowed over her hand, then to Miss Bingley, and then wrapped his arm around Mr. Darcy's back in a half embrace. In a voice just as deep as Mr. Darcy's, but without the softness, he said, "And what did you do to lure my cousin out of his lair?"

Surely the lighting in the room played tricks on her eyes. Though Mr. Darcy's face revealed nothing, his ears looked like they had been lit up by candles.

"Richard. As always, it is interesting to see you." Moving to the side to allow more room, he presented Elizabeth to his cousin. Colonel Fitzwilliam looked between Mr. Darcy and Elizabeth, an expression similar to a little boy who had managed to eat the last biscuit in the jar on his face. Mr. Darcy's ears would catch fire if they burned any brighter.

With a graceful bow, Colonel Fitzwilliam said, "I am pleased to meet you, Miss Bennet. Do you plan to stay long in town?"

"I am here at the whim of my aunt, so will stay as long as it pleases her." She smiled at the gentleman. He was not handsome like his cousin. He was rather plain, but he oozed charm through his pores, and Elizabeth could not help but like him instantly. Even Miss Bingley looked kindly toward him.

Dinner was announced, preventing further conversation.

Mr. Darcy held his arm out to Elizabeth, and she took it, her eyes on Miss Bingley to see her reaction. While she felt a measure of satisfaction in her small victory, she did not want to make enemies among Lady Rutledge's real family. She must give the impression of being a relative to appease Lady Rutledge's vanity, but she felt more and more like an impostor as Miss Bingley looked at her with something that could be nothing less than hatred.

Fortunately, Colonel Fitzwilliam extended his arm to Miss Bingley, distracting her long enough for Elizabeth to turn away and walk with Mr. Darcy into the dining room.

Candles flickered on their candelabras, and as Elizabeth looked down at her dress, she understood why Lady Rutledge had insisted on the shiny satin fabric under the net overlay. She sparkled with every step and, for the first time since Father's death, she felt a healthy hint of vanity. The only fault it had was of being short sleeved. There was no discreet hiding place for Mr. Darcy's handkerchief.

Mr. Darcy sat next to her after she was seated. She hoped Miss Bingley would not be so close that she could not ignore her glares. Obviously, she considered Mr. Darcy to be her property— as if he would agree to be owned by anyone. He did not strike Elizabeth as the type of man to be easily trapped.

She looked at him, trying to justify her opinion of him with what she had heard in the parlor moments ago. If she were to believe the comments of others, she would have to believe him proud— so proud that he would put his own wants above the desires of others at the cost of propriety.

"Why do you look at me so?" he asked.

Elizabeth wanted to look down at her lap, embarrassed at her indiscretion. But she forced her eyes to remain steady. There was no sense lamenting when she had been caught so plainly. Leaning back in her chair and tilting her chin toward him, she said, "I was attempting to discern your character, Mr. Darcy. I have not the privilege of understanding you."

"My character?" He shifted his weight in his chair and signaled to a servant to fill his glass of wine.

"Your character confuses me so that I do not know what to think. In my own experience, you have been the epitome of kindness and understanding. But I hear such reports about you which contradict what I have believed to be true." She searched his face. If only he would explain the contrary comments with a word. She would believe him if it came to that. Why should she doubt Mr. Darcy when she was better acquainted with him than the others who spoke against him?

Swirling the wine in his glass, he set it down. The muscles at his jaw tensed as if the answer pained him to declare.

"I have faults enough, but they are not, I hope, of understanding. I will not deny that there is some truth to it. I have been called proud. However," he paused so long Elizabeth had to take a breath, “events in recent months have helped me to see the error in my attitude. I was humbled in a most profound way and have vowed since to improve myself." He finally looked up from his wine glass. He looked as if he wished to say more, but after quite some time, he sighed instead and drank a long draught from his glass.

Her curiosity piqued as to the source of his great change in character, Elizabeth waited for him to expound on the subject. But with the frown on his face and the tension in his manners, she did not ask.

Finally, after some minute-long seconds had passed, she said in a cheerful voice, "Then I am grateful for the events which caused such a profound change. I think it an improvement over what you described yourself to be." Her mind catching up to her tongue, she felt the heat on her face at the compliment she so outspokenly gave him. Hopefully the candlelight would be merciful and cover her change in complexion.

Mr. Darcy grumbled some sort of reply she could not hear clearly over the conversations surrounding them in the room, deepening her curiosity all the more and strengthening her determination to understand the man next to her. Her compliment, instead of appeasing him or winning a smile, had only worsened the struggle she watched him fight. What an incredible man.

"You are much more forgiving of me than I am of myself, Miss Bennet, and I thank you for it. You deserve an amiable dinner companion and I am determined to do the duty justice." He forced a smile, flashing another dimple at her.

Her disappointment deepened. Was it a duty for him to sit beside her? Had his opinion of her changed now that he knew her to be a lowly companion, as Lady Rutledge had suggested?

Squaring her shoulders and setting her jaw, she determined not to be a bother. She would see if by the end of dinner, he would eat his poorly chosen words and wash them down with wine.

CHAPTER 17

Darcy glanced across the table. Though a candelabra served to cover his view slightly, Miss Bingley craned her neck around the obstacle to glare at Miss Elizabeth. He would have to be cautious. Miss Bingley could make her miserable.

He would keep his expression plain and his conversation polite, but he would reveal nothing which would worsen Miss Elizabeth's standing or make her the target of Miss Bingley's ire.

Sufficient time had passed for him to say something. He looked at Miss Elizabeth and the clear thoughts of moments ago scattered away from him. Candlelight danced across her face, and her eyes seemed to dance with it. They were filled with what looked like contained merriment and no small amount of mischief. Her eyes sparkled with it. Her dress shimmered at her every move, giving her skin a silky glow. She looked so soft. Her hair, twisted up and secured in a simple fashion, begged to be let loose. The tendrils most young ladies coyly left down to draw attention to certain features fell of their own accord to caress her cheek and graze the tender spot where her neck met her shoulder. Good God, this would be a long night. He nearly tipped his wine glass over when he reached for it— like the tea he had dumped over Bingley's tablecloth a few days before.

Figuratively dumping cold water on himself, stupidity making him mute, it was a relief when she spoke. "I wonder, Mr. Darcy, if it is only certain company which you consider it a duty to entertain or if your every action is controlled by such a deliberate sense of responsibility that you see even the most pleasant of tasks as a duty."

He groaned inwardly, careful to reveal nothing outwardly. If only he could learn to speak without giving offense, but he had wasted too many years unconcerned with how others reacted to his blunt speech and arrogant manners. He now found himself in the position of wanting to be kind, but being unable to show it lest he complicate matters for the very lady he would go out of his way to please.

"I think any man with a certain position in society and with people who rely on him for their livelihoods ought to take his responsibilities seriously lest others suffer from his neglect."

Her eyes dimmed, and he knew that he had, once again, spoken too plainly. Would he never learn?

Clearing his throat, he decided it best to get her to talk so that he might say less. "How would you define good company, Miss Elizabeth?" he asked, hoping to draw out a lengthy reply.

She locked eyes with him. He could not look away had he wished to. "My idea of good company is the company of clever, well-informed people, who have a great deal of conversation." She arched her eyebrow at him in a benevolent challenge. "That is what I call good company."

"You are mistaken," he said gently, "That is not good company. That is the best."

She smiled at his reply. Finally, something he said had pleased her. It was a different sort of pride which filled his breast and made him sit taller in his chair. He had made her smile. He could make her happy, even if only for a moment.

He needed to keep her talking, to ask another question, something safe or else he was in great danger of liking Miss Elizabeth too much. "How are you enjoying your new life with Lady Rutledge?"

"I hardly know yet. She is a puzzle, but I do not think she acts out of ill will. I have no doubt but that she gives Mr. Bingley much cause to worry." She chuckled and her face brightened. "But I do think that a little mischief where there is no malice gives a needed spice to a life which would otherwise be rather dull. What else is a lady of a mature age and great fortune to do?"

"Yes, but she did run over an officer in the park. Perhaps her refusal to wear spectacles to preserve her vanity did not stem from a sense of malice, but I doubt the officer would agree." Good. If they kept the conversation on Lady Rutledge, they were on safe ground.

Miss Elizabeth leaned forward enough that Darcy caught the intoxicating scent of jasmine. He closed his eyes and inhaled her perfume. His head whirled and he leaned forward to— Blast! So much for behaving himself.

Thankfully, she did not notice. In a lowered voice meant for only him to hear, she said, "That is not the complete story. The officer was walking with a young lady near the driving path when Lady Rutledge saw them. She observed the officer attempting to steal a kiss— a kiss which the young lady, by all appearances, was unwilling to give in so public a place."

The part of Darcy which had him leaning toward Miss

Elizabeth sympathized with the officer. The part of him who had a young sister to protect was appalled.

She paused to catch her breath. "You see, Lady Rutledge makes use of her poor eyesight, but I do not think we should be so quick to believe her deficiency. It does give her the freedom to act in ways which would not be so easily excused otherwise, but I feel that she used it well in this case."

Darcy leaned back in his chair. It was necessary for him to distance himself. "I ought to have known. Bingley does not know of this?"

"No, he does not, though I must tell him." She sighed through a frown. "I must tell him even though it will help him realize that my position here is unnecessary, and I will soon enough find myself back at my uncle Gardiner's."

"The idea of returning to your relatives is unpleasant to you now? Most ladies in your situation would much prefer it."

She nodded, her lips tightening. "Not unpleasant. But I have made my decision and must make the best of it now. Even if it lowers me in the minds of others." She searched his face as if she wished to know how she stood in his mind.

He kept his face neutral until he knew where he stood. Nothing about Miss Elizabeth was expected. In every way, she acted like a proper lady, but some of the things she said and, at times did, bespoke a more modern view, a view which he admired greatly.

Darcy had practiced his emotionless expression to perfection over the course of decades, yet this was the first time in his memory that it was so difficult to maintain. One look across the table reaffirmed his determination not to set Miss Bingley against the young lady who believed him to be so much better than he really was. He would prove himself worthy of her esteem.

Choosing his words carefully, he said, "My father used to

say, 'Give a girl an education and introduce her properly into the world, and ten to one but she has the means of settling well, without further expense to anybody.' It is a statement I have only recently begun to ponder. I had never considered that a lady might want to work."

She ate a spoonful of white soup, reminding Darcy that the utmost folly would be to neglect to eat at a dinner party.

Dabbing her shapely lips with her napkin, she answered, "When Father died, I had to see to everything. Mother did her best, but she did not know how to manage our stipend nor certain matters pertaining to the estate. Everything fell apart with Father gone." She shrugged her shoulders. "Somebody had to see to it. I am grateful that I knew what to do."

"While being occupied has definite advantages, it can also delay your grief. I could not properly mourn my mother until I had also lost my father and the effect was devastating," Darcy said softly, staring into his bowl of soup. When he looked up and saw the pity on her face, he regretted saying too much. He had told nobody of his feelings of loss. Not even Richard.

"You had a younger sister you needed to be strong for. I can only imagine the difficulties you faced."

He needed to change the subject. This was far too intimate. "Is that why you offered to live here? To keep busy?"

She nodded her head. "I made a choice and acted on it. It remains to be seen if I have chosen well or not, but I am at peace that, at least, it was my choice. If it bodes well, then I shall be content. If it bodes ill, then I only have myself to blame." She ate another spoonful of soup. "Of course, now that it is done, I shall do my best to ensure that it goes well." A determined grin softened the depth of meaning in her words. She was the sort of lady to take delight in a problem—even one of her own making.

"I can find no fault with that. Your reasoning sounds realistic, albeit a bit rash in its execution. You do not fear the opinions of others to intimidate or lower you?" If she had not thought about it, he certainly had.

She leaned toward him slightly, a delightful smile adorning her lips, "There is a stubbornness about me that never can bear to be frightened at the will of others. My courage always rises at every attempt to intimidate me."

Oh, how he wanted to trace her lips with his fingers. "I am glad to hear it."

"Besides, I do not want people to be very agreeable all the time, as it saves me the trouble of liking them a great deal."

Darcy held his breath to keep from laughing out loud and drawing the attention of everyone in the room.

"I often feel the same, but I could never have put it so well," he said, giving more attention to his soup before he acted on his impulses and embarrassed himself.

CHAPTER 18

By the time the last course was served, Elizabeth felt confident that Mr. Darcy no longer saw sitting beside her as a duty. Though his expression remained guarded, something she credited to the ever-glaring Miss Bingley from across the table as well as his natural demeanor, there were several times when she knew him to be smiling. His lips had not budged, but she saw it in his eyes. It was enough to satisfy her.

Her humor in high spirits and her stomach full of delicious fare, she decided that she would tell Mr. Bingley about the events of the park before the evening ended.

Lady Rutledge stood, signaling for the ladies to accompany her into the drawing room.

Mr. Darcy caught Mr. Bingley and Colonel Fitzwilliam's attention from across the table and motioned for them to move toward Lady Rutledge. Apparently, he saw no need for her to delay in telling the rest of the story. Her suspicion was confirmed when he looked at her to follow them. Of course, Miss Bingley joined their group at the head of the table.

"What is this?" asked Lady Rutledge in a hushed voice.

Mr. Darcy nodded at Elizabeth, and she stepped forward, knowing what she was expected to do. "Aunt Lavinia, apparently Mr. Bingley knows nothing of why you ran over the officer in the park. He ought to understand your motives, as should Colonel Fitzwilliam, do you not agree?" She spoke quietly and quickly, so the other guests would not hear.

Lady Rutledge raised her chin up in the air. "It pains me to be doubted in the first place. Let us not discuss this now. I must lead the way to the drawing room." She moved her skirt to the side and took a step away from the group.

Mr. Darcy said in a low, commanding tone, "Is it true that you merely sought to protect a young lady from the unwanted advances of the officer?"

She stopped mid-step and turned to face the group. "Why else would I dare run over an officer of His Majesty's Army in a public place?"

Colonel Fitzwilliam stood rigid. "You replaced his boots, Lady Rutledge. Why in heaven's name would you replace his boots when he proved by his actions that he deserved to trudge in the mud in his bare feet? I shall have a word with him as soon as I return to the barracks. He will learn that he cannot get away with such improper conduct."

With an impish smile, Lady Rutledge said, "Oh, my dear colonel, I do believe he already has learned that. Every step he takes in his new boots will serve as reminder enough."

Mr. Bingley asked, "You did not have them made too small, did you?"

Chuckles followed her as she started toward the door, shrugging off her nephew's question.

As she stepped by Miss Bingley, who smiled as heartily as the rest and arched her neck to flatter her bejeweled throat, that young lady reached out to her aunt and said sweetly, "How horrible of us to have doubted you, dear Aunt. With this knowledge, I daresay you are free to continue living as you did before... without a companion." She emphasized each last syllable so clearly, Elizabeth could not mistake her meaning. Nobody could have.

Lady Rutledge looked at Elizabeth fleetingly before shrugging. "Apparently so," was all she said as she led the way into the drawing room.

Elizabeth stood rooted to the ground. There had been something meaningful in Lady Rutledge's brief look, but she did not know the lady well enough to read it. Was she going to have to return to her uncle's house?

Allowing the other ladies to leave before her, she brought up the rear and heard the door close behind her as she continued down the hall to the drawing room.

So consumed was she in her own thoughts, she gasped when she felt a hand close around her arm and pull her closer to the wall.

"Hush! There is no need to alarm anyone," hissed Miss Bingley.

"What do you mean by this?" Elizabeth asked. She had no desire to talk to Miss Bingley.

"What were you speaking about so intensely with Mr. Darcy?" she asked, her grip on Elizabeth's arm tightening.

Wriggling her shoulder to loosen Miss Bingley's hold, Elizabeth stepped back and out of reach. "Of what import is it to you what we spoke of? It did not concern you."

Miss Bingley closed the distance between them, the lightly illuminated hallway casting shadows across her angry face. "You are nothing more than an exalted servant. My aunt has done you a favor by disguising you as her niece to appease herself, but your allowance is nothing more than a salary. Mr. Darcy might be polite toward you, but he is a gentleman and must be polite to everyone. He would never disgrace himself by showing a paid companion more attention than is absolutely necessary." She leveled her gaze at Elizabeth, an ugly smirk disfiguring her face.

Elizabeth's blood boiled at her unjust comments and insinuations. "Mr. Darcy is a gentleman, and I am a gentleman's daughter. In birth, we are equals... unlike others with their roots in trade who would improve their position in society by marrying one of their betters." She refused to allow Miss Bingley to rob her of her dignity.

Miss Bingley considered her with a cold, calculating glare which heightened Elizabeth's nerves. Had she reacted in a fit of temper like Lydia was accustomed to do, she would have felt better situated. But the coolness and composure Miss Bingley considered her with chilled her to the bone.

"You dare be impertinent with me? I can make you suffer like no one else," she said with as much composure as Elizabeth hoped to summon. Miss Bingley was the sort to triumph in another's weakness, and Elizabeth was not about to make her weaknesses so easily known.

Behind Miss Bingley, a figure walked toward them quickly. Her white maid's apron stood out in the dark.

"Miss Bennet?" she asked as she swerved around Miss Bingley. "Lady Rutledge requests for you to find a certain book in the library. She wants you to read for the ladies until the gentlemen join them."

"Which book am I supposed to look for?" Elizabeth asked, hoping it could be found in one of the sections she remembered.

"She requested that you get the tome of recently published poems by Lord Byron. Do you know where it is placed?"

Elizabeth scrunched up her face, trying to remember in which section of the vast library the poetry was located. "I will find it... eventually." Were it not for the smug presence of Miss Bingley, she would have hunched her shoulders at the task before her.

Flipping a ringlet over her shoulder, Miss Bingley dismissed herself to join the other ladies. "Do not make us wait too long, Miss Bennet. We require you for our entertainment." How she reveled in putting others down.

Grabbing a candle and striding to the library, Elizabeth skimmed over the titles at eye level and below as quickly as she could without burning anything with the flickering flame in her hand. What she would give for a gas lamp, but she did not want to take the time to find one or to light it.

When she had gone the full circle around the library, she sighed in disappointment. "Drat the tall shelves," she said under her breath.

"Is there someone here?"

Jumping away from the door, the candle in her hand fell to the floor. "Yes, someone is here. Someone you have scared half out of her mind! Who are you?" she demanded, in no mood to make polite conversation. She was now in a dark library with no way to find the book she had been sent for. She could already imagine the beady eyes of all the ladies as she walked into the drawing room after they had been kept waiting too long.

The light of a lamp passed the open door blocking her view and in walked Mr. Darcy with his cousin, Colonel Fitzwilliam. She relaxed instantly. Not only was the appearance of the gas lamp a relief, but she fully intended on using Mr. Darcy's superior height to full advantage. That he was there with the colonel was an added benefit. Between the three of them, they ought to find the book in no time at all.

"I am relieved to see you. I was sent here to fetch a book of poetry to read aloud to the ladies, but I cannot seem to find it and now am even less able to do so without a candle." She bent down to retrieve the stick of beeswax.

With a crack, her head crashed against something equally hard, sending her falling backward across the carpet.

Rubbing his head, Mr. Darcy rushed forward, tripping over his feet in his haste.

Still seeing stars, Elizabeth raised her hands up as if she had any chance in stopping the grown man from landing on top of her. He smelled divine— of clean linen and shaving cream. She was close enough to see a small indent in his chin. Lost in her observations and too slow in gathering her wits, she wondered if this was what heaven was like. That was, until an elbow connected with her ribs and she realized what a fool she was.

"My apologies," Mr. Darcy muttered as he scrambled to the side, the buckle on his shoes catching in the netting of her skirt and dragging her with him.

Elizabeth rolled, unable to free herself without tearing a gaping hole in her dress, and landed with her hand spread out against Mr. Darcy's chest in a gesture which would have appeared to be an intimate display of affection between young lovers were it done under any circumstance other than the present.

Her mortification complete, Elizabeth reached her hand out to free the lace of her gown from the buckle at the same time Mr. Darcy attempted the same. “My apologies,” he repeated.

No matter how she moved, she could not get away from him!

She reached once again, needing to distance herself before she perished in embarrassment. This time, Mr. Darcy caught her hands between his own. She looked down as his skin touched her own. This time, it had not been an accident. Mr. Darcy held her hands on purpose.

“Please, Miss Bennet, stay still while I attempt to detach your skirt.”

Feeling herself better qualified to deal with the lace on her gown, she opened her mouth to protest.

"Miss Bennet, I fear that if you try to help me, we shall end up worse off than we presently are. Please be still," he implored, only releasing her hands when she agreed.

A cackle in the direction of the gas lamp turned their heads. Colonel Fitzwilliam shook so hard, light flashed and bounced around the room. If he did not calm himself soon, they would lose their only other source of light with his brusque movements.

Elizabeth felt the heat steaming off Mr. Darcy, and if looks could kill, Colonel Fitzwilliam would have fallen from the sharpness of his cousin's glare.

CHAPTER 19

"Watching you is better than any comedy I have yet to see!" Colonel Fitzwilliam chortled between laughs.

Elizabeth, who had been taught from a young age to appreciate the absurdities in every situation, felt a smile spread across her lips and lighten her mood. When she heard Mr. Darcy grumble at his feeble attempts to detach her dress from his buckle, she could bear it no longer. Months' worth of laughter welled up inside her and burst through her. She laughed so hard, her sides ached. The colonel had sense enough to close the door and guffawed all the louder at her joining him.

Tears poured down her face and it became increasingly difficult to breathe, but Elizabeth felt as if a large weight had lifted from her. She wiped her eyes and checked Mr. Darcy's progress. He had finally freed himself of her dress, but sat next to her with his arms draped over his knees. He no longer looked at the colonel in anger, but had joined in their laughter, thundering nearly as loudly as his cousin.

If the library were not so far away from the drawing

room, Elizabeth would have been concerned that they would be overheard. As it was, she allowed herself the luxury of laughing without restraint.

When her cheeks hurt and she had to stop to catch her breath, she wiped her eyes again. "I have not laughed so well since… since I cannot remember when." Turning to Mr. Darcy, who leapt up to his feet and held a hand out to assist her, she said, "I know I ought to be embarrassed. Indeed, I was embarrassed only moments ago. But I cannot find it in me to continue so when you inadvertently gave me the gift of laughter. I had missed it."

He pulled her up until she stood before him. Her fingers tingled, and he held on to her hands a touch longer than he needed to. If he held her much longer, she might melt from the warmth spreading over her.

Finally letting go of her hands, he bowed deeply. "I am all too happy to oblige, though I hope that mention of this never leaves this room." He turned to glare at Colonel Fitzwilliam.

The colonel held his free hand up in innocence. "Me? Even if I were to blab your story all over London, nobody would believe me. The great Mr. Darcy, who has never been trapped or placed in an awkward situation, sprawled out on top of a handsome daughter of a gentleman in a dark, secluded library? Never." He clucked his tongue and shook his head.

Elizabeth went cold. Panic rose in her throat as she looked between the two gentlemen. She could never force a marriage nor be induced to accept a proposal given out of guilt. She admired Mr. Darcy greatly, but she would never take away his freedom like that. Not unless he gave it willingly. Mrs. Elizabeth Darcy… It had a nice sound…

Foolishness and vanity! She was worse than Mother and Uncle Gardiner! Mr. Darcy had given her no reason to suspect that he held her in higher regard than he did any other young lady of his acquaintance.

"Richard, I beg of you not to make mention of this outside this room. When we leave here, it is done," Mr. Darcy said in a low voice.

The colonel's face grew serious. "Darcy, Miss Bennet. You have it on my honor that I will divulge nothing of this incident. I am a witness to the fact that it was all one big, innocent accident." His hand over his heart in a solemn oath, Elizabeth almost resumed her laughing at his stance and the relief she felt at his promise.

"I believe you," she said. "Now, I must find that book. Please, will you raise your lamp and help me? I simply *must* return to the drawing room before Lady Rutledge sends another servant after me."

“Which book is it?” Mr. Darcy asked.

“Childe Harold’s Pilgrimage.”

“Lord Byron? Lady Rutledge has taken a romantic turn,” said Colonel Fitzwilliam. “It is new and will stand out against the older, worn books.”

They covered more ground with the brighter light of the oil lamp and eventually found the requested item. It was on a shelf so high, Mr. Darcy had to stand on his toes to reach it.

As he lowered the book, he voiced the same thought running through Elizabeth's mind. "I wonder why you were sent here to fetch a book Lady Rutledge knew you could not easily reach. She gave you no indication as to the book’s whereabouts?"

"I have not yet learned how her library is arranged, though I have spent some time in this room. She has only sent me to fetch novels, and I do not recall her telling me where she kept the poetry."

Mr. Darcy and Colonel Fitzwilliam looked at each other, their faces increasing in alarm. "We had best return to the gentlemen. And you had best make haste to the ladies. I have a sense that Lady Rutledge is up to something." Mr. Darcy spoke as he moved toward the doorway.

"Wait. Why did you come to the library?" asked Elizabeth.

"We were sent here to fetch a book for Lady Rutledge," he said in a dry tone.

"Oh dear." Elizabeth dreaded her return to the drawing room. She had kept the ladies waiting a good deal of time—time enough for Lady Rutledge to scheme up all sorts of mischief.

The gentlemen returned to the dining room and Mr. Bingley. Elizabeth pitied him. His aunt had him at his wit's end. Between her and his pernicious sister, Elizabeth understood his desire to live in the peace and quiet of the country. Too bad he had seen the need to return to town.

Clutching the book to her like a shield, Elizabeth opened the door to the drawing room and froze. The book of poetry dropped to the floor. She heard it land with a thud.

Darcy burst into the dining room and made a straight line to Bingley, who sat leisurely in his chair smoking a cigar. The nearer Darcy drew, the more Bingley's cigar sagged in his mouth. "What has she done now?" he asked, extinguishing his tobacco and standing.

"Perhaps we should join the ladies and see," suggested Richard.

Shoving his hands through his hair and rubbing his fingers against his face, Bingley stood. Darcy hoped that his growing suspicions were wrong and there would be nothing untoward in the drawing room.

Falling into step behind Bingley, Darcy flanked him with

Richard on the other side. He would need their support for whatever was to come.

The remaining gentlemen followed. Darcy had neglected to pay much attention to the other guests at the dinner outside of Miss Bennet and his own social circle, but he was pleased that it was a small number of individuals who would be affected. There must have been no more than twenty couples in total. Hopefully, they would be a forgiving lot.

They heard the cackles and overly loud voices before they even opened the door. Bingley paused, his eyes widening as the door flung open and his sister landed in the arms of Richard, who caught her around the waist before she landed on the floor at his feet.

Looking up with a toothy grin at Bingley, Richard said, "Tis not every day a beautiful lady flings herself at me." He chuckled as he attempted to help Miss Bingley to stand steadily on her feet. She swayed back and forth in an alarming manner until she flung one arm up in the air.

"You will see! In the end, I will triumph!" she said as she fell backward and Richard struggled to keep his hold on her lest she hurt herself by landing on the harp behind her. An indecorous snore escaped her lips and Richard dragged her as delicately as he could to the nearest chair where he deposited her. She stayed there, slumped and snoring.

Bingley and Darcy stood in the middle of the doorway lest the other gentlemen witness the scene. But they now had no option but to part and allow the men to see their wives and daughters in their current state. The ladies cackled at a whim, spoke in voices much too loud for normal conversation, and each and every one of them held a glass with a liquid much darker than any sherry Darcy had ever seen in their wavering hands.

Elizabeth stood next to Lady Rutledge, clutching the poems to her like it was armor. She encouraged Lady

Rutledge toward them with a look so fierce, Darcy was grateful not to be the one to receive it.

Lady Rutledge had the maid bring over the decanter holding the sherry. "Gentlemen, I fear I have made a horrible blunder. You know that I do not partake even of sherry, but I wanted to serve my guests the best. I heard that this is what is popular with the royal family, but I think I must have made a grave mistake. Here, Charles, try this." She took the glass the maid had poured and handed it to Bingley. Darcy did not need to taste it to know what it was.

Bingley sipped the burgundy liquid and groaned. "Aunt Lavinia, this is port. How could you confuse port with sherry? They do not look the same."

Placing her hands on her hips, she answered, "I told you already. I wanted to serve my guests something special. The ladies are always expected to drink sherry, and I thought that they might welcome a change. How was I supposed to know they would enjoy port so much?"

Bingley sighed, clearly not knowing what to say. The gentlemen rushed to the sides of their women, each in various stages of inebriation.

"Oh, I do hope that I have not offended anyone," said Lady Rutledge, her hand touching her cheek as if she had been slapped. So sincere was her apprehension that the gentlemen in the room were quick to reassure her that no offense was taken, but perhaps they had best take their leave.

They carried their women as quietly as they could manage to their carriages, and soon enough only the Bingleys were left with Richard, Lady Rutledge, and Miss Elizabeth.

“I am mystified by Caroline,” said Lady Rutledge. “She could not have had even half of a glass.” There was a lady who could not hold her liquor.

Looking at his sister draped over the chair in the dreamless slumber of one intoxicated, Bingley walked over to Miss Elizabeth. Dropping to his knees in an overly dramatic gesture, he raised his hands up as if in prayer. "Please. I beg of you to never leave her side again." He did not need to clarify of whom he spoke.

Darcy watched as the innocent guilt faded from Lady Rutledge's face to be replaced by one of pleased satisfaction. She had planned this all along. Now, if only he knew why….

CHAPTER 20

The distance was short, but Lady Rutledge ordered her coach to take Miss Bingley home, so that she might avoid being seen. The unanimously decided upon alibi was that she had taken ill, although Lady Rutledge recoiled at the possibility of it being said that the food served at her table had made her niece feel poorly. But all actions had consequences, and Lady Rutledge would make the best of whatever came.

When their last guest had gone, Lady Rutledge said, "Do you still have the book of poetry? I should like very much to have you read to me. This has been an agitated evening, and I need some calm."

She led the way up to her sitting room where she reclined on a couch and ordered some tea to be brought up.

Elizabeth sat in a chair near the couch, but her mind was too busy for relaxing poetry.

"May I ask you something?" she asked.

"Of course. You may ask me anything. Whether or not I choose to give an answer is another matter entirely."

Elizabeth's cheeks tightening into a smile, she asked, "How do you get away with what you do?"

Her question met with silence, but Lady Rutledge's head turned toward her, lending her an ear. It gave her the courage to continue. "I think I am beginning to understand some of your ways. What you did for the young lady with the officer was noble, if not a bit dramatic. But when his mother came, you gave her salt in her tea. It is something I would wish to do under the same circumstances, but as much as I might cut her with sly remarks, I would not have taken such drastic action. Surely, she knew you did it on purpose. And tonight..." She closed her eyes at the gravity of what could have happened.

"It is their fault for drinking so greedily when they ought to have sipped delicately like a proper lady." Lady Rutledge sniffed and raised her nose.

Elizabeth did not want her display of haughtiness. She wanted a real answer. "Your own niece conducted herself the worst of all. Do you not fear for her reputation?"

Lady Rutledge looked keenly at Elizabeth. "That girl cannot sniff a cork without getting dizzy," she snorted.

She would make light of it, but Elizabeth was not convinced. She held her gaze steady and waited.

"I can see that nothing will get by you, so I will be honest with you to the extent that serves my purposes," said Lady Rutledge, now perfectly serious.

Her purposes? Elizabeth shivered to think that she had more than one.

Smoothing her skirts, Lady Rutledge said, "It is my experience that people overlook a great deal when a mistake is made by a lady with a sizable amount of money. All of the couples invited this evening have benefited in some way from my patronage. Unless they want to be cut off entirely, they know better than to speak out against me or anyone associated with me. Besides, do you really think that the men will let it be known that their wives and daughters imbibed so heavily that they got a trifle disguised? That only reflects poorly on them, and their pride will prevent them from talking."

Elizabeth shook her head. "You planned this from the beginning, did you not? Whatever for?"

"I had an idea that your position here might be put into question by the very one who encouraged you to take it. I merely put to rest any doubts Caroline may have about me wanting you here. As to why I am interested in keeping you on, I shall not say. I only encourage you to keep your eyes and ears open to find out for yourself."

She did not know whether to be flattered or fearful to be involved in one of Lady Rutledge's plans. Her breath caught in her throat as she remembered the most important question. "Why did you send Mr. Darcy and Colonel Fitzwilliam to the library to fetch a book? You knew I was there. And for that matter, why would you send me to get a book in a library I am yet unfamiliar with?"

Lady Rutledge's eyes twinkled. The tea was served at that moment, and Elizabeth was on pins and needles while she waited for an answer— if Lady Rutledge deemed her worthy of an answer, that is.

"I have my reasons. You will have to trust me, as that is all I am willing to reveal."

Not one to give up easily, Elizabeth asked, "You will not tell me why you sent them? What role could I possibly have in your plans?"

"Much more than you need to know, dear. However, I am sure that you were grateful to receive their help, were you not? Mr. Darcy is quite tall and could easily retrieve a book from the top shelves."

Elizabeth recalled how he had stretched to his full height.

She had felt so small as he towered above her. And when he had fallen on top of her…

"Hmm. I wonder what else transpired in the library to bring you such pleasant thoughts."

Elizabeth wished she had her mother's fan to chase the heat away from her face and hide the silly smile that would not go away.

With a knowing aspect, Lady Rutledge said, "Fear not, dear Eliza. You are in need of laughter and a healthy dose of intrigue."

Sighing in relief at not having to explain what had happened in the library, Elizabeth's mind latched onto Lady Rutledge's words. Perhaps it was impertinent to ask, but she would not know until she tried. "How long did it take you to recover from your loss?"

"From the death of Alistair?" Lady Rutledge leaned her head back against the mound of cushions and placed her hand over her heart.

Sitting up as if recently coming out of a daydream to remember Elizabeth's presence, Lady Rutledge reached over to clutch Elizabeth's hand. "You do realize that losing the love of my life cannot compare to losing a father. It pales in comparison to the love you will feel for the man you marry. I lost part of myself when Alistair breathed his last. Only when I remember the magical life we had together does his memory make me whole again."

Elizabeth's heart skipped a beat at the prospect of a love as strong as Lady Rutledge had described: A love which transcended the grave. "You make me wish to avoid marriage and desire it all the more at the same time."

Lady Rutledge focused her gaze on Elizabeth's face. "You will find that there are many more happy memories than there are sad. You will gain in strength each day that passes until you become so strong that the sadness cannot overwhelm you. You become stronger even than your grief."

Blinking to keep her composure, Elizabeth said, "I long for that moment. Months have passed, and I long to be happy again. I miss the carefree girl I once was."

"If I am not mistaken, you caught a glimpse of that this evening," said Lady Rutledge, a twinkle in her eye.

Elizabeth looked into her lap, so Lady Rutledge could not coerce the story out of her.

"I take your silence as a good sign, Eliza." Lady Rutledge sighed deeply. "Do not long to go back. You must never do that. Who you are today is infinitely better than who you were yesterday or the day before. You must learn some of my philosophy: Think only of the past as its remembrance gives you pleasure."

And just like that, the conversation took on a frivolous turn. But Elizabeth was glad to have had it. She had to stop living over her mistakes and regrets from the past. They lent no happiness to her future. Father, above all else, would have wanted her to be happy. She ought not feel guilty for that. Had not Mr. Darcy told her the same?

"I am tired now. You can read to me tomorrow." Lady Rutledge dismissed her, and Elizabeth was glad for it. She had much to ponder.

~

DARCY, too, spent a good deal of time in reflection on arriving home. His actions and the events of the library should have caused him much more embarrassment than they did. That he was at peace with what had transpired— proud even— gave him much to ponder.

He had made her laugh until tears of joy poured from her face. He could even overlook Richard's remarks and elbow nudges the rest of the evening when he recalled how freely and innocently she had laughed.

He would have to take the utmost care around her now. The wall of grief which had surrounded her before had come crumbling down, leaving only a few bricks in place. She would have her moments, but she would be especially vulnerable, and he would see that nobody took advantage of her. He would keep a watchful eye over her— from a distance, like he would hope someone would do for his own sister. Only, his thoughts of Miss Elizabeth were hardly brotherly.

He looked at the stack of letters from Georgiana and from his aunt Matlock. How reassured he had been when his aunt had suggested that Georgiana go with them on a tour of the Lake District before joining him in London at the closing of the Season. What she needed most after her heartbreak was the company of a mature female with a calming influence. It was difficult to look at Richard and know that he possessed such a mother. The two could not be more opposite.

Pulling out a piece of cream paper, Darcy wrote to Georgiana. Should he give her a full and detailed account of the events of the evening? She already knew who Miss Elizabeth was, and she would be curious to know how the lady fared. She would keep his secret just as securely as he kept hers. His quill hovered over the ink pot, paused in midair.

CHAPTER 21

Elizabeth enjoyed restful slumber, replaying the scenario in the library time and again, watching it in her dreams like a theater performance. If others could see the images in her head, surely they would have roared as heartily as she had. Of course, she was not free to tell anyone about the incident. Except for Jane.

A wave of homesickness swept over Elizabeth— not so much for the home she had lost, but for the people in it.

She wrote to Mother first, careful what details she revealed and including nothing unpleasant to give her concern. She did not want to needle Mother's nerves.

Then, she started her letter to Jane. It brought her joy to relive once again the events of the past days, improprieties and all. Jane would be shocked and would warn her to be cautious lest her reputation suffer by association. While it was something to consider, Elizabeth was curious…

She had only just handed her letters to the butler when she was summoned by Lady Rutledge to the front parlor. They had a caller.

Elizabeth walked into the bright room to see Miss

Bingley tugging at the curtains. "Why could you not see me in the drawing room, Aunt? It is much too bright in here and makes my head ache abominably," she complained.

"It is not the brightness which ails you, Caroline, but rather the indulgence of too much drink. Let it serve as a lesson to you to sip daintily," said Lady Rutledge, tapping her spoon against her cup and letting it clatter against her saucer when she put it down. Miss Bingley winced and joined them at the table.

Grabbing her forehead and glaring from under her eyelashes, she grumbled, "Why must she be here?"

"She is my companion now and must go wherever I go. It is an arrangement you insisted on… unless you would rather take over the duty yourself?"

The look of horror on Miss Bingley's face at that moment revealed her feelings on the subject.

"Just as I thought," said Lady Rutledge. "Eliza is a fine companion, and I am so happy that you insisted that she keep an eye on me."

Miss Bingley grumbled under her breath at the ironic turn of events.

Recovering herself as much as she was capable, Miss Bingley drank her tea. Elizabeth waited until she could see her reaction from her first sip before dropping a teaspoon of sugar into her cup. Unlike Lady Rutledge, Elizabeth stirred gently and noiselessly set her teaspoon on the saucer.

"Charles told me what happened last evening, and I came by to express to you my immense displeasure, Aunt. How could you do that to me?"

"My dear girl, you were not the only one affected, and I daresay your reputation will remain untainted by it. It was an honest mistake after all."

Miss Bingley glared. "Honest mistake? You seem to have an inordinate amount of those."

"Life is only lived once, Caroline. Would you rather I live a dull one?"

"I would rather you not live one so lively."

"Never fear. I still intend to leave my fortune to you when I pass. My... mistakes, shall we call them... are not costly and will not diminish your inheritance."

Miss Bingley harrumphed and squirmed in her seat. "I would not put up with you otherwise," she mumbled.

"It is my eyesight which has been affected by age, my dear, not my hearing. I will overlook your comments as you and I are too much alike to agree all the time."

"So long as you have not ruined my chances of securing Mr. Darcy, I shall forgive you," retorted Miss Bingley stiffly.

Elizabeth could not imagine Mr. Darcy choosing to marry someone as haughty and supercilious as Miss Bingley.

Lady Rutledge said, "I found it interesting how you threw yourself at Colonel Fitzwilliam— quite literally."

"I tripped."

"Be that so, you landed in the strong arms of the colonel. He had to carry you over to a chair. He was a good sport about it." Lady Rutledge looked at Miss Bingley intently over the steam ascending from her tea cup.

Miss Bingley shrugged her shoulders. "The colonel is a dashing gentleman, I will give him that. Wherever he goes, he is welcomed by all. But he is only the second son of an earl— the heir presumptive. No amount of charm can make up for that deficiency."

"So he will most likely not inherit his family's title. He still comes from a good family of a higher social circle than ours. Darcy does not have a title," said Lady Rutledge flippantly.

"He does not need one. With an estate as grand as Pemberley and ten thousand pounds a year, he is the ruler of his own kingdom and in need of a queen." Miss Bingley looked pointedly at Elizabeth. "He is not the sort of man to marry the first pretty face to cross his path."

Elizabeth did not think he was of that sort either. She took it as a compliment that Miss Bingley thought her pretty and smiled at her.

To Elizabeth's satisfaction, Miss Bingley huffed and took a bite of her scone.

"Be careful, Caroline. Darcy is not the sort of man to be told whom he is to marry either," warned Lady Rutledge.

Swallowing quickly, Miss Bingley said, "Well, he certainly would not consider marrying beneath him."

"I believe you are right," replied Lady Rutledge, her eyes fixed on her niece.

The importance given to the circumstances of one's birth grated on Elizabeth's nerves. She had been fortunate enough to be born into a gentleman's family, albeit a gentleman of meager means. Never before had she been made to feel inferior, and she refused to accept it now. Miss Bingley, by the same standards with which she judged others, was only the daughter of a tradesman. All she had was money. Mr. Darcy had no need of that. What would he need in a wife? Elizabeth gave enough attention to the conversation at the table to be polite, but her mind pondered the question.

"Lady Rutledge knows how to throw a dinner party! I have not enjoyed such diversion since… since her last dinner party!" Richard crossed one boot over the other, giving every indication that his visit would not be brief.

Darcy set down his morning paper. He had the luxury of a free morning and Richard was always good company.

"Have you spoken with the officer about his conduct?" he asked.

"I did before I left. He is quite repentant and will not allow himself such freedoms again." He chuckled, adding, "I told him that if he attempted to woo a lady so brazenly, I would have Lady Rutledge run over his other foot."

They laughed together.

"Such impropriety in a public place. He ought to be ashamed. A lady's reputation is nothing to take lightly. If it is lost, she is the one to suffer," Darcy said gravely.

Richard grew serious. "Aye. Georgiana's near elopement with Wickham is as involved as I ever want to be with such an event. On a lighter note, I received a letter from Mother. She said that Georgiana grows happier every day. Her appetite has improved, and she participates in conversation more."

Darcy blurted, "I told Georgie what happened in the library."

"You did what?" Richard sounded shocked.

It had been impulsive— something Darcy seldom was. But he knew it would make his little sister laugh. If she laughed only half as enthusiastically as Miss Elizabeth had the previous evening, it was worth it to him. He knew Elizabeth would agree— Miss Elizabeth. "I know it was a rash decision, but I made no mention of the lady's name and stated explicitly that you were present. I did not tell her about the drunken scene in the drawing room."

"Good! If she shares this news with my mother, they will cut their trip short so that they might see with what sort of people we mix. Mother comes across as being calm, but if she suspected that I had fallen into bad company, she would not rest until she had set me straight." He grabbed the paper Darcy had set on the table and flipped through it energetically.

Annoyed that he had set his paper aside to attend to

Richard, only to have his cousin paw through it, he asked, "What do you search for?"

"I have been reading the advertisements lately. One finds the most interesting things... Take this, for example. These are my favorites!" He cleared his throat to better read in a dramatic voice.

Matrimony— A lady of an affectionate nature and great respectability is solicitous of an equally affectionate and respectable gentleman of middle-age with comfortable circumstances to marry. The lady is lonely and seeks domestic happiness with a life partner.

Crumpling the paper as he attempted to fold it in half, Richard said, "What do you think of that? You ought to take out an advertisement, Darcy. 'Wealthy landowner seeks female companionship...' or something to the effect."

Darcy snatched the paper out of Richard's hands before he made more of a mess of it than he had. "I would never consider doing such a thing. I have enough difficulty meeting strangers as it is, much less setting myself up for display like—"

"—like some monkey at an exhibition?" Richard guffawed, slapping his thigh at his own cleverness.

Glaring at him, Darcy said, "You are incorrigible. I ought to write to your mother and tell her how young women with healthy dowries throw themselves at your feet and yet, you remain unmarried."

Richard's smile disappeared. "You win, Darcy," he grumbled, his humor gone at the mention of his mother.

"You need not worry. I will not write to her, so long as you refrain from comparing me to savage animals." Not wanting Richard to leave in a bad mood, he added, "Whoever wrote the advertisement you read was quite clever. Did you notice how she made no mention of her age, income, appearance, or accomplishments?"

Recovering his humor once again, Richard chuckled. "Unless you call being affectionate an accomplishment. I daresay she will get countless replies and may pick whom she deems best out of the lot."

"It ought to be an accomplishment in a wife. What man would want to marry a block of ice where there should be the heat of passion? I want to marry a woman who would make me forget myself when in her arms; a woman who can ease my worries with a kiss and inspire greatness with a clever word; a woman whose laugh makes me forget what it feels like to be sad and whose curve of the neck makes my heart quiver to caress her; a woman whose scent brings me to my knees and makes me forget to be polite." His fingers dug into the sides of his chair, and he tried to control his breath.

Richard stared at him. "I refrain from teasing you on the intensity of your emotions, Darcy, for I could not have expressed what I want in a wife any better. A man can overlook a great many faults so long as there is loyal passion in his home." Wiping his hands against his breeches, he said, "I need a drink after that speech."

Darcy nodded over to the sideboard where a decanter sat surrounded by glasses. He was pleased to see that Richard poured a drink for him too. He needed it.

CHAPTER 22

A month free of disasters passed, and Elizabeth began to think that perhaps Lady Rutledge had run out of mischief. She hoped so. Miss Bingley did not visit often, the Season being underway and, no doubt, being otherwise more pleasantly engaged in her quest for social prowess.

Elizabeth had accompanied Lady Rutledge on her calls and outings, drives through the park where no pedestrians were endangered, and even to an orchestra performance, several plays, and the opera. They saw Mr. Darcy nearly every day, his tastes remarkably similar to those of Lady Rutledge's. Elizabeth now looked for him whenever she entered a room.

She found herself with time enough to write regularly to Mother and Lydia, who did not return the favor so often. Lydia was careless and easily amused in other activities, so she thought nothing of her lack of correspondence. But not hearing from Mother filled Elizabeth with guilt every time she thought of her. No doubt, she was upset at being forced to leave her home and begin anew.

Kitty and Mary had sent word, though the letter was

obviously penned exclusively by Mary who threw in bits of information about Kitty. Apparently, a young officer called often enough for both Mary and Aunt Phillips to expect that an engagement would be announced soon. Mary had no such romantic inclinations and contented herself with her work. It was what she most wrote about, and she was so good as to include a description of a business trip Uncle let her accompany him on to a nearby village. It made Elizabeth happy to know that at least some of her sisters were finding happiness in their circumstances. They chose not to live in the past, and her resolve to do the same strengthened every day.

Jane wrote often. Her letters were full of news from Aunt and Uncle Gardiner, as well as the children. They were letters penned to make Elizabeth happy, but it pained her to see what was not written. Jane had designated herself to the role of a nanny. She rarely spoke of meeting new people, and she had not attended any public balls. Elizabeth could not lay the blame on her uncle, knowing him to be a sociable man and keen at widening his social circles to the improvement of his business contacts and nieces' prospects. Elizabeth could only guess that Jane used Emma's slow recovery as an excuse to stay in. She would write to Aunt about it.

A knock, succeeded by the swishing of stiff, silk skirts, announced the arrival of Lady Rutledge to her room.

"Good morning, Aunt Lavinia," Elizabeth greeted her with a smile. She still did not think of the lady as her aunt in her own mind, but it had grown increasingly more comfortable for her to address her as such in private and public.

"I hope you are well-rested. We are to go to a ball this evening!" She clasped her hands together and swayed gently.

Elizabeth's heart leapt! "How lovely! I dearly love to dance." Perhaps, if it were not a private ball, she might see Jane. She had time to send a message to Gracechurch Street letting them know where she would be. It might be enough to lure Jane away from the house.

"Good. As my niece, I will encourage you to dance every set should you wish it. When I was your age, my card would fill up before I could cross the entry hall."

"Is there anything you expect of me?" Elizabeth asked, cautious not to forget her purpose in residing with Lady Rutledge. Even though the lady allowed her full freedom, she was still duty-bound to keep an eye on her.

"I shall tell you if anything arises, but the ball is to be held by the daughter of Lady Cassandra— one of my dearest friends. Her granddaughter came out this year, and the ball is in her honor. It should be a lavish affair, and I look forward to seeing Lady Cassandra as well as my most intimate friends."

Elizabeth's excitement diminished at the mention of the exclusivity of the private ball. She would not see Jane there. But she would get to dance— something she had not done for far too long.

"How lovely it must be to see your dearest friends. I will never go so far away from you that I cannot be easily called."

"Very well. I will have the maid get your best dress ready. Might I suggest that you rest before we leave? I plan to stay until the last of the guests have departed."

Much in the style of Mother. Oh, how she missed her.

ELIZABETH CHANGED into her best gown and twisted her hair into the stylish coiffure Kitty had spent hours teaching her so many months ago.

Lady Rutledge wore a blue silk gown. Sapphire jewels dangled from her ears and throat. A matching silk turban covered most of her silver hair.

From the moment they entered the residence at Grosvenor Square, Elizabeth felt like she was being watched. Not the flattering gazes of people admiring her new gown or curious about her identity, but rather the criticizing stares of judgment. Lady Rutledge seemed oblivious to it.

She followed Lady Rutledge inside and through the crush of people until she found the hostess of the party standing surrounded by her gaggle of friends. Lady Rutledge introduced Elizabeth to her friends, but she was soon forgotten as the ladies reminisced about the past and made comments about the other ladies in attendance.

A smooth voice behind her said, "Come, Eliza, let us take a turn about the room." The hair on Elizabeth's arms stood on end. But she could not refuse Miss Bingley in front of her aunt.

Lady Rutledge waved her off. "What an excellent idea, Caroline! You can introduce your long-lost cousin to your friends and ensure that she never lacks a dance partner."

With a coy smile, Miss Bingley linked her arm through Elizabeth's and together they set out across the room. Miss Bingley nodded and smiled at her acquaintances, of whom there were many. She slowed down at certain spots, as if she were displaying Elizabeth to certain groups. They would look at her and nod knowingly, then turn their noses up and talk amongst themselves, every now and again turning around with their eyebrows raised to see if she still stood there.

Elizabeth could not guess what Miss Bingley was about, but she would not allow herself to be affected by it. She held her head up and forced her shoulders down and away from her ears. When someone narrowed their eyes at her, she smiled back in her most becoming manner. She was satisfied to see quite a few confused expressions cross their snobbish faces.

Miss Bingley made little effort to speak, making only terse remarks about the size of the room or the number of couples dancing.

When they rounded a corner and saw Mr. Bingley speaking with Mr. Darcy, Elizabeth was relieved to see their familiar faces. As they drew closer, she also saw Colonel Fitzwilliam. His eyes crinkled up in the corners when he saw her, and it was a pleasure to return a smile sincerely given. She had endured enough fake ones in the past few minutes to last a lifetime.

"Charles, you simply must do me a favor. Eliza and I have walked through all the rooms, and she has yet for a gentleman to ask her to dance. I am in a state of desperation, for Aunt Lavinia requested that I ensure our country cousin at least one dance." She spoke in a voice loud enough for others to hear. A giggle escaped a lady from a group standing nearby.

Elizabeth clenched her jaw and felt the fist of her free hand tighten. It took everything she had, but she kept her complexion cool and her tongue still.

Mr. Bingley looked appalled. "How could that be true, Caroline? Miss Bennet is one of the handsomest ladies in this room!"

Miss Bingley sputtered unintelligibly, giving Elizabeth reason to hope that all was well in the universe and her cuts had not gone completely unnoticed. Before Miss Bingley found her eloquence, she was interrupted by Colonel Fitzwilliam.

Slapping Mr. Bingley on the back, he said in a merry voice, "That must be it, Bingley. She is so handsome, the men are afraid she will refuse them and thus, like the cowards they are, they do not even ask."

Elizabeth looked around to see who had heard. The colonel's voice had a bite to it and she could not help but feel the insult to the gentlemen who had overheard. Clearly, the colonel was not afraid of confrontation.

Oh, would this evening never end? She had not been at the ball for half of an hour, and she felt exhausted knowing that she could anticipate hour upon hour of Miss Bingley's cuts. And though his intentions were honorable, Colonel Fitzwilliam only added more kindling to the fire with his outspoken comment. Elizabeth felt dozens of eyes staring at her.

Stepping forward, Mr. Darcy extended his arm. "You must forgive me for asking before you are able to, Bingley, but I should very much like the honor of Miss Bennet's first dance in London. That is, if she agrees..." His eyes were so intense as he looked down at her, Elizabeth forgot how to speak. She could have kissed him then and there in front of everyone for his courtesy toward her, but she satisfied herself by extracting her arm from the vice-like grip of Miss Bingley and resting her hand on Mr. Darcy's forearm.

A huff of air escaped Miss Bingley as they turned toward the dance floor.

"Thank you," she said, the profundity of her emotions muddling the words which could express how deeply grateful she was for his kindness.

"It is my pleasure," he said, his tone much lighter than it had been moments ago.

They lined up with the other couples and the music began. Elizabeth still felt the eyes of multitudes watching her, but they could not bother her. Not when Mr. Darcy wanted to dance with her.

CHAPTER 23

Mr. Darcy was quite probably the most graceful dancing partner Elizabeth had ever had the pleasure to dance with. Unafraid that her toes would be trampled, she swayed and skipped as the music demanded it and soon forgot how unhappy she had been.

"You are an excellent dancer, Mr. Darcy."

"I am pleased you find me so, though I do think that you make me appear more skilled than I am. I do not practice often enough to deserve credit."

"You do not enjoy dancing?"

A painful expression crossed his face. "I try to avoid it."

Every time she met Mr. Darcy, she learned something new and surprising. How could a gentleman who danced as confidently as he did not enjoy it? With several minutes before them and nothing to lose, she asked. "I cannot fathom how you can possess such lightness of feet when you confess that you do not like to dance. Pray, tell me how that is possible."

"Any skill can be learned to exception under the correct

tutelage. Unfortunately, I lack the social skills which would encourage me to engage more in the activity."

He sounded so arrogant when his deeds toward her had been so chivalrous, the contrast made her laugh. "You are full of contradictions, sir. You profess not to like meeting people nor to have any skill in conversation, yet I have judged your character to be everything affable and considerate."

"You judge too easily, Miss Bennet," he said, his voice devoid of laughter.

She pondered his dry reply. She took no offense at it, for she did not believe it to be true. That Mr. Darcy errantly believed himself to be haughty and pompous must be the case. He had no reason to lie, nor did Elizabeth think him capable of duplicity.

Taking his statements against his own character, she challenged him. "A man's character is proved through his actions. I refuse to believe you anything other than what I have experienced for myself. Should everyone in this room speak against you, I would remember how you handed a stranger a handkerchief and how you asked me to dance when no one else would. Perhaps you acted against your better judgment. It would not surprise me to hear you say so, and thus I say it before you have the chance. However, I think that you are an honorable gentleman. And I thank you."

COULD she now read his thoughts? Knowing that he deserved her criticism made him desire her approval all the more intensely.

He nodded, trying to think of how he could reply. He wanted to change the topic, but she deserved more acknowledgment than a simple nod.

"Will your sister join you in town during the Season?" she asked. She was a mind-reader.

"She is with my aunt, Lady Matlock— Colonel Fitzwilliam's mother— touring the Lake District. They plan to join us in town in June."

"That is only just over a month away! How delightful to be reunited with your family."

He heard the longing in her voice as plainly as if she had stated it. "Do you miss your family?" he asked.

She smiled, her eyes glistening with the tears of one too long separated from the ones she held dearest. Georgiana had a much more difficult time adjusting after Father's death than he had. Girls were not trained to be independent from their families, leaving one home to marry into another without any time to be alone in the world. He admired Miss Elizabeth's gumption for setting out on her own so boldly without anyone to guide her in the path she had chosen. She was an extraordinary woman.

"I miss them a great deal— much more than I had thought possible. We are as different as night and day amongst ourselves, but we have always been together. Even though I have not always been the best daughter and sister, I know that they love me still." Her voice wavered ever so slightly.

"That is as it should be. If circumstances changed, would you reunite yourself with them?"

"If they would have me. They all seem to have moved on with their lives... as they should."

He made a mental note to remember that. With Georgiana and Aunt Helen coming to town in a month's time, the Bennets might be a welcome addition to their circle of friends. Darcy would find out what he could.

"You mentioned that you are different from your family?" He paused, knowing she would be happy to speak of her family as most people were.

"My eldest sister, Jane, is the gentlest lady I have yet to meet. She thinks kindly toward everyone and never suffers an ill temper."

"Her disposition sounds similar to that of Bingley."

She smiled. "Then you are fortunate to have such a friend. I am grateful for the good friends I have."

"Lady Rutledge has taken a liking to you, as well. Now that you know her better, do you like staying with her?"

"I am grateful she likes me," she said, her smile widening. "Otherwise, I know her capable of making me miserable. I have never met anyone like her."

Darcy sighed. "She is unique, but I hold her in high regard. She lives in a way which better suits her happiness and pays little attention to the expectations of others without neglecting her responsibilities."

"I had noticed that. Still, I can see how she would cause Mr. Bingley a great deal of trouble."

Chuckling, he bowed as the music came to an end. He watched her curtsy, a curl of hair bewitching him at the nape of her unadorned neck. He had never wished to wind his finger in a lady's hair so badly as he did that moment.

Someone bumped into him, nearly sending him across the small space separating him from Miss Elizabeth. He turned to see who the culprit was. Richard.

His cousin stood with a large grin on his face. "I apologize, Darcy. Sometimes I do not realize my own strength."

Darcy rolled his eyes. "What brings you here?"

Dropping his voice and stepping closer so that Miss Elizabeth might hear, he said, "I overheard the gossip and am here to put an end to it." Looking at Miss Elizabeth, he said, "Miss Bingley has spent the past week slandering you. She has let it be known that you were the one to suggest posing as a niece to preserve your dignity and set yourself up in Society." Putting his hand over his heart and striking a pose, he did his best imitation of Miss Bingley. "I am appalled at her presumptuousness in assuming a relation to our great family, so that she might marry into a fortune." He leaned in and said as softly as a man incapable of a whisper, "This will put a bur in her side!"

Miss Elizabeth giggled. "I know I should be offended, but I have decided that nothing will spoil this evening."

"Good. That is the spirit! Now," said Richard, extending his arm out to Miss Elizabeth, "may I have the honor of the next dance?" To Darcy he added, "Between the two of us, we shall see that Miss Bingley's plans are frustrated. Oh, how I take pleasure in bringing her down a notch! Look at her glaring at us!" he chortled.

Miss Elizabeth accepted his request, and Darcy departed before the music began. He was fairly certain that the other gentlemen would follow his and Richard's example so that Miss Elizabeth would never lack a partner for the duration of the ball, but he would ensure her one more dance. He strode across the rooms in search of Bingley.

ELIZABETH DANCED ALL EVENING, the gentlemen lining up to ask for their turn.

She danced until she could no longer feel her feet and her cheeks ached from her constant smiles. The evening improved greatly after her initial ostracism, but none of the men could compete with Mr. Darcy. Once again, he had come to her rescue.

Miss Bingley glared at her every so often, only a handful of her dearest friends surrounding her and talking behind their fans. She had lost her battle that night, thanks in good part to the colonel, who stood near Miss Bingley and beamed at her whenever she looked his way. He took great pleasure in frustrating her every move and even favored her with a dance. Miss Bingley struggled to keep her haughty pose in check, but there were brief moments when she appeared to genuinely enjoy herself with the colonel.

However, Elizabeth did not forget who had acted first. Mr. Darcy, without knowing the source of a ballroom full of snubs toward her, had asked her to dance. He had not hesitated.

Hobbling over to the corner with a view of the dance floor and an easy distance from the refreshment table, Elizabeth joined Lady Rutledge. On seeing her coming, Lady Rutledge patted the empty space on the couch next to her and made a comment which made her friends welcome her with smiles.

"I declare your first ball in London to be a great success," she said as Elizabeth eased the weight off her feet.

"I have never danced so much in all my life," said Elizabeth. To the grandmother of the hostess, she added, "Nor have I seen such an exquisitely decorated room. Your granddaughter will look back on this evening with much pleasure for years to come."

They chatted for some time until Mr. and Miss Bingley came over to bid them good evening.

As Miss Bingley leaned in to kiss her aunt, Elizabeth heard Lady Rutledge say, "Now that did not turn out quite as you expected, did it?" With the sweetest of smiles from a loving aunt, she told them to rest well.

Nothing escaped Lady Rutledge's notice.

CHAPTER 24

Miss Bingley did not call during the next couple of days. Not that Elizabeth missed her. She was too busy.

She still had not heard from Mother. If it had not been for Jane's reassurances in her letters, Elizabeth would have worried a great deal more than she did.

Elizabeth sat next to Lady Rutledge, reading aloud to her until their next social engagement, when Miss Bingley was announced.

She waltzed into the comfortable drawing room and sank down in a plush chair opposite her aunt, while doing her best to ignore Elizabeth.

"It is about time you called, Caroline. I had begun to think that you had left town. That would have been very unpleasant of you without telling me of it first." Lady Rutledge chided her niece in a sharp tone.

Arranging her skirts to the best effect, even though no gentlemen were present in the room to impress, she answered, "I have hardly been at home lately what with all of the demands on my schedule."

"I am glad to hear it. You have already made it through a few seasons without snagging a husband. I suspect that you will have better success this year."

Elizabeth swallowed hard to keep from laughing.

Miss Bingley feigned indifference, though the color in her cheeks deepened. "Yes, I have made significant progress on that front. Not that I have not been asked, mind you."

"Of course not, my dear. You are far too handsome to lack in suitors," agreed her aunt. "What you lack is good sense by insisting on marrying someone wholly unsuited to you."

Miss Bingley pursed her lips. "Who would *you* have me marry?" she snapped.

Lady Rutledge shrugged her shoulders.

A tap on the door preceded the butler's entry into the room. He carried a silver tray with some letters on it. Elizabeth expected nothing for herself, but she still peeked over the top of the tray to see.

"Two letters have arrived for Miss Bennet and the rest are for you, ma'am," he announced as he placed the tray in front of them. The first letter had the familiar handwriting of Aunt Gardiner. The other letter was from Mother. She stared at it, rubbing her thumb over her large, embellished letters.

She pressed them to her breast when she felt Miss Bingley's breath against her hand.

"Gracechurch Street? Do you have relatives there, Miss Eliza?" she asked.

Seeing no reason why she should not respond openly, Elizabeth said, "Yes. My aunt and uncle live at Gracechurch street. My eldest sister, Jane, currently resides with them."

"Is she the one I have heard you speak of so often?" asked Lady Rutledge. Leaning over to Miss Bingley, she added, "From what I hear from Eliza, she is a real beauty."

Miss Bingley's face soured. If only she knew how ugly she looked wearing that expression.

"Who is your other letter from?" asked Lady Rutledge.

"The other letter is from my mother."

"She lives at the address of a dancing school?" asked Miss Bingley.

Impressed with her eyesight and quick reading, Elizabeth said, "Yes. She and my youngest sister, Lydia, live in an apartment above one."

Miss Bingley rolled her eyes and inclined her head off to the side. "How charming, for sure," she said flatly.

"Perhaps we should invite them over for tea before long," suggested Lady Rutledge. "I admit to being curious about your mother. Do you resemble her a great deal?"

Elizabeth paused. She loved her mother dearly, but she could not easily speak of her. "My mother wishes for nothing more than security for her daughters."

"She wishes for you to marry?" asked Miss Bingley, one side of her mouth tilting up.

"I believe that most mothers wish for their daughters to marry," said Elizabeth, hoping that Miss Bingley would tire of the subject.

"How many daughters are there?" she asked.

"We are five."

"Have any of your sisters married?"

Growing increasingly uncomfortable, Elizabeth kept her answer brief. "No. Not one."

Her smirk widening, Miss Bingley said, "How difficult it must be for a mother with five daughters in reduced circumstances to be deprived of the joy of seeing them married."

Lady Rutledge harrumphed. "You ought to know about that, Caroline. You ought not criticize others for something you have been incapable of accomplishing yourself."

Elizabeth held her arms and legs still so that she would not squirm impatiently in her seat. She so badly wanted to dismiss herself and go upstairs to read her letters. Why had she thought that being a companion was such a wonderful idea? An act of madness, a decision made with emotion—that was what it was.

"Eliza, you may go up to your room to read your letters," said Lady Rutledge.

Elizabeth did not need any more persuasion than that. She made it up the stairs and down the hallway to her room in short time.

First, she read Mother's. The letters were difficult to read, being written in haste and with her flourished style of adorning each letter with unnecessary loops and marks. She and Lydia were kept busy with a multitude of callers and made more new friends every day. It was not the quiet life of a widow in mourning, but the diverting account of a young lady visiting town for the first time. Elizabeth poured over every word, written on both sides, hoping to find some information of substance. However, Mother only wrote of parties, her growing list of acquaintances, and her high hopes that her girls marry before the end of the year.

Elizabeth dropped her hands to her lap, the paper crumpling in her hands. What had she expected? Was not Mother acting precisely as she always had— with no other motive but to marry her daughters and take advantage of every social occasion set before her?

She tried to think well of her mother's happiness, but Mother acted as if she did not miss Father at all. As if she had already forgotten him. Elizabeth knew in her mind that her parents' marriage had long ago ceased to thrive on love. They had lived in indifferent complacency for as long as she could remember, but she felt that her father deserved more from his widow. Did he not? On the other hand, what was the purpose of living if it were not to be happy?

Frustrated and uncomfortable with the mix of emotions brought on by Mother's letter, she cracked the wax seal on

Aunt Gardiner's letter and settled into her chair to be delighted with her latest news.

A particular sentence caught her eye and she had to read it again. Sitting as straight as a board in her chair, she continued reading at a quicker pace. No, no, no! It could not be!

She started again, hoping that somehow she had misread the communication and her plans were not for naught. But there it was still. Jane was to accompany Aunt, Uncle, and the children to the coast for the improvement of Emma's health. They would be gone for a month.

Elizabeth felt like a child who had been promised an outing only to wake to rain.

CHAPTER 25

"You seem out of sorts, Eliza. What is wrong?" demanded Lady Rutledge. "Did your letters not contain good news?"

"Jane is leaving town with Aunt and Uncle for the coast. My cousin is recently recovered from a fever and the doctor suggested that the fresh sea air would improve her greatly. It is good, and I have no doubt but that Jane will benefit from the trip... but I had so hoped to see her."

"When is she to leave?"

"Today," she said, not bothering to straighten her slumping shoulders.

Lady Rutledge frowned. "How inconvenient. I have already sent an invitation to Caroline and Charles for luncheon tomorrow so that they might meet her. I even went so far as to include Mr. Darcy and Colonel Fitzwilliam to balance the table."

Jane would have enjoyed herself and surely with three single gentlemen present, she would catch the interest of at least one.

Her gut twisted and her fingers went cold. What if Mr.

Darcy preferred Jane? She was certainly more handsome, and she showed a much greater consideration for propriety than Elizabeth.

She pushed the dark thought aside, giving Lady Rutledge her full concentration. Maybe she would distract her out of her contrary mood.

Tapping her pointy fingernails against her chin, Lady Rutledge pondered. "I do not want to cancel our luncheon when it has already been planned. Do you suppose your mother and the sister with her would agree to join us?"

Elizabeth held back her initial joy. How would Lady Rutledge view her family? What would Mr. Darcy think of them? "They are in town, but my sister, Lydia, is much younger than Miss Bingley. I do not know that they could become such good friends as I suspect she and Jane would. Like most young people her age, she is... impulsive and... inclined to say the wrong thing."

She should have said that Lydia was a bore. That would have dissuaded Lady Rutledge. Contrary to what Elizabeth had hoped, the older woman brightened and she clasped her hands together. "Oh how lovely! It will be good for Caroline to be around someone who does not feel the need to seek the approval of others to the detriment of her own enjoyment of life. It is decided! Instead of your aunt and eldest sister joining us, we shall invite your mother and youngest sister."

Elizabeth, filled with anticipation and misgiving, asked, "Are you certain?"

"Absolutely. It is perfect. You can write to your mother right now and we can send it by messenger so that we may get her reply immediately."

Elizabeth's only hope was that Miss Bingley would be kind and Lydia would remain quiet.

~

"ARE you coming with us to the luncheon Aunt Lavinia plans for tomorrow, Darcy?" asked Bingley, moving a chess piece to the sounds of rustling newspapers and hushed steps in the library of the gentleman's club.

He shrugged his shoulders, uncertain how to reply without sounding too eager. "I should like to go very much, but I must see if I am available at that hour." The truth was that he longed to see Miss Elizabeth again.

"Make yourself available! Aunt said that the purpose of her luncheon is to introduce us to Miss Bennet's eldest sister, Miss Jane Bennet. Is that not a lovely name?" Bingley rested his cheek against his hand and sighed.

"Are you so determined to fall in love that you would become infatuated with a name? Come, Bingley. Love is not a trifle sentiment to be taken so lightly." He had seen the expression Bingley wore before. Several times, in fact. "Checkmate."

Dropping his hand, Bingley bunched his eyebrows together. "You insult me, Darcy. Have I not made it through over a month of the Season without declaring myself in love? No, I am decided that I shall be more selective in my choice of a wife. I am no longer of an age to indulge myself in harmless flirtations."

"Flirtations are never harmless," Darcy said.

"Perhaps not for someone like you. You are much too serious for it. I, on the other hand, have had to learn that kindness is oftentimes mistaken for flirtation by young ladies looking to abandon their single state. I cannot manage to act unkindly, and thus it behooves me to marry before I am trapped by someone for whom I have no particular regard. I should much rather choose my own wife, you know."

Darcy chuckled. "You have become wise of late."

Bingley smiled at the compliment. "Wisdom by association, Darcy."

They sat in silence for some time, which was odd for Bingley. He was not the sort of man to lack words or get lost in his thoughts.

"I do think that I shall know her when I see her," Bingley said finally.

"You believe in love at first sight?" asked Darcy. He would not discredit Bingley so quickly. He still remembered the first time he saw Miss Elizabeth. Not that he was in love, mind you. He admired her greatly. That was all.

"I cannot be for certain, never having experienced the sensation to that degree. I have thought several ladies agreeable at first sight, but I cannot say that I loved them. I would like to think that each of us has the ability to connect to the emotions of a lady in such a way as to understand each other from the beginning. The ideal would be that she reciprocates, of course, or else I would have to lead a life of misery being ignored by the one woman I felt a profound attachment to." His romantic idea, once elaborated on, waned in intensity. As so often happened in the novels, he went from the height of elation to the depths of despair.

Darcy, not wanting his friend to suffer long, said, "While I do not agree with the whole of the idea, there is some truth to it. Otherwise, why do some experience matrimonial bliss independent of the amount of time spent in courtship? I have found that, oftentimes, the married couples who married after a brief courtship are just as happy as those who have known each other their entire lives."

"That gives me hope, Darcy. All the ladies with whom I grew up are either already married or are…" Bingley shivered in repulsion. "I would never insult a lady by implying that she was… unfortunate in appearance… but suffice it to say that there are no ladies of my early acquaintance whom I would consider marrying."

“There are ladies who increase in beauty on further acquaintance,” suggested Darcy.

“And there are others who worsen,” sighed Bingley.

"Let us pray that you are able to discern which camp the lady of your choice falls into before you marry her."

The first time he had seen Miss Elizabeth, her face was stained with tears and her eyes had been swollen and red. It was not the sort of encounter to inspire romantic feelings. Yet, his heart had stirred— with admiration.

She had been handsome to begin with, but their lively conversations and her outspokenness— even when she was wrong— had adorned her until Darcy believed her to be the handsomest lady of his acquaintance.

Abruptly, he rose from his chair, startling Bingley.

"I apologize. There is some business I remember that must be seen to. I will not be able to accompany you tomorrow and will send my regards to Lady Rutledge. I wish you a pleasant luncheon and hope that Miss Jane Bennet is everything you hope her to be. Good day, Bingley."

He left the room before Bingley could ask him what his business was about or attempt to dissuade him in any way. He knew what he must do for Miss Elizabeth, and he would not leave any detail up to chance.

CHAPTER 26

The morning crawled by. Elizabeth had gone to bed disappointed the night before and her humor only worsened as the day progressed.

Mr. Darcy had called the previous afternoon, but they had been out taking a drive in the park. Elizabeth loved the opportunity to be out of doors and she dearly missed her daily long walks, but she would have encouraged Lady Rutledge to stay in had she known that he would call. He would be unable to join them for luncheon.

So, she prepared herself to receive Mother and Lydia, her excitement only dampened by the threat of Miss Bingley's critical eye.

She descended the stairs to the parlor where a round table had a checkered cloth laid over it so that it resembled an indoor picnic. Cucumber sandwiches, assorted cakes and biscuits, strawberries, and other treats to delight the senses covered the surface. Lydia, always one with a healthy appetite, would be in raptures. There was a large, crystal bowl of lemonade in the center with cheerful, yellow slices of lemons floating in it.

"It looks lovely," said Elizabeth to Lady Rutledge, who fussed with an arrangement of flowers at the other end of the table.

"One should take pleasure in everything one does. I look forward to meeting your mother, and all the more so because I sense some hesitation on your behalf."

Elizabeth sighed. "Does nothing escape your notice?" she partly teased.

"I make it my aim to notice everything. Never worry, Eliza. Charles has a tendency to think everyone agreeable, Colonel Fitzwilliam is an amiable gentleman, and Caroline... She might present some difficulties, but she is not truly malicious. She only pretends to be when it suits her."

Elizabeth doubted that. "It is a pity that Mr. Darcy could not join us. She is always on her best behavior when he is present."

Lady Rutledge dismissed his absence with a wave of her hand. "These busy men with their large estates and many responsibilities.... It is only because his sister is so soon to join him in town that he has stayed. Otherwise, he would do as he always does and deprive everyone of his company by hiding himself away at Pemberley. Not that I blame him. Pemberley is the sort of place one would never wish to leave."

For Lady Rutledge, who was accustomed to surrounding herself with luxuries to speak so of the grandeur of Pemberley, Elizabeth could hardly imagine what it was like. She had never been that far north. Perhaps Lady Rutledge would wish to go when the *beau monde* left town.

The Bingleys arrived along with Colonel Fitzwilliam a few minutes before the hour agreed upon.

They were received in the drawing room until all of the guests arrived. Only Mother and Lydia remained. Elizabeth looked at the clock again.

"Dear Caroline, I am sorry that you will not have the

pleasure of meeting Miss Jane Bennet today," said Lady Rutledge. "I saw no need to say anything before, as we are to receive Mrs. Bennet and her youngest daughter, Miss Lydia, today in her place."

"What a pity," said Mr. Bingley, looking genuinely disappointed before he remembered himself. “Not that I do not look forward to meeting your mother and other sister…,” he said to Elizabeth.

Miss Bingley rolled her eyes at her brother’s sincerity. "That is a shame. I rather anticipated meeting her. Did she give a reason for her absence?" she asked her aunt.

"She is out of town. Apparently, my invitation crossed paths with a letter from Mrs. Gardiner stating that they were to leave for the coast. It is unfortunate, but we shall invite her again when she returns to town. Colonel Fitzwilliam," Lady Rutledge turned to the colonel. "Did Darcy give a reason for his absence? All he told me was that he was called away for business."

Colonel Fitzwilliam shook his head. "I know nothing more, but you know how he is. It could very well be that he did not want to come."

Elizabeth did not want to believe it. Could it be that he did not care to see her?

Miss Bingley twisted her shoulder and arched her neck. "I dare say you are correct. Mr. Darcy will not be convinced to do anything he does not wish if he is not tempted." She looked at Elizabeth levelly. "Besides, he spent a good deal of time with Charles and me only yesterday. He mentioned nothing of our little gathering today."

The colonel puffed out his chest. “I see that I chose my words poorly. In no way did I intend to imply that he found the company offered by Lady Rutledge lacking, and I doubt that you mean to infer as much against your own aunt, Miss Bingley.”

Her nostrils flared, and Elizabeth watched in delight as her complexion turned a rosy shade of pink.

Continuing, the colonel said, “Darcy is fond of Lady Rutledge and finds Miss Elizabeth to be excellent company.”

It was Elizabeth’s turn to puff out her chest, but she refrained from doing so. A lady should not gloat so openly.

The entry of Mother and Lydia into the parlor stole the wind from her sails. They were late.

Lydia bounced in as she always did, the ringlets around her face bobbing up and down as enthusiastically as she did. Mother put a hand on her shoulder to calm her.

Before introductions could even be performed, Lydia spoke to anyone who cared to listen, "I do apologize for making us late, but you see, there was a bonnet in a shop window. It was divine, and I simply had to have it. I would bring it in to show you, but the butler insisted that I leave it with him." She pouted.

Elizabeth rushed over to them as quickly as her feet could carry her and before any other proclamations could be made. She placed herself between them, linking her arm through theirs on either side, and made introductions. Lady Rutledge looked pleased and proclaimed their visit to be like a country spring breeze. Colonel Fitzwilliam looked amused. Mr. Bingley looked overwhelmed. Miss Bingley looked smug and self-satisfied.

"Charmed, I am sure," she said, inclining her head at their curtsies. "What a pity Mr. Darcy could not be here. I am certain your family would leave him with quite the impression," she added with a haughty twist of her mouth.

Elizabeth would have none of her sarcastic comments. Miss Bingley’s unforgiving attitude toward her family made Elizabeth feel like a cat with its claws out, ready to pounce at the next insult.

Mother spoke. "It was a pity we did not meet you or Mr.

Darcy while you were at Netherfield Park, Miss Bingley. My husband had so recently passed away, and we were unable to make any calls. How fortuitous that we should now meet again in town."

"I am sorry for your loss, Mrs. Bennet. How distressing it is to lose one you have held dear for so many years... and with five unmarried daughters," said Lady Rutledge, instinctively understanding Mother's chief concern in life.

Mother leaned in toward Lady Rutledge, her face as serious as it had been on the day of Father's burial. "It is my greatest concern, Lady Rutledge. How well you understand my predicament." She eyed Mr. Bingley and the colonel so openly, the gentlemen shuffled their feet.

Their discomfort was short-lived, for they soon made way to the elegant table.

Lydia skipped into the room, clasped her hands, and spun in a circle like a little girl. "How delightful. Mother, have you ever seen such a beautiful table?" She fingered a cucumber sandwich before Mother reproved her for touching the food before everyone sat.

Elizabeth wondered what had come over Mother. She expected such behavior from Lydia. But she could not remember a specific time when Mother had corrected her. It was a welcome change, and Lydia withdrew her hand and sat impatiently until Lady Rutledge signaled that it was time to partake of the offerings spread before them.

"Have you met many new people since your arrival?" asked Lady Rutledge politely.

Mother's face flushed in excitement, but her fan was nowhere in sight. Nor did she reach for it. "Oh, it has been a delight to be here and such a welcome change after what we have been through. It is enough to make me forget how things were."

Forget? How could she forget so easily?

Shoving the food into a bulge in her cheek, Lydia said, "And we have ever so many gentleman callers." She looked back and forth between Mr. Bingley and the colonel and giggled.

Mother waved her napkin at her. "Shush, dear, and chew your food," she said under her breath. In a louder voice, she said, "Indeed. I did not think that it would be so easy to make new friends, but we find that we have more than enough to divert us. It is everything I dreamed it could be." She dropped her eyes down to her lap, her face flushed.

Elizabeth was torn. While it pained her to see how easily Mother put the past— and Father— behind her, she was happy to see her looking so well. She smiled at her, attempting to communicate to her mother what she could not say in front of the others seated around the table.

Mother must have felt her warm gaze. She reached under the table and squeezed Elizabeth's hand. When she looked up, it was Elizabeth she looked at. Mother was the picture of contentment, and it was so good to see her— and happy, at that. Perhaps Mother did not need anyone to look out for her after all.

"How helpful that your brother lives here. I only met Mr. and Mrs. Gardiner recently, and they are a charming couple. Surely, they have presented you to some of their friends," Lady Rutledge said.

Swallowing the lump in her cheek, Lydia interrupted, "Oh, no. All I did was place an advertisement in the newspaper."

She looked so pleased with herself against the disbelieving stares around the table. Elizabeth was at a loss for words and wished the floor would swallow her whole. Her humor helped a good deal, but Colonel Fitzwilliam looked as amused as Miss Bingley looked high and mighty. Fortunately, it was the colonel who found his tongue first.

"What an excellent idea! I love to read the advertisements. Just the other day I read an exceptional example of one from a lady. Without giving her age, station in life, or even hinting at her circumstances, she solicited a gentleman to marry. The only recommendation she gave was that she is affectionate."

Mother blushed, and Lydia bounced in her chair. "I helped to write that!"

"That was your work?" asked the colonel, clearly impressed.

Elizabeth sat silently, trying to comprehend what she had heard. Mother wished to remarry? So soon?

Mother beamed at Lydia. "She is a clever one. When I told her my idea, she quickly got to work, and the response has been better than I had imagined."

“Apparently, there are many gentlemen in London in want of affection,” mocked Miss Bingley.

Elizabeth still waited for the floor to open up, but she had no such luck. She squeezed her eyes tightly shut, wishing to become invisible, but that did not work either.

The colonel's clap opened her eyes. "Well done, I do say!" he said as he applauded their creative, though unrefined, way of meeting people.

Miss Bingley huffed from across the table. "How can you applaud such a breach in propriety?" she snapped at the colonel. "No one in polite society would act so beyond the pale." She looked around the table for support, settling on her aunt.

Elizabeth held her breath. What would Lady Rutledge think of her mother and sister's bold ways?

"Why, dear, do you assume that ladies and gentlemen in polite society would never use a popular means of communication to further their ambitions? They do it all the time. I admire Mrs. Bennet for her honesty."

"They may do such things, but they do not proclaim it

openly! They keep it private," insisted Miss Bingley. For once, Elizabeth agreed with her, but she would not give any indication of it.

Lady Rutledge furled her brow. "Would you have her refuse to admit having written the advertisement once it became known?"

Her challenge met with silence.

Colonel Fitzwilliam added, "Precisely! Which is worse: admitting to putting an advertisement in the newspaper when pressed or brazenly lying about it just to keep up appearances?"

Miss Bingley opened her mouth to speak, but seemed at a loss for words. After several false starts, she finally said, "I would not ever be in a position to know. I would never consider such an indecorous course of action." Satisfied with her answer, she raised her head in her superiority over everyone else in the room.

The colonel was not impressed. "The problem with some people in society is that they give too much import to the opinions of others."

Miss Bingley's eyes snapped at him. "I know of others who would share my opinion. Mr. Darcy, for example." Her eyes trailed over to Elizabeth.

A sea of turbulence battered her stomach. What would Mr. Darcy think of her family? Elizabeth could not care less what others thought, but his opinion had become very important to her. Would he think ill of her family and cease to be her friend?

CHAPTER 27

Now that Darcy had determined to arrange an outing which would allow Miss Elizabeth an enjoyable evening with her family in a place where all would be at ease, the universe conspired against him. Urgent letters arrived requiring his immediate attention, and he spent a good portion of his afternoon at the solicitor's office making decisions he would have postponed if at all possible.

He called at the address for Mrs. Bennet only to find her out. He called at the home of the Gardiners to find that they had left town and were not expected to return soon. His plans off to a rocky start, he returned home exhausted and surly. To make things worse, he had not seen Miss Elizabeth all day.

Only a book would put up with him when he was out of sorts, so he hid away in his study, pouring himself a drink and settling into his leather chair with a novel Miss Elizabeth had recommended. Engrossed in the reading, it irked him all the more when a knock at the door and a visitor was announced.

Richard breezed past the butler, charging into Darcy's

study like the intruder he was. Darcy glared at him in the hopes that his overly cheerful cousin would take his hint and go away.

Sitting across from Darcy, crossing his ankle over his knee, and helping himself to the decanter on the table beside them, Richard began speaking. If he had noticed how unwelcome his presence was, he ignored it.

"You missed all the fun this afternoon, Darcy. Never have I met such diverting people before!"

"You do not get out enough," growled Darcy.

"Miss Jane Bennet and Mrs. Gardiner were unable to attend Lady Rutledge's luncheon, being out of town..." Richard continued with an explanation of their absence, a point which Darcy already knew. "...Mrs. Bennet and Miss Lydia Bennet came in their place, and what a treat it was for all of us at the table. All of us excepting Miss Bingley, that is." He stopped to chuckle, and Darcy's impatience grew now that his cousin finally had something interesting to relate.

"What were they like?" he asked to get Richard talking again.

"Mrs. Bennet is a handsome widow if I ever saw one. One would never guess that she has borne five daughters. She is of a merry sort and brutally honest— to the point of making herself an easy target for ridicule."

Darcy furled his brow. "What of the other daughter?"

The colonel paused for a considerable time. "I got the impression that she has been allowed her way much too often. She came across to me as a spoiled child, immature in her ways. Her childlike manners were endearing to a certain point," he said, in an obvious attempt to justify her poor behavior. "It grew evident to me that Mrs. Bennet is new to correcting and guiding her, which makes me curious as to why she would change her treatment of her daughter after fifteen years of what can only be described as negligent."

Such a contrary report of Mrs. Bennet did nothing to clear Darcy's confusion as to her character. He had been under the impression, from the comments of others, that she was known for being silly. What Richard told him suggested, at the least, that she was trying. Perhaps her change in circumstances had served to her benefit in some way.

"I have asked Miss Elizabeth previously about her family, and she has only spoken freely to me of her eldest sister."

Richard nodded. "I think that I now understand why. However, I must give Miss Elizabeth credit. Though her mother on occasion and her sister on several occasions said things appalling enough to make anyone shrink in shame, she did not. We know Miss Elizabeth to be a lady in every sense of the word, but she is not ashamed of her family. In fact, when Miss Bingley made trite comments, I thought that the glares in her direction might catch her on fire. Her loyalty transcends their failures, and that is worthy of admiration." Richard looked intently at Darcy. "Do you not agree, cousin?"

Richard was fishing for information which he had no right to know. Nor was Darcy inclined to tell him. Noncommittally, Darcy nodded and said, "Quite. Now do tell me what they said that was so shocking. Was it one truly appalling statement, or were there several slightly appalling comments?"

"Miss Lydia managed to astonish everyone with each uttering of her mouth. But Mrs. Bennet only truly shocked me with one acknowledgment of something her imprudent daughter said. Do you remember the advertisement I read some mornings ago about the lady soliciting a husband?"

Darcy knew what Richard was about to say before he could say it. His heart hurt for Miss Elizabeth. How would it make her feel to know that her own mother could not mourn her husband for a full year before seeking another? That her father could be so easily replaced would be bitter to swallow.

As he remained silent, Richard continued. "Mrs. Bennet placed the ad. She even boasted at how successful it had been in bringing several callers to their doorstep and how many new friends they have made as a result of it. Fortunately, I sensed in Mrs. Bennet some level of sense, and I do think that she is choosy with whom they associate— to some degree."

"For Miss Elizabeth's sake, I do hope so. Mrs. Bennet is playing a dangerous game, but I do wish her success all the same."

Richard lounged back in his chair, looping his hands behind him as if he would never leave. Darcy's mind was taken off his own concerns, and he wondered how Miss Elizabeth had become the decisive, opinionated, mannerly young lady she was. She had not been given much direction in her formative years— that much he knew. His admiration for her grew more still, so much, in fact, that he would continue with his plans despite the obstacles he had encountered just to see her face glow with delight. He had not made one decision since departing Netherfield Park that did not take her into consideration.

His pulse raced, and his stomach tied into knots. The discomfort only lessened when his mind conjured up an image of Miss Elizabeth with her silky hair, soft skin, beguiling smile, intoxicating laugh, and intelligent eyes. She had the power to make him both miserable and gloriously happy. And she had done so without guile or disguise. His life revolved around her, and he could no longer fool himself. What he felt for her went far beyond admiration. He loved her. Purely. Deeply. Ardently.

Reaching up to tug his cravat, then to push his fingers

against his pulsating temples, he reached for his drink and downed the amber liquid in one toss of his head.

"Darcy? Are you well?" asked Richard, leaning forward in his chair.

What a sight he must seem.

Deciding that the best way to conceal the truth of his emotions was through honesty, he admitted, "No."

Richard poured him another drink. "Shall I fetch your doctor?"

Taking the glass proffered, Darcy said, "I thank you, but I do not need a doctor for what ails me."

Richard gave him a quizzical look he would have to keep, for Darcy was not about to satisfy his curiosity. This was the worst possible moment for him to realize his true feelings for Miss Elizabeth. He loved her. He loved her so much, it would be the worst torture to be near her knowing that she was not free to accept an offer of marriage. Not while she was under the thumb of Lady Rutledge. Not until she came out from under the shadow of guilt she felt for her mother and sisters— a loyal devotion she stubbornly clung to with her adorable tenacity.

He did not realize that a groan had escaped him until Richard said, "I shall call the doctor. You are giving me cause for concern." He leaped up and strode to the door.

"Richard, stop! I tell you that I do not need a doctor," he insisted.

When Richard did not stop, he knew he needed to give him more information or else risk disturbing the good doctor while he was dining with his family or enjoying some other activity much more worth his time.

"I have come to a realization, that is all, and it has… disturbed me."

Richard turned, his hand on the doorknob. "A realization? What sort of realization? You are never disturbed, Darcy, and that you should be so affected means that it is something of tremendous import."

Darcy nodded gravely. "It is of the greatest import." He would continue with his plans. He would do anything and everything to delight Miss Elizabeth. Elizabeth.

She may not be free to return his love yet, but that would not stop him from doing everything in his power to win her heart as surely as she had won his.

Richard turned back, a perceptive contemplation on his face. Walking over to Darcy, he slapped him on the shoulder and chuckled. "One moment, you look ill, and now you have the largest, stupidest grin on your face. I see it has got you too."

ELIZABETH WAITED the remainder of the day for Lady Rutledge to comment on her mother and Lydia, but she said nothing. By that evening, Elizabeth was convinced that had Lady Rutledge called Mother and Lydia silly outright, it would have been preferable. Her imagination was much worse than any truth could be.

The next morning, an invitation awaited them at the breakfast table. It was from Mr. Darcy, inviting them to join him and a party of close friends to an outing at Vauxhall Pleasure Gardens. Elizabeth noticed that a private note was included with the invitation. Lady Rutledge read it, then folded it as she looked up at Elizabeth. Too bad it had not been for her.

"How gracious of Darcy to arrange for an outing. The weather has been fine lately, and I dare say that it will hold out until tomorrow. Have you been to the gardens before, Eliza?" Lady Rutledge nibbled at a slice of buttered bread.

"No, I have not had the pleasure yet." She was excited to

go. It meant an entire evening in Mr. Darcy's company.

"With your relatives living in London? I find it difficult to believe that they have not thought to take you. They seem so attentive." Lady Rutledge clucked her tongue at their negligence.

"They are attentive, but the weather is not so gracious. My previous visits have been during the winter months when the gardens are closed due to the rain. Apparently the ladies of the *ton* do not like to ruin their slippers or muddy their hems just to walk through the glorious landscape," she defended, a picture of Miss Bingley attempting to do so lightening her mood.

"Indeed. We will leave early enough to have time to wander around and partake of the many entertainments available before nightfall." She tapped her spoon against her teacup, her bottom lip tucked behind her teeth and her eyes looking at something far off. She was scheming. "You know, we could go up in the balloon." Her eyes wandered to the distance again, flickering to Elizabeth now and again.

"Did Mr. Darcy mention who else he has invited? His sister has not yet joined him, has she?" she asked, anxious for any news of the gentleman.

"No, she will not arrive for another two weeks. It is a pity she will miss the excursion, but if I know Darcy at all, I am confident that he will make it up to her. My nephew will be there, of course, as will Caroline and Colonel Fitzwilliam. He mentioned a couple of other names, but you need not concern yourself with them." She flicked her fingers in the air, emphasizing the insignificance of the others invited. Nor did Elizabeth care. *He* would be there!

Elizabeth ate her breakfast in silence while Lady Rutledge pretended to read the paper. She could not help but note to which section Lady Rutledge gave the utmost attention. The advertisements.

CHAPTER 28

Elizabeth woke to a cloudless, azure sky. The sun shone like a giant daisy. She hummed as she dressed, taking care to wear a light coat in which to ensconce Mr. Darcy's handkerchief. Lady Rutledge had been uncommonly quiet since receiving the invitation, thus piquing Elizabeth's curiosity and filling her with unnerving excitement. All would be well. Mr. Darcy would be there. And she had learned that Mother and Lydia would be too.

Lady Rutledge had the forethought to send her carriage to Mother's apartment so that they might ride together.

"I am so glad the weather has held. The hot air balloons will be out, and I have longed to go up in one. Darcy will have everything arranged, I am sure," Lady Rutledge looked like a little girl as she peeked out of the window of their carriage.

"Today is the kind of day where dreams come true. Could it be any more glorious?" commented Elizabeth.

Lydia squished Elizabeth, piercing her leg with her elbow in a futile attempt to look out of the opposite window. "Why are all the things worth seeing out your window, Lizzy? I cannot see a thing!" she whined. Elizabeth moved over to allow her sister a better view.

"Perhaps if you would bother to look out your window, you would find equally fascinating things to look at," Elizabeth suggested.

Mother was strangely quiet during their drive across the Thames to the Vauxhall Gardens. Elizabeth was grateful she only had to soften the comments of one of her relatives, and contented herself with Mother's rosy cheeks and lively eyes that she was happy with their excursion. Mother looked at each carriage and person they passed by with keen interest.

They arrived just after the Bingley's carriage which carried the rest of their party.

Mr. Darcy immediately came to them, leaving Miss Bingley alone with her brother and Colonel Fitzwilliam. The colonel smoothly stepped into his vacated place and offered his arm to Miss Bingley, who hesitated to take it. He graciously offered his other arm to Lydia, who accepted all too eagerly and hung on to him as if he were the only male she had seen in a fortnight, and would ever see again. Miss Bingley tightened her grip on the colonel's arm and batted her eyelashes up at him when he looked at her in surprise.

Mr. Darcy offered his arm to Mrs. Bennet, a gesture which Elizabeth appreciated more than if he had offered her his arm. Lady Rutledge pushed Mr. Bingley toward her and Mother found herself in the flattering position of getting to choose which gentleman to accept. Her cheeks flushed and at Lady Rutledge's encouragement, she accepted Mr. Bingley's extended arm.

Elizabeth went to walk with Lady Rutledge, but she took her nephew's free arm.

That left her and Mr. Darcy. Yes, this was the perfect day. He held his arm out with a welcoming smile.

"May I escort you in, Miss Elizabeth?"

She smiled at his use of her name, though her eldest sister was not present. It felt friendly, though the way he lingered on the syllables in her name gave rise to an emotion she dared not allow herself to feel. Hope.

"Please forgive me for not offering earlier. I assumed that Lady Rutledge would want you to walk with her."

"Lady Rutledge does everything possible to ensure that I am seen to be treated the same as her own niece. I do not understand why she insists on upholding the farce as she does after what happened at the ball, but she does. There are many things she does that I do not quite understand."

Mr. Darcy chuckled. "I have known her for most of my life, and she remains a mystery to me. I wonder what she has schemed for our party today."

Elizabeth laughed. "I have been wondering the same thing."

"Lizzy! Lizzy! Look at the balloon!" shouted her sister several paces in front of them.

Elizabeth nodded, then turned her head hurriedly back to Mr. Darcy.

“We had best join them. How would you like to go up in a hot air balloon?” he asked her.

Breathless in excitement, all Elizabeth could do was nod enthusiastically.

Lady Rutledge looked pleased with herself. “Did I not tell you, Eliza, that Darcy would have it all arranged?”

Behind her, Elizabeth saw the large woven basket with the silk balloon floating up in the air. A gentleman with a thick mustache and long side whiskers opened the wicker door and motioned for them to join him inside.

"He will take us all up if we want. The day is so fine, we shall be able to see all of London from a bird’s eye view,” said Mr. Darcy.

Mother refused to ascend. "I will keep my feet on the

ground where God intended them to be. If I were meant to fly, he would have given me wings. Thank you, Mr. Darcy, but my nerves would give me a fit. It will give me much more pleasure to watch from the safety of the solid earth."

A group of dandified gentlemen walked by. Lydia, too, felt that her time was best spent on the ground.

At their refusal, Miss Bingley flounced her way to the open side of the basket. "I am unafraid and think that experiencing the closest thing to flight a harmless diversion."

If she did not take care to lower her nose, she might trip over the edge of the basket, which floated a few inches from the grass. Thanks to the colonel's attention, she ascended without mishap.

Mr. Darcy looked at Elizabeth. She smiled, and together they joined the colonel and Miss Bingley in the basket. Mr. Bingley decided to stay behind to attend to Mother and Lydia.

Lady Rutledge was the last to enter and the gentleman with the whiskers closed the door, securing it tightly.

The basket jolted as the sandbags holding them down were thrown overboard. She felt a warm hand cover hers and laughed when she saw Mr. Darcy's expression.

"I apologize, Miss Elizabeth," he said, moving his hand away as swiftly as one would from a flame.

Elizabeth was not sorry. How divine it would be to have Mr. Darcy hold her hand because he wanted to. Waves of energy coursed through her arm, and her hand tingled from his brief touch. She wished the balloon would move abruptly again. Elizabeth nearly giggled as she realized how brazen her thoughts toward Mr. Darcy had become.

Her little sister waved and blew her a kiss. At least Elizabeth assumed it was for her.

Mr. Darcy had moved his hand, but he was still so close, she could touch him with a flinch of her little finger. Peeking at him from the corner of her eye, she traced his firm jawline all the way to the small cleft in his chin. He was taller than most men. In an embrace, her head would rest right over his heart. She felt the heat rise in her face at her intimate thoughts. The light, summer breeze did nothing to cool her as the balloon rose in the sky. Mother and Lydia were soon the size of ants.

"Caroline, are you well? You are dreadfully pale," exclaimed Lady Rutledge.

Elizabeth turned from her spot overlooking London to look at Miss Bingley. There was a green tinge to her skin, made all the more notable against the strawberry hue of her hair. Beads of sweat covered her upper lip.

Miss Bingley stiffened her spine and in a false sense of bravado, said, "I am well. It is merely the effect of the change in air." She attempted to release one of her hands which gripped the side of the basket so tightly her knuckles were as white as her face, but her gesture was brief and forced, and soon she returned to clinging with her other hand to the side.

"I find the air refreshing, and I see it has lent a rosy sheen to Eliza's cheeks. Are you afraid of heights, Caroline? Had I suspected as much, I never would have suggested that you join us." Lady Rutledge stepped closer to her niece, shaking the basket as she did so.

Miss Bingley's semblance strained in panic.

Lady Rutledge froze. "Perhaps I had best stay where I am. No need to make things worse."

Colonel Fitzwilliam, who stood closely on the other side of Miss Bingley, said in a soothing voice, "If you look out over town, you will soon forget that only a thin basket separates us from plummeting to the ground." His eyes smiled and, for a moment, Elizabeth thought Miss Bingley might have courage enough to release the side of the basket to smack the colonel on the arm. But though her expression changed from one of fear to anger, she did not release her hold on the side.

Motioning with his hands, the colonel pointed out certain areas of interest. He even spotted the location of her home in St. James in an effort to distract Miss Bingley.

It warmed Elizabeth's heart to see how attentive the colonel was to Miss Bingley in his attempt to lessen her anxiety. Lady Rutledge joined him in pointing out different landmarks. Miss Bingley's anxiety, while it did not lessen, did not worsen with the help of Colonel Fitzwilliam and her aunt.

Mr. Darcy stood silently beside her. His relaxed hands and healthy complexion proclaimed him unaffected by the tremendous height they were at. He seemed to be lost in his thoughts.

"Have you been up in the balloon before, Mr. Darcy?" she asked.

"I never had the desire to ascend before. Now, I think that I shall return with Georgiana. She would love this."

Looking toward Miss Bingley, who was occupied listening to Lady Rutledge and the colonel distract her, she said, "It feels more secure than I had thought it would hanging in the air in a large basket with nothing to hold us up but the thin silk of the balloon. Do you come often to the gardens with your sister?"

"The last time I came was with Georgiana. She wanted to see the fire balloon."

"Fire balloon? A balloon like this one?" Her alarm grew as she looked up at the flame propelling them upward and pondered the possibility of it catching the silk on fire. If Miss Bingley thought of it, she would lose what control she had.

"Do not worry yourself. There are no people in the fire balloon. It is merely a balloon which is filled with fireworks. When it has ascended to a certain height, it is lit, filling the night sky with color. As a grand finale, the balloon then goes up in flames. The spectacle is so great, it can be seen all over London."

"Lady Rutledge says that they will have fireworks here tonight."

A whimper from the other end of the basket made them turn to see Miss Bingley melt into a puddle inside the basket. She wrapped her arms around her legs and rocked herself.

Mr. Darcy addressed the whiskered gentleman. “Is there any way to cut our excursion short?”

“It will not be the first time, sir, nor the last.” He reached up to lower the flame. “It takes longer to get down than it does to get up, but I will do my best.”

Miss Bingley’s skin was as pale as paper. She shook like a leaf on a blustery day.

“Stay in place, lest you shake the basket,” commanded Colonel Fitzwilliam. He slowly knelt down until he sat beside Miss Bingley. She wrapped her arm around his and buried her face into his shoulder. He patted her hand and spoke gently into her ear, swaying to her rocking motion. It was not proper, but it was the deed of a true gentleman. Which reminded her…

“Mr. Darcy, I must apologize to you for not returning your handkerchief sooner.”

“Think nothing of it. You needed it more than I did.”

“Still, it has been long enough since you lent it to me. I ought not keep it any longer.” She pulled it out of her sleeve.

A gust of wind blew it from her fingers and she watched breathlessly as it floated down into the gardens to be swallowed by the vegetation below. She rubbed the inside of her sleeve, but nothing was there. Mr. Darcy’s handkerchief was gone.

CHAPTER 29

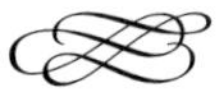

"Miss Elizabeth, I do own more than one handkerchief. Please, do not worry yourself." To prove his point, he pulled out another linen square with his initials embroidered on it in shiny, white thread. Unlike her, he kept a good grip on it and returned it safely to his pocket.

"It has been so long with me, I feel as if I have lost a friend," she peered over the edge to see if the dot of white could be discerned from their descending height. She skimmed over the crowds of people and stopped when she identified Mother. She stood arm-in-arm with a gentleman Elizabeth did not recognize. "Who is that?" she asked, pointing. "Did you invite him?"

"I do not know him personally, but Mrs. Bennet did ask if a friend of hers might join us. I could not deny her."

The balloon could not descend quickly enough.

On closer inspection, the gentleman standing between Mother and Lydia as if he had a right to stand there was older than Elizabeth had thought initially. His thick, dark hair had no silver streaks running through it, but his face was marked with the lines of a man of as many years as Mother. They curved upward around his eyes, casting a friendly demeanor even before he smiled to reveal perfect, white teeth.

Mother made introductions immediately and Mr. Angelo Carissimi bowed deeply, the smile never abandoning his face.

After acknowledging everyone in their group, he bowed over Elizabeth's hand. "Miss Bennet, I am particularly pleased to make your acquaintance. Any daughter of the charming Mrs. Bennet is a welcome friend to me."

His appearance decidedly foreign, it surprised Elizabeth to hear him speak without an accent. Even more surprising was Mother's reaction to him. She looped her arm through his and simpered like a maiden in love.

"We have some happy news, dear," Mother said when she could pull her eyes away from Mr. Carissimi. "We are engaged!"

Elizabeth felt her heart drumming in her ears. She did not know the man who would take Father's place, and she doubted that Mother knew him very well either. She had not been in town long. Objections sprang to her tongue.

"But your mourning is not finished," she said, hoping not to sound as contrary as she felt.

Clucking her tongue, Mother said, "It is close enough, Lizzy. Men marry soon after losing their wives, and I see no reason to postpone our engagement when I am so happy."

Elizabeth could not argue with her mother over that point. Mother did look happier than she had seen her in many years. Even with Father.

It was difficult to say, but she felt she must. "I am happy for you." She looked between Mr. Carissimi and her mother.

Lady Rutledge stepped forward. "Are you a relative to the Carissimi establishment at Pall Mall?"

Miss Bingley gained some color to her pallid face when she heard the last name. “The chocolate house?”

Mr. Carissimi smiled his affirmation. "My grandfather began our family business with lace and wine. It was my idea to include chocolate with its endless variety of delightful confections to further entice our patrons. Have you had the pleasure of sampling one of our truffles, Lady Rutledge?"

With a contented sigh, Lady Rutledge said, "Indeed I have. Although my niece gobbles them up before I have much opportunity to eat my fair portion."

That brought some color to Miss Bingley's pale cheeks.

With a chuckle, Mr. Carissimi said, "Then I shall have a box sent to your home to remedy the situation immediately." Looking at Miss Bingley, he inclined his head and added, "Perhaps I shall send one to your home as well, signorina."

Elizabeth watched Mr. Carissimi closely as everyone chose their walking partner. Mr. Darcy offered her his arm. She had only just taken it when Mr. Carissimi joined them with Mother.

"Please excuse me, Mr. Darcy, but might I suggest a trade? You see, I have put Miss Bennet in the awkward position of not knowing the gentleman who is to marry her mother. It is my hope that we shall become friends, but conversation is required to achieve such a worthy aim."

Mr. Darcy looked at Elizabeth and only stepped away from her when she agreed. Mr. Carissimi’s manners were polite and friendly. She had no reason to refuse him. Hesitantly taking his arm, Elizabeth was more concerned about Mr. Carissimi's entry into the Bennet family than what Mother might say to Mr. Darcy.

Mr. Carissimi patted the hand she placed on his arm as if she already were his daughter. "Please do not be alarmed, Miss Bennet. I assure you that my intentions toward your mother are honorable. She is a lovely woman, and I aim to make her very happy. You have no way of knowing whether or not you can trust my word, so I encourage you to ask me anything you wish."

His forthright honesty allayed some of her fears, and more questions than she knew how to ask flooded her mind. But one stood above the others. "Do you love my mother?"

"I do."

"You cannot have known each other very long. How is that possible?" She waited for him to bristle up in offense, but he did not.

Patting her hand, he answered softly. "I am not a young man who does not yet know his own mind. I will leave it to her to tell you the circumstances of our meeting, but I knew within only a few minutes in her company that she was the special lady whom I would choose from amongst thousands to spend the rest of my life with. She is everything I desire in a wife, and I will do everything in my power to live up to her expectations and ease her worries."

Mother's expectations? What would Mother want in a marriage, if she could choose? She certainly had not expected much with Father. This man, Mr. Carissimi, seemed to care enough about Mother to concern himself with her expectations. Elizabeth struggled against her tendency to like him—but he was very likable.

He patted her hand again and, oddly enough, it seemed as if he had always been around to do so.

"Do you plan to live in London?" she asked, listing her questions up in her head now that the mud in her mind had cleared.

~

"I CONGRATULATE you on your recent engagement, Mrs. Bennet," said Mr. Darcy politely. He did not want to ask too many questions, but he sensed that they would be answered whether he asked them or not. He was pleased with how civilly she treated him after refusing his company for so long.

There were apples in Mrs. Bennet's cheeks, and her eyes sparkled in the dimming evening light. Would Elizabeth resemble her mother as the years passed? It would not be a bad thing.

"Thank you, Mr. Darcy. How kind of you to say so. I am in a better position to take care of my daughters now— should they need my help. And I am so very happy. Happier, in fact, than I have been these many years..." Her voice trailed off and for a brief second, her semblance saddened.

Clearing his throat while he thought of a more cheerful question to bring her out of her past sufferings and into the joyous future, he asked, "Do you plan to live in London?"

"Indeed, we do not plan to stay in London. Alfonso has an estate outside Bath. I have always wanted to go to Bath. I went once when I was a girl, and I imagine that it is much changed."

Darcy nodded, and the gesture was sufficient for Mrs. Bennet to carry on in her conversation.

"Alfonso has a son and two daughters of his own. The eldest son has taken over the family's business, so we are free to retire into the country— although I suspect that I will give him reasons enough to frequent Bath and London." She smiled contentedly. "How lovely it will be when we can travel as we see fit." She lowered her voice and looked pointedly at Elizabeth. "She would never admit her father's faults, but he never once took me to town— even though I dearly wanted to. My girls' education was not properly conducted. It is mostly my fault, I know, but when every effort of mine to see that my daughters study under the masters in town was hindered, I gave up. I can see so clearly now what an injustice

I did to my girls. At least, with my marriage, they will have more time to settle."

Darcy stared in amazement at the woman beside him. Was this the same silly creature he had been told about by Mr. Bennet?

Not one to remain serious for long, an impression Darcy was relieved to see verified, Mrs. Bennet continued, "But I will make the most of it! That is my determination. You see, Mr. Darcy— and I have no shame in admitting as much to you when you already know my methods— I met Mr. Carissimi through my advertisement. I came to London with the sole purpose of marrying as soon as it could be arranged. I took care to select a gentleman who would be kind to not only me, but also to my daughters. It is my wish that they join us at his estate. There are many marriageable young gentlemen about Bath, and I am in a better position to promote my girls properly as Mr. Carissimi's wife. He has been most agreeable."

Now in possession of much more information than he was entitled to, Darcy did his best not to appear too interested in her conversation. What plans did she have for Elizabeth? Did she know how tender his regard for Elizabeth was? Did Elizabeth feel the same?

He did not realize that he had been staring ahead at the object of his affections until Mrs. Bennet tugged on his sleeve. "Of course, Mr. Darcy, if you think that my Lizzy stands a better chance at securing a happy future here in London, I shall not even make mention of quitting to Bath..." She looked up at him, her eyebrows arching so high, her pupils dotted them as question marks.

There was one matter he must hear from Mrs. Bennet's lips before he would allow himself the joy of asking for Elizabeth's hand. Keeping his expression steady, he said, "You must do what you think is best for all of your daughters,

Mrs. Bennet. I do not expect you to do any less for Miss Elizabeth. Am I to understand, then, that you have forgiven me?"

Her bewilderment stunned him cold. “Forgive you, Mr. Darcy? Whatever for?”

His fingers turned to ice. “For the wrong I committed against Mr. Bennet. I wrote a letter, which Mr. Phillips ensured me that he delivered, detailing what had transpired between us on his return from Hunsford before his death.” This was a disaster! If Mrs. Bennet was unaware of what the wrong he had done Mr. Bennet, then Elizabeth did not know of it at all. He forced himself to breathe slowly.

“Mr. Darcy, what happened in the past is done and gone. I see no reason why you should torment yourself over one who is deceased these many months.”

“Mrs. Bennet, I—” he started.

“Mr. Darcy, I must insist. I have no desire to speak of Mr. Bennet nor hear any news regarding him. He is gone and we have continued on. In the time we have known you, I have yet to see you act with anything but the greatest consideration for others. If forgiveness is what you seek, then consider yourself pardoned and let us speak no more of the subject when today is a day for merriness.”

They neared the dinner boxes and the waiter he had made arrangements with welcomed them. “Mr. Darcy, please come. I have reserved the finest dinner box for you and your party.”

Darcy followed his direction in stunned silence, mechanically filling his part as the host of their gathering. He needed to talk to Elizabeth.

THEY FILED into the dinner box made to fit a group of their size. The night descended over them, but the lamp at the table illuminated a lovely painting of milkmaids dancing to the tune of a peg-legged violinist. They looked carefree and gay.

Elizabeth looked at Mother, who sat next to Mr. Carissimi. She looked as cheerful as the dancing figures in the painting.

Painful as it was, she had to acknowledge that there was the possibility that Mr. Carissimi would be a better husband to her than Father had been. She could give him the benefit of the doubt and assume that he was sincere. He certainly appeared to be. Even Lydia, who sat on his other side, hung on his every word. Could he be the source of the positive changes Mother had made in her treatment of Lydia?

Thinly sliced ham, cold meats, chicken, cheeses, salads, custards, tarts, cakes, puddings, wine, beer, cider, and arrack punch were dexterously arranged on the table before them, and Elizabeth partook of the spread before her with a lighter heart. She felt Mr. Darcy's gaze upon her, and she smiled her thanks and appreciation for the trouble he had gone to. No other dinner box had such a fine spread, and it was not every day one could enjoy a ride in a balloon.

"— finishing school?!" shrieked Lydia from across the table, pulling Elizabeth out of her reverie.

"What is this?" she asked, having missed what had led to Lydia's outburst.

Lady Rutledge leaned in and whispered in her ear. "Apparently she is to stay in town to attend a ladies finishing school after the wedding." Dropping her voice even lower, she added, "Personally, I think she stands to benefit a great deal from such an education. I applaud your mother."

Crossing her arms and sticking out her bottom lip, Lydia complained, "I refuse to stay behind at some stuffy school while you go to Bath and have all the fun."

Mr. Carissimi said, "It is not a decision your mother made

lightly. You will be in the same school as my daughter Isabel so that you will not feel alone. You will join us in Bath for your holidays, and we will do our best to see to your diversion on such occasions."

Lydia's forehead bunched up. "How am I to be the first among my sisters to marry if I am stuck in a stuffy, boring school?"

"Eat, dear. It does no good to fret on an empty stomach," soothed Mother. Fortunately for everyone at the table, the orchestra began playing. Between the good food and the lively music, Lydia forgot her current plight enough to pay heed to Mother.

CHAPTER 30

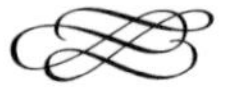

A whistle blew and dozens of servants sped out into the gardens to light hundreds of glass lamps hanging from the trees. It was as if the heavens of a clear night had descended upon them to surround them with stars. The flickering flames danced their reflections inside their glass orbs, twinkling like a scene out of the Arabian Nights. If she closed her eyes, Elizabeth could smell the exotic spices in the warm air.

The music played softly, and the ham tasted like none other in its superiority. Even the rum punch, of which she partook sparingly, burst with flavor in her mouth. Laughter and merry conversation filled the air, and Elizabeth opened her eyes and heart to enjoy every moment. It was difficult to imagine, in such a place, that she had ever been unhappy or sad. She watched the others at the table. Mother and Mr. Carissimi conversed with Lady Rutledge, Lydia remained stubbornly cross despite their magical surroundings, Mr. Bingley was engaged in a lively discussion with Colonel Fitzwilliam, Miss Bingley alternated between arguing with the colonel and trying to include Mr. Darcy.

Mr. Darcy sat at the other end of the booth, but the distance did nothing to lessen the intensity in his eyes as he gazed upon Elizabeth. She could not read his stormy expression, but her skin prickled all over her body in response to it.

The occupants of the boxes surrounding them soon emptied and an impromptu ball formed in the open grass before them. It was lovely to see the ladies, dressed in their finest evening gowns, parading before them on the arms of gentlemen proud to be seen with them.

Mr. Bingley, never one to give up an opportunity to dance, asked Mother if he might have the pleasure of a dance. She was delighted to be asked— even though Lydia took it as a personal affront that her mother should be asked before she was.

Everyone in the box thus paired up and dispersed across the lawn, Mr. Darcy asked in a low voice, "Would you like to take a turn around the lawn with me?"

She could not deny him. "Of course, Mr. Darcy."

They walked a short distance within view of the hundreds of dancing couples. The crowd gave them a certain measure of privacy. Pride filled her as she rested her hand on his steady arm. Of all the ladies present, he had chosen her.

Darcy hated himself for what he had to do. It was entirely his fault that Elizabeth's night— a night he had planned specifically for her enjoyment— would be ruined. He had watched her all evening. Her smile reached her eyes; incandescence added to her beauty. He sighed. Just as he felt confident of her favor, he would have to shatter her favorable opinion of him.

He led her to the edge of the crowd, first securing her a glass of lemonade. It would raise too many eyebrows if they were seen disappearing off into the maze of paths through the garden, and he would do nothing to put her reputation in question— especially where he was concerned. She may never want to see him after she knew how dishonorably he had acted toward Mr. Bennet.

Her eyes searched his face for answers. He could delay no longer. She deserved the truth.

"Please know that over the past months, I was convinced of your knowledge of what I must reveal to you. Every detail of my proud indifference was penned in a letter I addressed to your mother and which was delivered on my behalf by your uncle, Mr. Phillips. Only tonight did I find out that Mrs. Bennet did not read it."

"I am not surprised to hear that. Surely, Mr. Darcy, whatever you wrote about cannot be so grave."

"I fear it might change your opinion of me. You see, I met your father at Rosings the week before the Meryton Assembly."

"You told me as much when we first met by the stables in Meryton."

"He went to speak to Mr. Collins, who happens to be the rector at my aunt's estate. After spending the night at the Hunsford rectory, he was to leave the following morning— the same morning I would leave for Netherfield Park." He breathed deeply and continued. "Mr. Collins was as desirous of ridding himself of Mr. Bennet's company as Mr. Bennet was in leaving Mr. Collins. However, a wheel of his carriage was in need of repair. Knowing that I was to leave for Hertfordshire that morning, Mr. Collins came to consult with my aunt about the possibility of Mr. Bennet traveling with me in my carriage. I was in the room with my aunt when he suggested as much in a roundabout way."

Darcy clenched his fists together and willed himself to continue.

"I knew what he wanted, and yet I chose to ignore it. I did not want any company in my carriage— especially that of a stranger whom I considered beneath me. In short, I could not be bothered."

Elizabeth's eyebrows bunched together as she searched his face. "You refused to extend kindness to a stranger? That does not sound like you," she said in a whisper he heard as loudly as a shout over the music and chatter of the crowd.

"I am ashamed of how I acted."

She chewed on her bottom lip. "What else happened? Our coach did not return home until the day after Father arrived. He never told me what happened, but his good humor ran contrary to everything you just told me."

That took Darcy by surprise. He wanted to ask at that moment how that could have been so, but too much had happened between those two points that needed to be filled in. "It was just outside Hunsford that I saw your father. His face was a startling shade of purple. He was bent over with his hands on his knees, attempting to catch his breath. The coach lay at an appalling angle, having lost one of its wheels. How it did not topple over completely, I do not know, but I am grateful for Mr. Bennet's sake that it did not."

Elizabeth gasped, raising a hand up to cover her mouth. "He said nothing of an accident, though I noticed him limp. He said that the rain affected his joints and… I believed him." Her eyes brimmed, and she blinked furiously to hold the tears back. "What a horrible daughter I am," she said more to herself than to Darcy.

His chest constricted and his heart squeezed in his chest. He held his hands together before they could reach up to caress her cheeks. "Do not blame yourself when you are in no way at fault. My conscience has plagued me since I saw what my neglect had caused him to experience. He was fortunate not to suffer any great physical injury from the accident, but his aspect concerned me greatly. He clutched his chest and pulled at his neck cloth like it choked him. I pressed him to allow my aunt's physician to see him. I could see no external injury, but I was convinced that his heart had been affected greatly. He refused and, not feeling that I had the right to insist further, I offered to convey him to Longbourn— something I ought to have done to begin with. Mr. Bennet may not have died had I not worsened his condition by my thoughtless neglect."

Elizabeth closed her eyes and nodded her head as if pieces of the puzzle came together and she could see a more accurate picture. What did she think of him now that she knew?

One small tear trailed down her cheek and the brave lady attempted to smile at him. Dare he hope that she could forgive him?

"Lizzy! Lizzy!" a shrill voice cut through the tension surrounding them, turning several heads to look toward the originator of the cry.

Mrs. Bennet came running toward them. Not a ladylike walk, but the run of one unaccustomed to the exercise. Her eyes were wide with panic.

Elizabeth reached her arms out lest she be rolled over by her mother. "What is it?" she asked, placing her hands on Mrs. Bennet's arms to still her.

"It is Lydia. We cannot find her anywhere! I suspect that she has been kidnapped!" Her voice carried over the crowd of dancers, and the number of people listening in on the scene before them grew exponentially. They whispered among themselves, yet not one individual offered help.

Indignant that they would gossip amongst themselves while doing nothing, Darcy stepped forward. "When did you last see her?"

"I left her in the dinner box to dance with Mr. Bingley

when he asked. I daresay she was none too pleased that he did not prefer to ask her. I had assumed that someone else in our party would have asked her to dance. She is a pretty little thing and a very accomplished dancer."

Mr. Bingley caught up with Mrs. Bennet, bringing Mr. Carissimi and Richard along with him. Behind them still were Lady Rutledge and Miss Bingley. Every member of their party was present except for Miss Lydia. Darcy immediately scanned the dancers before them while he continued to ask questions. "Did none of you ask Miss Lydia to dance?"

Richard said, "I danced with Lady Rutledge."

Mr. Carissimi said, "I asked Miss Bingley for a dance after Miss Lydia refused me. At the time, I thought it was her way of showing me how much she disapproved of our decision to send her to a finishing school." Looking to Mrs. Bennet, he said, "I am so sorry, my dearest. I will do everything possible to find her and, with the help of our friends, she shall be brought home safely." He looked at Darcy, who only interrupted his survey of the crowd to nod to the gentleman.

Richard said, "We should organize a search of the park. Darcy, you take the south end with the entrance. I will take the north. Bingley the east, and Mr. Carissimi the west."

It was a good plan, and the gentlemen had already walked a few paces away when Elizabeth protested. "And where do you suggest we ladies look? I will not be left behind when my sister could be in danger." A tendril of hair hovered over her eye which she puffed away from her face with an exasperated breath. Her fists were balled up on her hips, and Darcy wanted to embrace her and kiss the top of her head so badly, he had to clasp his hands together to prevent himself from acting on his impulse.

"She is right, Colonel. I would much rather help than wait here twiddling my thumbs. However, the gardens are not a safe place for a lady to wander about alone at night," said Lady Rutledge.

Mrs. Bennet's eyes bugged out in her concern. "I will accompany Mr. Carissimi. I cannot remain idle while my girl is lost."

Mr. Carissimi whispered reassurances in her ear and patted her hand resting on his arm.

Before anyone else could make any suggestion otherwise, Lady Rutledge said, "I want to go with my nephew. You can arrange yourselves as you see fit." She looked between Richard and Darcy. "Caroline is wearing some jewelry, though, so might I suggest that whoever she accompanies should take extra care to protect her from harm?"

Richard stepped forward. "Nothing untoward will happen to Miss Bingley in my company. I will ensure her safety."

Not wanting to lose any more time, Darcy set off across the park with Elizabeth.

Elizabeth had to run to keep up with Mr. Darcy's long strides, but he did not slow his pace. She would have run anyway.

"LYDIA!" Elizabeth called at the corner of every bend and turn in the paths they encountered. Her eyes searched every shadow and hiding place frantically.

Her head ached and she struggled for breath, but she pressed on. She fought to push her thoughts to the side. They would have to wait. Right now, her sister needed her. The gardens, though pleasurable, were not a good place for a young lady to wander through alone. Pickpockets and riffraff were known to lurk in the darkness.

After entering every nook and cranny in their path, they

were no closer to finding Lydia than they had been before their search. Had anyone else in their party fared better?

"Would she have tried to walk back into town?" asked Mr. Darcy, shoving his hands through his thick hair.

"It is worth looking into. I cannot pretend to understand Lydia's reasoning, but she was upset when she left."

"You believe that she ran away?"

"I think it more likely than for someone to have kidnapped her."

What would Lydia have to offer besides her youth? Sure, that might be enough to tempt some, but there were too many other young ladies at the park with wealth and rank who would make more profitable targets than Lydia. Mr. Darcy did not ask for her reasons. He did not need to. He knew their circumstances.

The void in her stomach deepened, but she pressed on. Without another pause to comment, she hastened toward the entrance of the gardens to the bridge crossing the Thames.

Carriages scraped across the stones and, in the middle of the bridge, a lone figure stood leaning her body over the edge to look at the water.

"Lydia!" Elizabeth cried, rushing across to meet her.

Her feet stopped when Lydia saw her and leaned forward all the more.

"Lydia, stop! You will fall!" she shouted, moving once again with her arms out toward her sister.

She was close enough to see Lydia's expression as she spoke. "Come no closer, or I will cast myself into the river."

What insanity had overcome her sister? "Lydia, you are overreacting! Do not do anything rash!"

Her face crumpling up like a child's in a tantrum, Lydia dangled one arm over the edge while the other grasped onto the ledge. "Nobody cares about me anyway. I was supposed to marry first, not Mother. Now I have to go to a stuffy school with a bunch of girls whom I know I shall hate. It is not fair!"

Elizabeth stepped forward.

"Stop, Lizzy! I should die if you try to stop me."

"Lydia, think! You shall die if you jump off the bridge. Let me help you." Desperation made her lunge forward and reach for Lydia. She was too late.

Elizabeth felt the soft fabric of her dress run across the tips of her fingers as Lydia tipped over the edge of the bridge and vanished from sight.

CHAPTER 31

Darcy ran to the edge of the water. He could not hear what was said, but the precarious tip of the girl over the ledge of the bridge convinced him of the possibility of some drastic action. His boots got wet, and he reached down to wrangle them off without averting his gaze.

He heard a scream from the bridge, and the slap of Miss Lydia's body as she hit the surface of the water. Plunging into the Thames, the cold water flowing past him as he swam in broad, resolute strokes out to the middle, Darcy prayed he would reach the girl in time.

It grew increasingly difficult to see her in the murky water. His only aid was the light glow of her white dress, but the muddy water nearly swallowed her up. His arms burned under the weight of his clothes, but he kicked harder. She made no effort or struggle in the water, but slipped down so far into the depths that he could no longer see her.

He looked up at the bridge. Elizabeth shouted, but he could not hear through the water rushing past his ears and the gasps of his own breath. She pointed and he dove. He waved his arms back and forth as he pushed himself deeper into the Thames, searching for her.

Something soft tangled in his hand. Pulling on it, he reached along its length. It was heavy.

The need to breathe consumed him. One more second. He opened his eyes but he might as well have been blind. One more second. Only one more second. The pressure in his chest ached as he let out his last breath in a stream of bubbles up to the surface.

Needing to breathe before he added to the number of bodies in the Thames, he tangled his other hand in what he could only hope was Miss Lydia's hair and kicked with all his might until he reached the surface, pulling what he gripped in his hands with him.

His lungs were on fire and his eyes burned, but the relief he felt when he saw the moon reflect off Miss Lydia's pale skin far surpassed his discomfort. Leaning so that he could float on his back, he pulled Miss Lydia up so that her mouth was clear of the water and paddled as furiously as one arm and feet entangled in the fabric of her dress would allow him.

Elizabeth was at the shore, the bottom of her skirt soaked in river water, when he finally felt ground under his feet. He stood and balanced Miss Lydia in his arms as he slogged through the mud in waterlogged stockings. Finding the closest dry spot, he laid her on her side and pumped her limp arm up and down.

"Dear God, help us," Elizabeth repeated until he joined in her prayer.

Dread pierced down to his bones. She was not responding. A crazy bit of news he had read came to mind. With nothing to lose, he pinched her nose and lowered his mouth to breathe into hers.

She coughed, spitting out the filthy water of the Thames. Her eyes remained shut, but she breathed.

He leaned back and let Elizabeth curl her sister up in her arms, rocking her back and forth, and bathing her face with tears.

Darcy had never felt heavier in his life... not even when he had so nearly lost his own sister in ruin.

Through the weight of the moment, he searched around them for someone he could use to send a message to the rest of their party. He could not leave Elizabeth in her present state, nor would he ask her to leave Miss Lydia under his care while she fetched them alone.

His legs trembled as he stood and stepped closer to the bridge where he would have better success summoning some help. He walked behind Elizabeth's back, allowing himself the luxury of trailing his fingers so near her, he could sense her warmth. When she reached up to clasp his hand, he thought his legs would give out on him. He melted into her palm, though he remained upright by some determined force beyond his own strength.

"You will not leave us..." she started, her eyes wide.

"Never," he forced through his tightening throat. "I will never leave you."

The air grew thick like the weather during a thunder storm. When the pop of fireworks over the gardens began, they hardly seemed strong enough to compare to the beating of his heart and the energy coursing through his veins.

Elizabeth pressed her cheek to his hand, sending chills throughout his entire body. Through his rugged breath, he said, "I must find someone to fetch Mrs. Bennet."

Elizabeth released him, and he flexed his fingers before balling them into a fist to fill the empty space where her hand had been.

Stopping the first person he saw, he offered a sum for the lad to search through the gardens for Mrs. Bennet. After giving a brief description of her and Mr. Carissimi, he returned to the shoreline and stood watching over Elizabeth and her sister.

She rocked her steadily, one hand busy rubbing against Miss Lydia's wet arm and pale cheek. She breathed and coughed occasionally. Her eyelashes fluttered when Elizabeth spoke softly to her.

"She will recover," said Darcy, trying not to think of how another tragedy would affect Elizabeth.

Never stopping her swaying movement, she looked up at him with the calm assurance of someone in charge of a situation. It was exactly as he had seen her the day of her father's funeral. Her strength of character through adversity filled him with awe.

He did not know how the brazen act of Miss Lydia would affect Elizabeth— Lady Rutledge scoffed at propriety, but even she must have her limits— but he knew that she would come out fighting. He would be close should she need him. Or want him.

The ardor of his love for Elizabeth fanned the flames in his heart. Not even his wet clothes dampened it.

Wrapping his arms around himself to keep warm, he tensed his muscles before they quit working completely. The surge of power he had experienced only minutes before began to wear off, and he felt cold. His shoulders wished to sag under the weight of his sopping coat, but Elizabeth needed him to be strong for a while longer. He would not let her down as he had before.

Shrieks and the scrambling of high heeled feet in the dust sounded behind him.

"Oh, my Lydia! My dear, dear, foolish girl!" Mrs. Bennet exclaimed as Mr. Carissimi struggled to keep her from falling in the loose gravel and dirt descending to the shore.

~

Mother yanked Lydia out of Elizabeth's arms, leaving her empty and cold. The water from her dress had soaked into Elizabeth's, and she shivered without the warmth of Lydia's body next to her.

Mr. Darcy looked like she felt. She could see the effort it took him to stand upright as he rubbed the arms folded across his chest. He had saved her sister's life.

Mr. Carissimi stood beside him, wisely giving Mother some time with Lydia until his carriage was brought closer and he could convey them safely home. Joining them, Elizabeth wished that she could climb into Mr. Darcy's arms so they could warm each other.

"How can we ever repay you, Mr. Darcy? You saved Lydia and mere words cannot express my gratitude," she said, needing to say something.

Mother spoke from behind her, so that Elizabeth twisted to see her. "Yes, Mr. Darcy. Thank you so much for rescuing my little girl."

Elizabeth looked at Mr. Carissimi, who regarded Mother tenderly. Elizabeth could not doubt the depth of his admiration for her.

Mr. Darcy's eyes lingered on her, not even leaving when Mother spoke. His confession had seemed so important to him minutes ago. How could he doubt his honor when time and again he proved by his actions that he was everything a gentleman ought to be?

Mr. Darcy's speech cast him as an arrogant man with little or no regard for others, but his actions portrayed him as the best of men.

Elizabeth felt so divided, her skin was the only thing holding her together. She wished she could cry, scream, and laugh uncontrollably. She must keep her composure. Mother did not need another hysterical daughter, and the last thing

Lydia needed was to see the responsible sister lose her fortitude before her eyes.

She looked at Mr. Darcy, who had sent the boy to find the rest of their party, so that they could leave. Mr. Carissimi had already sent for his carriage in which he would convey Mother and Lydia home.

Even with his coat sagging and his boots off, Mr. Darcy took command. His presence brought some comfort to Elizabeth, even if an evil little voice in her mind nagged that he only helped because he felt guilty. She could never do him the injustice of believing that guilt was his sole motivator, but she did not have much to recommend herself. The seed of doubt, once it took root in her heart, crushed her soul.

Her shame deepened as her understanding grew. All those months at Longbourn when they could not afford beef, tea, or repairs to a tenant's home, miraculously, a basket would show up outside the kitchen door and they quit receiving complaints from their tenants. Elizabeth had not given it much thought, but it had to have been him. Mr. Collins would never be so thoughtful toward them— not even with the influence of Charlotte. It had been Mr. Darcy all along.

She could not remember a time she felt so low. She was really, truly alone. Mother was leaving her to begin a new life. Jane was happy with Aunt and Uncle Gardiner. Lydia, if she allowed herself, would be much improved with the association of other young ladies better prepared than she. Mary was happy with Uncle and Aunt Phillips. Kitty was very soon to be engaged. Everyone in her family had moved on. Except herself. She had isolated herself from her family in order to pretend to be part of another one. And through it all, he had been there like an anchor.

Elizabeth saw the glint of Miss Bingley's shiny gown sparkle off the glow of the moon and heard the boom of

Colonel Fitzwilliam's baritone and the concerned exclamations of Mr. Bingley and Lady Rutledge. Elizabeth prayed that Miss Bingley would act as civilly as she had the rest of the evening.

Watching her closely, Elizabeth stood next to her mother, who now had a slightly recovered Lydia in her arms.

Taking in the scene before her, Miss Bingley said, "My, my. Some do know how to steal all the attention." She clicked her tongue and shoved her pointy nose into the air.

Elizabeth's blood boiled, and she clamped her mouth shut to keep the words bubbling up inside her from spilling out.

CHAPTER 32

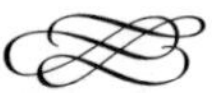

Elizabeth's jaw ached with the force she used to keep her mouth shut. Her head pounded.

Miss Bingley scoffed at her silence. Looking from Lydia to Elizabeth, she asked, "What did she do? Topple over the side of the bridge?"

Mr. Darcy, in a tone as cold as the Thames, said, "What has transpired this evening is nothing to poke fun at or take lightly. We should all go home. The carriages should arrive at any time." He looked apologetically at Elizabeth, as if Miss Bingley merely voiced the thoughts of everyone in their group. To his credit, Colonel Fitzwilliam dropped her arm and stepped away.

"Well, I would never resort to such dramatic behavior only to make myself the center of attention. An accomplished lady need not stoop so low." Miss Bingley assumed her haughtiest air.

That was enough.

Trembling with anger, Elizabeth stepped so close to her the toes of their slippers touched. "No. Proper ladies prefer to get soused on port and pass out in their aunt's drawing room."

She knew she should regret her words, but she did not care. She saw the change in Miss Bingley's complexion along with the sounds of her huffs. She looked like a fire-breathing dragon. Nary budging an inch, Elizabeth would slay her with her sword-like tongue should she make any more comments against her or her family.

Lady Rutledge's voice pierced through the silence, and Miss Bingley broke eye contact. "That is sufficient. At this point, I hesitate to call either of you a lady. Let us make haste to our homes before we are seen like this."

Elizabeth resumed her place behind Mother. Surely, Lady Rutledge would allow her to see Mother and Lydia home.

Colonel Fitzwilliam, seeing Mr. Darcy's state, rushed over to assist her with Lydia. He picked her up like she weighed no more than a feather. Mr. Darcy held out his hand to assist Mother up from the ground.

Mother brushed off her dress, thanking the gentlemen for their graciousness.

When Elizabeth tried to loop her arm through hers, Mother shrugged her off. "No, Lizzy. You chose your place, and you must keep it." She looked past Mr. Carissimi and his carriage to Lady Rutledge, who was already being handed into her waiting coach.

Mother's comment felt like a slap in the face. Was this her reward for defending her family?

Leaning out of her carriage, Lady Rutledge called for her. "Eliza, come."

Elizabeth hated being called Eliza. She hated being called like a dog. Even worse, she hated how she was obliged to obey.

~

ELIZABETH FELT isolated from the world. A week passed, and she had seen no one. Mr. Darcy had not called.

She received a note from Mother informing her that Lydia was fully recovered and only suffered from a runny nose of which she hoped she would be cured before she was expected at the finishing school the next day. Mr. Carissimi had purchased a special license, and they would have a quiet wedding in a matter of days. She had nothing else left but to wish them happy. She did not know if she would be allowed to attend Mother's wedding. Lady Rutledge had hardly spoken to her since their evening at Vauxhall Gardens.

When they took their meals together, the only sound was of the cutlery against the china dishes and their own chewing. Lady Rutledge's silent stares and pensive ruminations were excruciating, and Elizabeth wished Lady Rutledge would say something… anything… no matter how disapproving or unflattering.

She should have kept quiet against Miss Bingley's insults.

Elizabeth received a letter from Jane that morning. She read it in the library, letting the sunlight pour over the pages and warm her through. Jane had returned early from the coast with Aunt, Uncle, and the children. Emma was much improved, as was she, and Aunt had plans to attend some of the public balls they had been invited to with the intention of introducing Jane to potential suitors. Elizabeth sensed Jane's excitement and nervousness through the pages, and her heart warmed for her. Jane was so beautiful, she was sure to be a sensation wherever she went. She did not suffer from bouts of temper and an uncontrollable tongue. Nor would she act impulsively and cause herself to live a life of misery with no escape.

A maid tapped on the open door, cutting Elizabeth's self-condemnation short. "Lady Rutledge has requested to see you, miss."

Folding Jane's letter and hiding it where Mr. Darcy's handkerchief used to rest, she followed the maid upstairs to Lady Rutledge's sitting room.

Lady Rutledge laid her newspaper down and looked up at Elizabeth. Even after the maid left, she sat contemplating Elizabeth without a word.

If her intention was to intimidate, then she did not know Elizabeth's character well enough. Elizabeth raised her chin and returned her stare, locking eyes with Lady Rutledge.

Finally, she spoke. "I am going to send you away, Eliza."

Elizabeth was not surprised. Still, her pulsed slowed, and she felt the blood drain from the top of her head down to her toes. "When?" she asked.

"I would send you away immediately, but Charles would only insist that I find another companion, and I would rather avoid that. It is my intention to carry on as I did before my brother and sister-in-law left for the New World — without a nanny keeping watch over my every move." Her words snapped like a whip, and Elizabeth felt her cheeks sting.

"When do you expect them?" she asked, proud that her voice held steady.

"Any day now. Their journey was not to be a long one. I advised them against it, but they were determined to go." She waved her fingers, bored with the details. "As it is, I do not feel that I can give you a recommendation. You are not well-suited as a companion."

"May I ask why, with so little endeavor for civility, I am thus dismissed?" The answer would be as severe as her question, but she needed to know.

Lady Rutledge leaned forward, captivating Elizabeth's gaze with her intensity. "My mission in life is to see my niece appropriately settled. I had thought that you would be a wholesome influence on her and distract her from a certain gentleman I believe to be unsuitable for her— a purpose you fulfilled for a time."

Elizabeth crossed her arms. She would never answer for Miss Bingley's faults. Those were hers and hers alone.

"This I could forgive, but your defensive attitude toward your relatives' conduct has discouraged Mr. Darcy at the same time it cast a negative light on Caroline in front of Colonel Fitzwilliam. I feel the need to do something drastic to see where their true emotions lie."

Miss Bingley would look bad without her help. She was as selfish as Lady Rutledge claimed her not to be.

"I apologize for not fulfilling my role in your game to your expectations," she said, stabbing her tongue with her teeth at the sound of the sharpness of her voice.

"What makes you think it is over? I have such high hopes for you." She looked genuinely sad, puzzling Elizabeth. With a scoff, Lady Rutledge continued, "You appear surprised that a single-minded woman such as me should take an interest in you."

Single-minded? Was that how stubbornness was defined in her day? "I am. From the day I took up residence here, I have felt like little more than a pawn."

Lady Rutledge shrugged her shoulder. "And so you are. But it is time for you to join your mother. I shall be able to convince my brother of the futility of my being forced to have a companion as soon as he returns."

"If it was so distasteful to you, why did you agree to it?"

She huffed, clearly done answering impertinent questions. "What can I say? I love my nephew and knew that he would have no peace unless I played along."

Further puzzled at her acceptance of Mr. Bingley's concerns against her will, Elizabeth responded, "That was kind of you to do so on his behalf." With a curtsy, she bowed her head, "I thank you for allowing me to have a part in it. It was diverting."

The lady's face softened considerably. "You may go now. You will want to write to your relatives. I took the liberty of meeting with your mother, and she agrees with me that this is for the best. You will join her in Bath."

Thus dismissed, Elizabeth turned to leave the room, her limbs numb. Would she be able to see Mr. Darcy again before she was forced to leave?

She had just crossed the doorway when Lady Rutledge said, "I think you will be all right, Eliza. You must trust me."

If she had been confused before, she was fully bewildered as she returned to her room. Her mind in the clouds and her vision blurry, Elizabeth rounded the corner and smacked into the butler, sending the silver tray with a package wrapped in brown paper clattering to the floor.

"I am so sorry," she said as the butler scrambled to put everything back in its proper place. Once she assured herself that he was well, she went to continue to her room to begin writing her first letter. She would write to Uncle Gardiner.

"Miss Bennet, this is for you," the butler called from behind her. He pushed the tray in her direction.

"For me?" She had only received frequent letters from Jane and Aunt Gardiner, and the occasional message from Mother and Mary. She had no reason to expect that they would send anything for her.

"Who is this from?" she asked.

The butler, his stoic face revealing nothing in his expression, said, "A messenger boy delivered it. If there is a note, it might be inside."

Not satisfied, Elizabeth asked, "Was there nothing in his dress or speech to indicate where the messenger came from?"

"He was not dressed as a household servant would be, and the only words he spoke were those I repeated to you."

"Thank you," she said as the butler continued to Lady Rutledge's room with what appeared to be some invitations.

The weight and thickness of it felt comfortable and familiar in her hands. It had to be a book. She cradled it in her arm as she continued to her room.

Unwrapping the paper, her breath caught in her throat and a sob escaped. Hurriedly, she hugged it to herself, swaying back and forth with it in her arms, petting the cover as if it were a precious kitten.

Lowering the worn leather volume and sitting on the chaise by the window, she carefully opened the cover to the first page and traced her fingers over the letters written within. A teardrop landed on the page, blurring the name she could not stop staring at. Wiping it from the page and sniffing to prevent herself from ruining such a precious document, she dabbed her face with her sleeve.

She lifted it out of the paper. There was a note scribbled in large, loopy handwriting on the inside of the brown paper.

To my dearest Lizzy,

I am ashamed to say that I only found this journal as I began packing for my new life with Mr. Carissimi. It seems unfaithful of me to have it now— especially when you stand to benefit the most from what is inside.

Look through every page, my girl, and know that while I have at times reacted wrongly, it was done out of my concern for you.

Yours Always in Affection,
Mother

. . .

ELIZABETH FOLDED Mother's note neatly, setting it next to Jane's on her writing table. Slowly flipping through the pages of her father's journal, a loose paper fell to the floor. It was an unfinished letter addressed to her. She stopped breathing as she read Father's final words.

CHAPTER 33

Darcy stood against the wall in the large ballroom, trying to recall why he had decided to come against his better judgment. Several reasons had been presented to him, all of them rational and expected of him as a gentleman in society, but only one had convinced him. Elizabeth was to be there that night. He had not seen her in a week, being indisposed with a cold in his head. He did not want her to blame herself every time he sneezed, which had been often.

He rocked up on the balls of his feet to better skim over the tops of the heads in the room. He had picked the perfect position with a view through the grand archway to the entry door where people filed into the already cramped rooms. He had refused every implication of a dance, not wanting to miss her.

Georgiana nudged him in the ribs. "You look like a crane standing like that. Or a giraffe with its neck stretched to reach the highest leaves on a tree branch," she teased. She knew who he looked for. He had no secrets from his little sister.

“Like Richard?” He pointed his forehead across the room to where their cousin stood in a similar posture.

“Precisely,” Georgiana laughed, but soon covered her mouth with a horrified expression in her eyes. “He is not…? I mean… He does not…?”

Darcy knew who Richard waited for, and it was not Elizabeth. “You need not worry on that account. He assured me that his sights are set elsewhere.” He did not tell his sister what a relief it had been to hear his fear rebutted.

"I hope Miss Elizabeth likes me. Otherwise, it was silly of me to suggest to Aunt Helen that we return to town two weeks early. Do you think she will like me?" asked Georgiana, her voice trembling in her shyness.

"How could she not?" he looked at her long enough to see her relief at his assurance before returning his sight to the door.

"You must really love her," she said, her pointy chin tilted up to meet his eyes.

"I will not diminish the power of such sacred words by saying them before they must be said and to who should hear them, Georgie."

She smiled brilliantly. "It is as I thought. Nothing else would persuade you to come to a public assembly with its overcrowded rooms— much less convince you to bring me with you. I like the changes in you that Miss Elizabeth has brought on. You seem… softer."

Darcy was spared from having to reply when the Bingleys entered the room. All of the Bingleys. Bingley held his mother's arm, and Miss Bingley walked with her father. Her dress was a touch more sedate than normal, complimenting her features instead of overwhelming them.

Richard practically ran over to greet them, smiling wider than usual to the Bingley parents.

"Am I seeing what I think I am seeing, brother?" Georgiana tugged on his arm in case he had not seen.

Darcy chuckled. He would not have guessed it either had he not asked forthright.

"Miss Bingley is the object of Richard's affections. According to Richard, she is 'determined to leave her ambitions and improve her character.'" Darcy chuckled at his cousin.

"But why her?" Georgiana covered her mouth apologetically. "I do apologize for speaking out, but I know your opinion of her."

Darcy would have laughed at her sensitivity, had she not been so genuinely apologetic. "I reacted the same initially. She has done everything possible to make herself look undesirable to him, but all he sees is her potential and tenacity." He patted her hand and she relaxed.

"Potential?" asked Georgiana.

"He sees what we do not, Georgie. However, I do agree with him that once he gains her loyalty, she will make a devoted wife. If he can love Miss Bingley despite her flaws, then who are we to speak against the match?"

"Richard is romantic and honorable. But do you really think he is in love with Miss Bingley? She is so..." She blushed, closing her mouth on her unfinished sentence.

"That she is, but you know Richard. He always has enjoyed a good confrontation. She represents a challenge to him, and he is determined to win her. From what I see, he has met with some success."

Sure enough, Richard extended his arm out to Miss Bingley. She accepted. He walked with a bounce in his step, his chest puffed out, and his head held high— as if he were escorting the Queen herself. Miss Bingley flounced across the floor, looking pleased to be seen with the distinguished officer. Darcy smiled to himself. They would manage well.

That Richard would conquer the battle before him was not in doubt.

Georgiana squeezed his arm. "Is that her?" she asked, looking up at him anxiously.

He had been so distracted by Richard and Miss Bingley, he had looked away from the door.

She wore a simple muslin dress, adorned with nothing more than her brilliant smile and sparkling eyes. She needed no feathers, brooches, or jewels when her very person exuded radiance and life. Especially tonight. There was a lightness about her he had not seen since their time together in Lady Rutledge's library.

His heart rose up into his throat at the sight of her. Breathing through his nose and out his mouth, he felt his whole body break into a sweat when her eyes met him across the length of the room.

ELIZABETH SENSED him before she saw him. It was as if her eyes were pulled by magnets, the draw was so intense. And there he stood, arm in arm with a beautiful girl who looked to be the age of Lydia. Please, Lord, let her be his sister. She tried to recall past conversations for a description of her or any mention of when she was expected in town— anything to ease the wrench in her gut at the sight of the angelic creature beside him.

"Stay with me, Eliza. I intend to keep an eye on Caroline tonight, and I need your help," Lady Rutledge said through the side of her mouth as she smiled regally to the ladies and gentleman crowding around them.

The music started for the beginning of another dance, and Elizabeth searched the figures for Miss Bingley. She was not there.

"Aunt Lavinia, Mr. Darcy is over there. Perhaps he has seen Miss Bingley?" she suggested, hoping to allay her fears before they grew within her and spoiled her evening completely.

Lady Rutledge's lips pursed together. "Not yet. A lady must never approach a man, but must patiently see if he will approach her."

What was she talking about? Elizabeth sighed, and with one more glance over her shoulder, she looked at Mr. Darcy before they passed by the grand archway in their search for Miss Bingley.

After a few discreet inquiries, they found her surrounded by a circle of young ladies. Each seemed more determined than the next to dress more extravagantly than the other— except for Miss Bingley, who looked elegant in the midst of her garish friends. Elizabeth would have rolled her eyes at their vanity and snobbery, but Miss Bingley saw them and waved them over, welcoming them to her group with open arms.

Elizabeth looked behind her. Surely, Miss Bingley's gesture was not meant for her. There was no glass in her hand. She had not imbibed too much.

Touching Lady Rutledge on the elbow, Elizabeth inclined her head toward the waiting group of young ladies.

"Oh, how delightful! You found her. Let us join them. Caroline and I had a lengthy discussion about her comments outside the gardens, and she is anxious to make amends."

This would be interesting.

When they drew closer, Miss Bingley took Elizabeth's hands into her own and welcomed her with a smile that did not appear to be fake. Pulling her into the center of the group, she introduced her to all of her friends. Elizabeth recognized some of the names. Others were new to her. They smiled sweetly at her, making her all the more confused. She responded as was expected of her, all the while bracing herself for the ridicule to come.

Looping her arm through Elizabeth's, Miss Bingley said, "Miss Eliza has become a dear friend of mine of late, and I just know that once you get to know her, you will feel the same."

Elizabeth saw the reactions of disbelief among the ladies who had less control over their expressions than the others.

With a pious tone, one intrepid lady asked, "I was under the opinion that you did not much care for your cousin." She drew out the last word, emphasizing it.

Miss Bingley's retort was so immediate, she must have practiced it. "And who told you that?" she asked in a silky voice.

"Miss Minerva Oliver told me she heard it from Mrs. Woodly who heard it directly from you." She snapped her fan shut and tapped it against her hand. If she was a friend of Miss Bingley's, she was not a good one. She took too much delight in contradicting her in front of others.

Miss Bingley waved her fingers through the air. "I am surprised at you for believing everything you hear from Mrs. Woodly." She scoffed and turned toward Elizabeth and her aunt.

Lady Rutledge, pretending to have not heard the entire exchange clearly, said, "Who did you say? Ah, Mrs. Woodly? You know, dear," she said in a confiding voice loud enough for all to hear, "you can only believe half of what she says."

Elizabeth would have burst out in laughter at how well Miss Bingley and Lady Rutledge caused the ladies in their group to doubt what they knew all too well had been said.

"Let us not stoop to harmful gossip. We are above that," suggested Miss Bingley, looping her arm through Elizabeth's and pressing it to her side. She added, "Anyone who repeats even the slightest criticism against my cousin will answer to me directly."

Elizabeth did her best imitation of Mr. Darcy's neutral expression. That must have been some conversation Lady Rutledge had with her niece.

Miss Bingley's friends did not look completely convinced, but a few did smile nervously at Elizabeth, and she did not feel like such a pariah.

A booming voice behind her, who could only be Colonel Fitzwilliam, said, "Here is your lemonade, Miss Bingley." Addressing the rest of the group with a graceful bow, he continued, "I only apologize that I did not bring sufficient with me for the rest of your friends."

Pleased to receive the attention of a charming colonel, the ladies gushed while Miss Bingley looked as proud as a peacock. Elizabeth watched her closely, seeing how her fingertips covered the tips of his and lingered a fraction of a second longer than they needed to. Could it be? Had the colonel turned her affections? He would be a worthy opponent— er, match— for her.

As if she could read Elizabeth's thoughts, Lady Rutledge spoke. "Let us circulate, Eliza. There are still many other people I wish to see, and I am sure that the colonel would rather dance with my niece than converse with us."

Colonel Fitzwilliam laughed. "I like how you think, Lady Rutledge!"

Miss Bingley smiled again. She really was quite handsome.

Elizabeth willed Lady Rutledge to return to the room they had just passed. Maybe Mr. Darcy would still be there. But it was not to be. Continuing forward, they entered a room set aside for refreshments. A splendid table was laid out, and several couples milled about.

"There they are. They sent word to me yesterday that they

had arrived, but I did not expect to see them here." Lady Rutledge pulled Elizabeth further into the room, passing the tables flowing with lemonade and punch.

They stopped in front of a couple who looked to be close in age to, if not a bit younger than, Mother. The gentleman had a large, copper mustache with streaks of silver through his hair. His wife had fair hair the same color as Mr. Bingley's. Elizabeth did not need to be told who they were.

"Brother, Susanna, you did not tell me you would be here tonight," chided Lady Rutledge as she kissed them each on the cheek.

Mr. Bingley Senior— Elizabeth had to have some way of keeping the misters Bingley straight in her mind— laughed as easily as his son often did. "Lavinia! How glad we are to see you again, my dear sister." Looking between her and Elizabeth, he added, "You have not been making much trouble, have you?" He managed to look cheerful through his furrowed brow. Elizabeth could more easily understand the origins of Mr. Bingley's easy temperament.

"Not much, John. Your son has made certain of that." Pushing Elizabeth forward, she presented her to her brother and sister-in-law.

Mr. Bingley bowed gallantly. In a serious voice, he said, "I do hope, Miss Bennet, that my sister has not been too much of a handful. She keeps me on my toes on a good month, and I worried that she would pose a problem for my son, who is not so experienced as I am in her methods."

Mrs. Bingley's eyes grew wide, and she nodded solemnly in agreement.

Elizabeth laughed gaily. She liked the Bingleys.

"Lavinia," said Mrs. Bingley, "you know our expectations of Charles. I hope he has not been too busy keeping an eye on you that he has neglected to seek a wife." Her final words faded down into a whisper and her eyes darted about to prevent any eavesdropping ear from hearing her plain speech.

"Never fear, Susanna. He got Miss Bennet to stay with me until your return."

"Until our return? How did this come about?" asked Mr. Bingley.

"I think it important for you to understand the version of truth I have spread. Miss Bennet is a niece of mine— a distant cousin to your children." Did she really just wink?

"Lavinia, you know how much I disapprove of your 'versions of the truth,' as you call them," said Mr. Bingley Senior, doing his best to look stern.

She shrugged her shoulders. "We are all descendants of Adam. I need not go into inquiries or details about how distant the relationship is between Miss Bennet and me, but you have to admit that the details of our relationship is nothing but a matter of degrees."

Rolling his eyes and puffing out his reddened cheeks, he addressed Elizabeth quietly. "If I may be so bold, might I inquire if you are in need of another position? I am well aware of the circumstances by which a young lady might agree to live as a companion for one so troublesome as my sister."

Lady Rutledge interrupted before Elizabeth could answer. "It is very like you to concern yourself for another, but I have better plans for Eliza. I have done my best to secure Miss Bennet's future, and I thank you not to disturb my hard work." She gave her brother a pointed look.

Better plans? Secure her future? How was dismissing her securing her future?

Mrs. Bingley stood on her toes and looked about the room. "Speaking of securing futures, I want to find Charles. Shall we go to the ballroom?"

Finally! Hopefully Mr. Darcy would still be there.

The music broke when they entered. Mr. Bingley came over to them after returning his dance partner to her seat. They stood just inside the archway near the door. Mr. Darcy walked toward them, the fair-haired girl on his arm.

More guests entered, and their group fell silent as Mr. Bingley stepped forward, his mouth open in awe. “She is heavenly,” he said, clearly unaware of anyone else in the room.

Elizabeth looked away from Mr. Darcy to see whom he spoke of so reverently. Covering her mouth with her fingers to keep from squealing in her immense joy, she went to Jane.

CHAPTER 34

Elizabeth embraced Miss Bennet with an enthusiasm Darcy hoped to be the recipient of soon.

"Mr. Darcy, how good to see you here!" Mr. Gardiner greeted as he joined them. Turning to Mrs. Gardiner, he said, "Are you not glad we came, dear?" Turning back to Darcy, he added, "This is the sort of event we generally avoid, but Lady Rutledge insisted we come. Our Janey would not miss seeing her sister for the world." How interesting. Lady Rutledge had insisted that he be present also.

Grateful for the familiar manners and friendly speech of Mr. Gardiner, Darcy presented them to his sister. Georgiana's eyes fixed on Miss Bennet, who smiled in return at her curiosity.

"Have you met my nieces, Miss Jane Bennet and Miss Elizabeth, yet Miss Darcy?" asked Mr. Gardiner amiably.

"My brother and I saw Miss Elizabeth come through the door a couple of minutes ago with Lady Rutledge, but I have yet to be introduced to her. I do so look forward to meeting her. I have heard nothing but kind things said about Miss

Elizabeth." Georgiana's cheeks flushed pink, and it surprised Darcy that she spoke as much as she did.

Mrs. Gardiner stepped closer to Georgiana, leaning in to speak as if she would share a secret with a friend. "I can assure you, Miss Darcy, Elizabeth is everything good. She has a way of brightening a room with her laughter." A flicker of sadness crossed her face.

Georgiana understood. Reaching her hand out as if she would touch Mrs. Gardiner's arm, but stopping short, uncertain of herself, she said, "Losing a dearly loved parent will alter a person's character for a time. I suspect that even Miss Elizabeth is not immune to grief, but if happiness is in her nature, she will soon return to it."

Her mature words stunned Darcy. Had she noticed such a change in him when their father had died? The look she gave him answered that she had.

Tipping up on her toes, Georgiana whispered into his ear, "She is lovely, William."

Indeed she was. It had not taken long for him to believe Elizabeth to be the handsomest woman in all of England, but tonight… Tonight, he had to remind himself to breathe. The vision before them glowed as if the stars had descended from the heavens to illuminate her steps. The luminaries— bewitched by her body and soul just as he was— twinkled in her eyes, returning the spark of which her father had spoken.

Elizabeth hugged her sister with no concern for who may see her public display. Her eyes glistened with joy as she turned to face him, leaving Miss Bennet with the enamored Bingley and his parents.

Darcy finally answered the pinching squeeze of Georgiana's fingers against his arm and introduced her to Miss Elizabeth.

Lady Rutledge, an ostrich feather towering over her silk turban, floated over to them.

"My dearest Darcy, how good of you to allow your sister to accompany you this evening." She grasped Georgiana by the shoulders, giving her air kisses and making Georgie blush.

As soon as Lady Rutledge released her, she looked expectantly at Darcy. Elizabeth had a large grin across her face. A charming dimple graced her left cheek, and Darcy wondered what other delights adorned her that he did not know of yet.

Elizabeth's dimple deepened, and he felt Georgie relax at Elizabeth's sincere pleasure in meeting her.

To Darcy's surprise, it was Georgie who initiated conversation. "I am so happy to finally meet you, Miss Elizabeth. I have heard so much about you, I feel that we are already the best of friends." She blushed at her outspokenness, and Darcy feared that she would withdraw into her shell after her moment of boldness.

Elizabeth reached out and touched one of her hands, holding it like she would one of her own sister's. "And I am equally delighted to meet you, Miss Darcy."

Georgie's complexion calmed, as did she.

Darcy had almost forgotten the presence of Lady Rutledge, something inexcusable in her eyes. Her eyes had narrowed into slits as she considered them, looking back and forth between him and Elizabeth. Would she resent him if he acted on his heart and swept Elizabeth away? He nearly chuckled out loud when he thought that he really did not care. He knew whom he wanted to spend his life with, and nothing and no one could stand in his way. Not even Lady Rutledge.

Georgiana looked up at him, expecting an answer to a question he had been too distracted to hear.

"I apologize. I was lost in my thoughts. What did you say?" he asked.

She looked at him strangely. "My brother lost in his thoughts? That is very unlike you, William."

He would have apologized again, but she looked from the corner of her eyes to Elizabeth and smiled devilishly. "They must have been pleasant thoughts if I read the expression on your face correctly."

Dear Lord, she had become more outspoken than he had believed possible. It was a welcome change, but he hoped the lighting in the room would disguise the heat he felt choking his neck and running up into his face.

An impish glint in Lady Rutledge's eyes told him that his body had betrayed him. The best he could do was admit the truth and hope that someone would change the subject. "They were the best of thoughts," he said simply, doing his best to glue his eyes to his sister at his side instead of the cause of his lack of composure in front of him.

"Would that we all be blessed with such pleasantries, Mr. Darcy. No doubt, your sister's presence is a good influence," said Elizabeth, emanating sunshine.

Grateful for the excuse, he pounced on it. "You have read my mind, Miss Elizabeth. There is nothing like being reunited with a beloved sister after too much time apart."

Georgiana shushed him. "It has only been a short time since we last saw each other. After all the trouble I caused, I thought you would be grateful to be relieved of me for a spell."

His pulse quickened. She referred to her near elopement with a childhood friend, something she would never speak of casually in front of a stranger. He looked at Lady Rutledge, who was more interested in watching him than his sister. All the better. She could probably be trusted with a secret, but he would not put her to the test.

Elizabeth said, "I know what you mean about being apart from your siblings. I miss my sisters dearly and should love to be reunited with them— no matter how troublesome they may be at times," she said smoothly, glossing over Georgiana's comment.

Georgiana's face turned a scarlet shade of red. Squeezing her hand, which gripped his arm, he said, "I had the honor of meeting Miss Elizabeth's mother and youngest sister on a recent excursion to Vauxhall Gardens. Unfortunately, our excursion was cut short— a mishap I should like to remedy by returning on another occasion."

Lady Rutledge decided to join in the conversation. "It was a pity to cut our excursion short." Leaning closer to Georgiana, she said, "Eliza did not get to see the glass house, the Chinese pavilion, or the music house." She looked pointedly at Darcy.

Georgiana's eyes lit up, and she forgot her blunder of earlier. "Oh, William, do you think that we might arrange another excursion to the gardens? I have not been in such a long time, and Miss Elizabeth really must see the glass house!" She continued in a dreamy voice, "It is the most beautiful place. Imagine," she said, spreading her hands before her, "the entire building is made of glass so that you can see the stars through it. It is the most romantic place."

"It sounds absolutely lovely, and I should like to see it someday," Elizabeth said longingly.

Looking up at him, Georgiana asked, "Could we not go very soon?" She tugged on his arm just as she had done so many times as a little girl when she was excited about something.

He looked up at Lady Rutledge, knowing that Elizabeth would never be allowed to go anywhere without her permission. "I think we can arrange something. I shall let Georgiana help me, since she has such strong opinions on what we should see there," he said.

Lady Rutledge pinched her lips in thought.

Elizabeth said, "I am sad to say it, but it will have to wait if I am to join you. You see, this is my last week with Aunt Lavinia before I return to my mother."

Darcy felt like the floor had opened up, and he fell through an endless abyss. "She has quit London already, has she not?"

"She and Mr. Carissimi married, and she invited me to join them at his estate."

Georgiana asked, "Is it far? Perhaps they could join us?"

Elizabeth's smile contradicted her sad eyes. "They left yesterday. His estate is outside Bath. Mother asked me to join them; otherwise I would have given her more time to settle into her new home before intruding."

Darcy narrowed his eyes at Lady Rutledge, who held his stare firmly. Why was Elizabeth leaving? Why could she not stay with the Gardiners?

Georgiana bunched her cheeks in thought. "Since I already have permission of sorts to arrange an outing at Vauxhall Gardens, I do not think my brother would deny me the privilege of inviting you over for tea tomorrow." She still looked up at him for his consent, which he readily gave. It thrilled him to see her making decisions and acting on them like a responsible young lady.

Tipping his head forward, Darcy said, "I think that is a marvelous idea."

Too excited to stand still, she bobbed up and down on her toes a couple times before settling. "Please come for tea tomorrow. I should love to entertain both of you." She looked expectantly at Elizabeth and Lady Rutledge.

Lady Rutledge answered, "I have a previous engagement, but I would hate for Eliza to miss the occasion. Her presence is not required where I am going, so I shall send her in my carriage."

Georgiana tried not to look too pleased, but Darcy saw

through her politeness. Her relief at not having Lady Rutledge present was too great.

Elizabeth, too, looked surprised but pleased. Her eyes flickered over to him, and he wished he could think of some excuse to join them. But morning tea was for ladies, and he would not intrude on Georgiana's plans. Unless he could conjure a perfectly reasonable explanation for his presence…

"I see people I want to introduce Eliza to before she leaves me. Do you not agree, Darcy, that now that my niece is free, she ought to strengthen her acquaintances?"

"Free?" he blurted.

The feather in Lady Rutledge's hat twitched. "Of course. She is under no obligation to me and may go where she pleases, although I did arrange for her to join her mother in Bath. There are sufficient single gentlemen there to keep her entertained. She will be snatched up before the end of the season, I daresay."

Not if he could help it! Darcy knew Lady Rutledge's game, yet the hair on his arms and neck stood on end.

Nothing could prevent him from missing Georgiana's tea on the morrow.

CHAPTER 35

Elizabeth waited in the drawing room with Lady Rutledge. She still had half an hour before the coach would convey her to Darcy House, but in her excitement, she had been ready to leave for the past hour at least. She liked Miss Darcy.

If only Lady Rutledge had let her make her own arrangements, she could have continued in London. Lady Rutledge had been silent against her questions since last evening.

"How good of Caroline to befriend you like she has. And did you notice that she danced with Colonel Fitzwilliam not once, but twice?" commented Lady Rutledge.

"Several people noticed. You must be pleased with yourself. The gossip is that they are very soon to be engaged." Even more shocking had been Miss Bingley's kindness to her during the entire course of the evening. She did not openly apologize, but every word and action implied it.

"I started that rumor," said Lady Rutledge with a self-satisfied smirk.

"Why am I not surprised? Does everything you plan come to fruition?" teased Elizabeth.

With a devilish look, Lady Rutledge said, “Let us hope for your sake that it does.”

Elizabeth wondered what Lady Rutledge had up her sleeve, but she dared not flatter herself that she would care enough about her future to involve herself in it. Or would she?

Finally, the coach was ready, and it was time to go.

"Have a lovely time at tea, Eliza." Lady Rutledge arched her eyebrow, the corner of her mouth turning slightly upward.

Over the crowded, cobbled streets the carriage traveled. Elizabeth felt her nerves growing as the distance to Darcy House shortened. She hoped she might have the opportunity to see Mr. Darcy and allay him of his fears. He should not hold himself responsible for Father's death. Even if she did not see him, she had every intention of making mention of it somehow to Miss Darcy. Elizabeth did not want to leave London without giving her reassurances. It would not be fair after all Mr. Darcy had done for her and her family.

The carriage slowed to a stop and she took a deep breath as she descended the step and went to the front door held open by a butler. She was seen into a butter-yellow parlor where the sun shone through the windows. It was warm and welcoming with the aromas of fresh bread and sweet jam wafting from the table.

Miss Darcy rose to meet her, holding her hands out to take hers. "Miss Elizabeth, I am so happy you could come. Please forgive my negligence in inviting any other ladies, but I do not have many close friends of confidence in town, and I do so want to know you better."

Her innocent timidity endeared her further to Elizabeth. "I am honored, Miss Darcy. Would it be too soon for me to beg of you to address me by my name?"

Miss Darcy's smile assured her that she welcomed the

intimacy, and she pulled her chair forward to sit closer to Elizabeth.

What would her name sound like on Mr. Darcy's lips? How would his name sound on hers? Fitzwilliam? William? Fitzwilliam seemed too stuffy. William. Now, that suited him much better.

"If I am to call you Elizabeth, please call me Georgiana."

"I would love to. Do you spend much time in London, Georgiana?"

Georgiana twisted her fingers together. "I prefer the quiet and peace of the country, but I begged my aunt Helen to cut our tour short, so that we might join my brother earlier than planned. It is only a shame that you must quit London so soon."

"I am sad for it as well. Had I been allowed to make my own arrangements, I would have stayed with my aunt and uncle Gardiner, whom you met last night. As it is, Mother expects me in Bath, and I cannot disappoint her. Do you travel much to Bath?" Elizabeth asked hopefully.

Georgiana shook her head. "My brother has gone with me before, but we prefer to stay at Pemberley. I wish you could see it! If ever you travel in the direction of the Lake District, I hope you visit us there. You would love our library." She stopped short, as if she had said something she should not have uttered. Covering her hand with her mouth, she said, "Dear me, I did not mean..." Her face reddened, and she stared at her lap.

Elizabeth could not prevent the smile from coming any more than she could prevent her complexion from deepening to match Georgiana's, judging from the heat in her cheeks. Georgiana looked pained, and her eyes wandered around the room in search of something, landing on anything except Elizabeth.

If Georgiana already knew of the incident, where was the

harm in laughing about it? It truly was a ridiculous scene and, though it shocked Elizabeth that Mr. Darcy would admit to it to his sister, she was not surprised that they shared an intimacy only enjoyed by the closest of siblings.

"You heard of that, did you?" she asked with a chuckle. "Your poor brother did his best to act as a gentleman ought—of that I must assure you. It was a conspiracy of candles and lace which caused his fall. Quite literally."

Mr. Darcy entered the room just as she and his sister burst into laughter.

With a large smile on his gorgeous face, he walked to stand beside where his sister sat. “I would ask what the source of your merriness is, but I fear the answer.”

"Brother, how fortuitous you should join us. I have something I want to show to Elizabeth, and it would be horribly rude for me to leave her alone. Will you stay here and keep her company until I return? I shall not be away long."

Elizabeth could think of half a dozen other ways Georgiana could retrieve whatever it was that needed retrieving without leaving her alone in the room with Mr. Darcy. But the opportunity to speak to him without overhearing ears was too great to pass up, so she did not protest, but rather watched for his reaction.

"Very well. Leave the door open, and ask a footman to stand there until you return." Propriety seen to, he waited until Georgiana left before he spoke.

His forehead furled and his eyebrows bunched together. "Miss Elizabeth, I do not want to seem insensitive to the news I confessed to you at Vauxhall Gardens, nor the events which followed—"

"You could hardly have mentioned it at the ball, Mr. Darcy. Really, you need not concern yourself," she broke in, wanting to ease his discomfort.

He lowered his head, shaking it. "No, I could not. I discuss many things with my sister, but that is not one of them."

The look of pain on his face made Elizabeth want to make him laugh— anything to lighten his guilt. "Yes," she said with a chuckle, which forced his head back up to meet her eyes. "Georgiana, apparently, is aware of our awkward exchange in Lady Rutledge's library. I shall always remember that occasion when I am in need of a laugh."

The corner of his mouth curled up, but it spread no further.

Leaning forward in her seat, not wanting him to miss a word of what she had to tell him, Elizabeth said, "Mr. Darcy, I thank you for your honesty. It has helped me to understand your character. But I must allay your concern over your part in my father's death— if indeed you played any part at all. You owe nothing to my family. You owe nothing to me." She held her breath.

He spoke slowly and deliberately. "You ease my conscience greatly, but I will not change my behavior toward you unless you wish it."

"I do not wish you to act out of guilt on my behalf."

"You believed me to be kind and thoughtful when the truth is that I have lived most of my life unconcerned with how my words and actions affected others. I deserved your criticism, yet even when others spoke ill of me, you refused to believe them." He shoved his hand through his wavy hair. With a shrug, he said, "I had to live up to your expectations of me. I could not disappoint you."

CHAPTER 36

Darcy held his breath. Surely she must know how his heart burned when he was near her, but something bothered her. He felt it.

"I am honored that you value my opinion. I treasure yours. You have offered reassurances which put my heart at ease. Let me do the same for you, and let us be forever rid of the guilt and regret which has loomed over us."

She had his full attention. "My father traveled to Hunsford to speak to the heir apparent because he knew his health was failing. At the time, I did not realize the extent of it. Otherwise, I would have… Oh, there are so many regrets of which I must learn to let go. I would have embraced him harder before he left and harder still when he returned home. I would have told him how much he meant to me. I would have thanked him for imparting to me what knowledge he could. I would have asked him how he expected me to act on the sad event of his passing. I have been haunted over the past months, thinking that I have acted against his will— not for how my happiness has been affected, but rather how my mother and sisters have suffered because of it."

He reached out to her. He wished to impart some of his strength to help her shoulder the burdens she carried, but he pulled back before he touched her. Now was not the time. Patience, man. Clasping his hands together, he said, "Any loving father would put the interests of his daughter ahead of his own expectations."

Her fingers twitched and she clasped them together. "I know that now." She pulled a folded up paper from her sleeve. One side of it was covered with writing, but it bore no marks of ever having been posted. "Father liked you."

His body felt limp with relief. Mr. Bennet approved of him.

Elizabeth continued, "Mother sent me his journal and I found a letter in it. He wrote it to me. It is unfinished, but it is enough." She unfolded the letter, smoothing over the creases delicately with her fingers. Her eyes looked like glass, reflecting the unshed tears floating in them.

"Mr. Bennet spoke so highly of his daughter— his Lizzy, he called you repeatedly," Darcy's words stuck in his throat, and he forgot what he had meant to say. The look Elizabeth gave him as he uttered her name discomposed him completely.

"He wrote about that. He wrote that he had never met a gentleman with a better listening ear. He was happy to have some time in the company of a sensible gentleman after his visit with Mr. Collins, whom he described as the most ridiculous of men."

Darcy nodded. He shared a similar opinion of the clergyman.

Her face flushed. "He said that if any of his daughters were to marry Mr. Collins, he would never speak to her again."

"How sensible of him— and of you to have refused Mr. Collins' offer," he commented, hoping to lighten her embarrassment.

With a sigh, she relaxed into her chair. "How I needed to know that! I have been living with the horrible burden of being responsible for the break-up of my family. We lost our home because I could not force myself to love such a man, and I refuse to marry for anything other than the deepest love."

Breath escaped Darcy. She could not possibly know how deeply her words affected him.

"That is how it should be. I have always viewed marriage as a sacred bond not to be taken lightly."

Her lips parted, but she remained silent, contemplating him. They sat in silence, knowing that they had spoken too plainly, but wishing to speak plainer still.

SHE HAD ALREADY SAID TOO much. What she really wanted was to give Mr. Darcy the letter and let him read it. But the letter spoke too frankly about how good a match he would be for her, so she dared not. She fiddled with the edge of her sleeve, so happy and yet so lonely.

She looked at the door, hoping Georgiana would step through before she asked what she so badly wanted to. Did he love her as ardently as she loved him?

"Miss Elizabeth, you have given me the best gift today. I have been haunted by the consequences of my ungentlemanly behavior, and I have spent the past months trying to make atonement."

Hope flickered in her breast like a tenacious spark in a dying fire. Looking at his face intently, she said, "You are free of any obligation you believed yourself to be under. Thank you for your kindness toward me and my family, but you owe us nothing. You never did." Her throat was so dry, it stuck together, and she had to whisper. Her eyes stung. So many times, she had held back her tears. So many times, she had suppressed her emotions to avoid causing a scene.

She tried to smile. She could never tell him how her heart broke more at the thought of losing him forever than it had at her father's death.

Breathing through the knot in her throat, she looked down so that he would not have to see. Crying was an ugly business, and she was no longer under the assumption that she could fool him.

Elizabeth squeezed her eyes shut, trying to force back the intensity of what she felt. When she opened them again, a white handkerchief hovered by her face. Mr. Darcy was on his knee before her, offering her his handkerchief just as he had so many months ago. An eternity ago.

With a sob, she reached for the soft linen. His hand did not leave it, but followed the handkerchief to her cheek where he gently caressed it.

"Elizabeth," he pronounced her name in his velvety baritone.

He went to move his hand, but she clutched at it, pressing it against her face.

"I love you," he said in a voice meant only for her to hear.

She wanted so badly to believe him, but she would not allow him to suffer an attachment extended out of pity. Dabbing her eyes and raising her head, she asked, "Why?"

She looked into his eyes, wishing she could read his mind, desperate to understand his heart.

He lowered his hand from her cheek to hold her hands in his. The warmth in his touch enveloped her with security like a soft blanket. "I began loving you before I even met you." He sighed and shook his head, running his other hand through his hair. "Mr. Bennet poured out his concerns in our carriage ride. He was distraught and feeling unwell. His desperation made him speak openly, and he shared details about his faults toward his family that I doubt he had dared think even to himself before. It did not take long for me to notice that one subject in particular lightened his heart and calmed him more than any other." His eyes were so inviting, Elizabeth felt like she could drown in them. "It was you. Whenever he spoke of you, a tenderness came over him and calmed him. So, I asked him questions about you to keep his mind off his discomfort and on a beloved subject. The woman he described so honestly was the lady I had always dreamed I would marry. Over the past months, I have watched you and have come to realize that you are so much more than your father described."

If it were possible to melt, she would have. His words embraced her soul as wholly as his hands caressed hers.

He did not budge or flinch a muscle when Georgiana walked back into the room. He only smiled and looked at Elizabeth in the eyes. He was so beautiful, her heart ached, and her hand started to sweat.

"Will you marry me? Do you love me?" he asked. The uncertainty in his voice made her want to laugh and kiss him so firmly on the mouth, he would never doubt again.

Biting her lips, she said, "I love you, William. I love you more than I ever believed possible."

Georgiana froze in place, her hands clasped in front of her chest.

"Will you marry me?" William asked, more confidently.

Wrapping her arms around him and burying her face in his neck, she said in his ear, "Yes."

She was so happy, she might have floated up into the heavens had he not wrapped his arm around her and leaned his cheek against her forehead. He did not release her hands, which still grasped onto the handkerchief… that blessed, wonderful handkerchief which had begun everything.

CHAPTER 37

ONE MONTH LATER

Elizabeth and Darcy arrived at Pemberley early in the morning. The sun had yet to dry the dew on the green grass, and the birds still picked at the earth for their breakfast.

The grounds belonged in a fairytale. Every blade of grass grew in its proper place. Every tree in the forest belonged and added to the splendor of Pemberley. The rose garden they passed had perfectly trimmed bushes and luscious blossoms where butterflies and bees gathered.

The carriage stopped and William handed her out. "There is something I want you to see before anything else. It is a surprise." He shuffled his weight, and he bunched his chin. He was nervous.

She gave him her best smile. "I love surprises!"

Together they went into the house, greeted by the household staff, who missed their master and were happy to welcome their new mistress. He answered a few questions regarding Georgiana, who would arrive the next week with the Matlocks. But William did not slow his pace as they walked on the polished black and white squares of the entrance hall and past the grand staircase with its shiny bronze stairwell.

They passed several doors before he stopped. Moving behind her and covering her eyes with his hands, she held her breath as she heard him open the door and felt his body against her as they moved forward into the room. They took several steps inside.

"I did not understand my motives at the time. All I knew was that I had to have them. Now I understand." He let his hands drop from her blinking eyes. "I did it for you."

The familiar smell of book binding and worn leather filled her senses. It was one of the largest libraries she had been in— even larger than Lady Rutledge's. She looked around her, thinking that heaven could not be more beautiful.

“Oh, William, it is breathtaking!” she exclaimed, spinning through the room.

“Do you still feel guilty for refusing Mr. Collins?” he teased.

She punched his arm.

William pointed to the books in front of her. “Look in front of you.”

She took a step forward to see better, then paused. She knew. The books were too familiar for her not to recognize.

Slowly, reverently, she ran her fingers over their smooth covers. She pulled out a volume and read father’s thoughts written in the margins. “How did you get these?”

“When Bingley left Hertfordshire, I made my way to Brighton, where Mr. Phillips told me the gentleman who had purchased your father’s library resided. I convinced him to sell it to me.”

Spinning around to face him, her chest heaved to catch her breath. "You bought father's library when you hardly knew me? You dear, wonderful man!"

She rushed back to William, nearly toppling him over when she jumped up to wrap her arms around his neck. He scooped her up and she felt her feet dangle over the floor as he swayed her back and forth, sprinkling her face with kisses. She ran her fingers through the curl of hair at the bottom of his neck and let herself feel the happiest she had been since the day they had married.

"Oh, William, will I always be this happy?" she asked, kissing the cleft on his chin.

He set her down and she caught her breath.

"I will see to it," he promised.

Flattening both hands against his chest, he tipped her chin up so that their eyes met.

"There was a time when I thought I would never be complete again. But you have healed me. Love surpasses grief, and now I cannot imagine how I lived before you. You are my family, William."

Perhaps grief is the price paid for loving so deeply, but it was also the greatest gift she had ever been given, and its power was so far superior, she could now think with fond memories of her dear father. He had not been a perfect father by any means, but he had loved her unconditionally. Through all his faults, he had left her one legacy which stood out above all others. He had taught her that love was worth waiting for. Love never fails. As Elizabeth looked into her husband's eyes and felt his tender embrace, she knew that he had been right.

THE END

Can't get enough of Darcy and Elizabeth? Read on to find your next book!

Follow Fitzwilliam Darcy as he overcomes various challenging roles on his path to love.

Read all the standalone books in the Dimensions of Darcy series here!

Can curiosity and crimes lead a young lady to the altar? Join Elizabeth Bennet as she finds out!

Read all the standalone books in the Mysteries & Matrimony series here!

Darcy and Elizabeth form a formidable investigative team as they work together to bring enemies to justice and forge unbreakable bonds with their newfound family.

One-click the complete Meryton Mystery series here!

A hidden letter that rocks the Darcy cousins' world. Will it ultimately lead them to their own happily-ever-afters?

One-click the complete Darcy Cousins series here!

THANK YOU!

Thank you for reading *Love Never Fails.* I hope you enjoyed reading it as much as I loved writing it. Please click here to leave a review — I read all of them!

Want to know when my next book is available? You can:

* Sign-up for my newsletter
* Follow me on Twitter
* Like my Facebook page
* Follow my Author page on Amazon

ABOUT THE AUTHOR

When Jennifer isn't busy dreaming up new adventures for her favorite Austen characters, she is teaching English, reading, perfecting her doughnut recipe, or taking her kids to the park.

Her wish is to continue to write sweet romances with happy endings for years to come.

She currently lives in Ecuador with her husband and twins. All of them are fluent in Spanglish.

Right now, Jennifer is imagining a new way to bring our beloved Darcy and Lizzy together so that they can enjoy another Happily-Ever-After.

OTHER BOOKS BY JENNIFER JOY

Single Titles

Earning Darcy's Trust

Win, Lose, or Darcy

Sweet Contemporary Romance

Written in the Stars: Starlight Terrace Proposals #1

Made in United States
North Haven, CT
04 August 2023